BAREFOOT IN GENESIS

MORE THAN CHANCE BK 4

BARBARA LANDON

Dedicated to El Shaddai my God Almighty, All-Sufficient God.

CONTENTS

INTRODUCTION

I meet you today at your kitchen table. When I arrive the smell of coffee fills the air and the sound of praise music fills my ears. Immediately my soul thrills at the excitement of what Master desires to teach us through these last chapters of Genesis. Quickly we arrange our bibles, our coffee, and our notepads on the table before us. You reach for my hands and over our bibles we open our hearts and minds to our Master.

As we bow before Him our minds fill with His majesty in creation and the daily adventures we found there. With my mind soaring, I think of Adam and Eve, and the lessons for our lives. The Garden of Eden and the peace we found there.

Noah and the smile on his face when he greeted his LORD. My soul floats with the memories of scripture describing the ark and the families and animals saved by God's hand. However, I cannot remember the ark without knowing the sounds of those left outside the door, sealed by God Himself and my heart breaks for them. Noah's family will forever hold a cherished place in my heart.

I am surprised as I consider the genealogies, which I complained at studying, but today cherish. The lessons and the memories are vast. Our God found such interesting and fun ways to teach us His word.

The years of traveling with Abraham and his family. The heartaches and the joys. The excitement of watching God create a Righteous man of Abraham.

Sarah, Hagar and Katurah the women in Abraham's life and the lessons we glean from them.

The Tower of Babel and the fear I experienced.

Abraham's sons Isaac and Ishmael and how we began to see how they effect our present-day world.

Jacob's entire life lay out before us as we witness his becoming a Righteous man of God.

Esau had a testimony for us that brings understanding to our hearts.

With open hands we bow before you Master
ready to learn more of You.

I am ready!

WHO IS JOSEPH?

Genesis 37:1-7

1. Now Jacob dwelt in the land where his father was a stranger, in the land of Canaan.

2. This is the history of Jacob. Joseph, being seventeen years old, was feeding the flock with his brothers. And the lad was with the sons of Bilhah and sons of Zilpah, his father's wives; and Joseph brought a bad report of them to his father.

3. Now Israel loved Joseph more than all his children, because he was the son of his old age. Also he made him a tunic of many colors.

4. But when his brothers saw that their father loved him more than all his brothers, they hated him and could not speak peaceably of him.

5. Now Joseph had a dream, and he told it to his brothers; and they hated him even more.

6. So he said to them, "Please hear this dream which I have dreamed:

7. "There we were, binding sheaves in the field. Then behold, my sheaf arose and also stood upright; and indeed your sheaves stood all around and bowed down to my sheaf."

Not aware of time or place; you and I awaken to find we are no longer in the land of Esau. Somewhat confused we peek out the door of our shelter to find ourselves back in the camp of Jacob. You respond with an amazed WOAH! And I respond by asking what year it is. Master greets us, encouraging us to prepare for our day. His presence and the uncertainty of our surroundings draws us quickly to our knees before Him.

As always, our security is renewed in the touch of His hand.

We praise Him for always being here for us and for the recent journey to experience Esau's family. You thank Him for the day He has set before us and we nod in agreement that whatever it is; we will praise Him. We ask His grace and guidance as we have learned that the words 'whatever it is" will be amazing! We praise Him for this meal of fresh fruit, flat bread, and goat cheese. I thank Him for the wonder of my feet that do not show the wear of walking this land barefoot. The fact that He renews and restores me moment by moment for this journey blows me away!

When we have finished our morning routine, Master invites us to walk with Him. Excitedly, we rise as He reminds us that Abraham is a stranger in this land, this is not his home. Getting our bearings, we understand that we are back with Jacob in the land of his father Abraham in Canaan. The fact that he never had an earthly home is both amazing and pleasing. As we consider this, Master adds that He was and is Abraham's home. I still do not quite understand this so I ask if we can talk more of this, He assures me that we will.

He reminds us that this land is the same land we talked of in **Genesis 17:8 "Also I give to you and your descendants after you the land in which you are a stranger, all the land of Canaan, as an everlasting possession; and I will be their God."** Then He reminds us that this is where El Shaddai changed Abram's name to Abraham and introduced him to the covenant of circumcision. This is also where Yahweh told Abraham, again, that Sarai will give him a son and Abraham laughed because he was old.

The surrounding fields of wheat are nearly ready to harvest, and corn fields will soon offer their best bounty. Master quickly turns our attention to Joseph, the firstborn son of Rachael and Israel, the eleventh son of Israel. Joseph is a teenager now; our scripture tells us he is seventeen. Our scriptures also tell us that Israel loves him more than the older boys who were born of Bilhah and Zilpah. We have seen before the tragedy this favoritism can cause as we remember the relationship between Ishmael and Isaac.

We crest a low hill and see the sons of Israel tending to the flocks in the valley below. The once lush valley is showing signs of flocks having grazed here and there is less vegetation that I remember. Tending the flock is a big job and requires all their participation. Master points out that Joseph is there with them. As we walk Master shares that Joseph makes it his business to report back to Israel all the activities of his brothers. This reporting always causes strife between them, but it seems very 'family like' to us and with that alone we do not see a problem. We assume that because of the favorite child status Israel favors Joseph's reports over his brother's explanation nearly every time. He points out that the problem however does not lie with the reporting. The problem is that Israel loves Joseph more and displays it openly. Israel has even made Joseph a costly **"coat of many colors"**.

You ask why this 'coat' would be such an issue. We remember this story from Sunday school, and at the time this coat seemed like a fun thing for Joseph to receive. You ask if there is symbolism in this coat that we do not know. He shares with us that this coat is more than a colorful garment. It indicates honor or perhaps even position. You ask if Israel is indicating Joseph is set apart to receive the headship of the family and therefore the inheritance.

Indicating that we need to slow down and learn, Master leads us to better understanding. He tells us the same word for robe is mentioned one other place in scripture in **2 Samuel 13:18 Now she had on a robe of many colors, for the king's virgin daughters wore such apparel. And his servants put her out and bolted the door behind her.** We understand that Tamar will be wearing a robe that is called by the same word as Joseph's robe. In this passage of scripture, the robe is used to set her apart from others. In the case of Tamar, the robe is not a glorifying thing, it draws attention to her as being different.

Master listens as we reason what we currently know from our studies of God's Word. Some bible translations describe Joseph's coat as having long sleeves and hanging to the calves or ankles. Not reasonable for a working man. Another version translates it as a decorated or ornate tunic, or sleeveless and another says that it is various colored. From the people around us we conclude that man does not know how to dye wool and dying linen is expensive. Most 'coats' are made of wool which naturally ranges in color from very dark gray to white. With this understanding we assume the wool coat Joseph received was a variety of gray tones. You offer that this wool coat would probably also be used for sleeping because of the warmth it will provide. We are not now certain what it is about this coat that strikes such anger in His brothers, but we can see that it does.

As we continue reasoning, Master listens with delight while as we recall what we have learned. We know from our own day that a Hebrew leader who wears tassels on his robe is set apart as the leader of a group. These tassels are called ornaments. Joseph's robe does not mention tassels, but it does say that it is "ornate" which may mean tassels.

I mention that the men we have seen are wearing an underlying tunic. This tunic is usually a light tan color and made of linen from flax. Most men wear what we would call a 'maxi-kilt' extending to the calf and worn over a shorter kilt that is usually pleated. You add that they do not always wear a shirt but when they do, they are wearing a simple square with the sides sewn up leaving holes for arms and a hole for the neck.

Master interjects into our understanding that when the brothers see this coat, they cannot ignore the favoritism from Israel anymore. They can no longer be civil to Joseph and they begin to plot against him. Master compares his brother's hatred with the same Hebrew word used when Leah was hated by

Sarah. This hatred is bitter and hostile.

We continue walking through the fields, feeling the tops of the wheat stalks with our hands. You ask, "Why would Joseph tell his brothers his dream when they are already so hostile toward him? With this question we all stop walking as Master pulls the head off a stalk of wheat. At seeing His gesture, I do the same and you stoop down to pick up a rock from the rich soil.

He explains to us that man feels great excitement, and sometimes pride, when he hears from his God. Sometimes his excitement gets away with him and he voices the message before considering if it is a public message or a private one. To that I ask, "Which type of message is Joseph's?" Without answering me, He faces us and peels away the outer shell of the seed. Then continuing, he reminds us that since the time of Jacob God has chosen dreams to appear to man. As a result, all dreams are taken seriously and considered a message from God.

We begin walking again as Master pops the first couple seeds in His mouth. As He does so, He points out that now, not only is Joseph Israel's favorite son, he is also set apart as special with this new coat. He cautions us not to forget that God has really appeared to him in a dream. You add that this is not just any dream. Our scripture says that Joseph's older brothers will bow down to him. This is not endearing news for any older brother.

Master guides us to considering the type of man Joseph is:

1. Certainly he is favored and protected from birth.

2. He is younger than eleven brothers and his labors, if any, are light.

3. He tells others how he sees things, right or wrong. He is a 'reporter'.

4. He reports details precisely and regularly.

5. He has high self esteem and is comfortable in his position with his father.   6. He does not consider whether

or not what he says hurts others.

7. He would be a typical teenager in our day.

With a determined throw, your rock flies as you declare, "Nope, I don't like him. Someone needs to teach him some manners."

Master suggests that we not judge him so quickly. You somewhat confrontationally suggest that Joseph is seventeen years old, so this is a lifestyle. Matching your passion, Master suggests that we not forget that these brothers are the same ones who slaughtered a whole city, including women and children, then plundered all the cities goods as told in **Genesis 34:27-29**.

Master continues that Joseph is the man Yahweh has chosen for an incredibly special mission. We must reserve our uneducated opinions as we have much to learn about Joseph and his brothers. The picture and influence of their lives will go way beyond this family struggle.

With that you concede and thank Him for enlightening us. Breathing a sigh of relief, I relax. I was concerned at your confronting our Master. However, as we continue walking, I consider the thought that He did not mind being confronted.

HATED AND REJECTED

Genesis 37:8-19

8. And his brothers said to him, "Shall you indeed reign over us? Or shall you indeed have dominion over us?" So they hated him even more for his dreams and for his words.

9. Then he dreamed still another dream and told it to his brothers, and said, "Look, I have dreamed another dream. And this time, the sun, the moon, and the eleven stars bowed down to me."

10. So he told it to his father and his brothers; and his father rebuked him and said to him, "What is this dream that you have dreamed?" Shall your mother and I and your brothers indeed come to bow down to the earth before you?"

11. And his brothers envied him, but his father kept the matter in mind.

12. Then his brothers went to feed their father's flock in Shechem.

13. And Israel said to Joseph, "Are not your brothers feeding the flock in Shechem? Come, I will send you to them." So he said to him, "Here I am."

14. Then he said to him, "Pleases go and see if it is well with your brothers and well with the flocks, and bring back word to me." So he sent him out of the Valley of Hebron, and he went to Shechem.

15. Now a certain man found him, and there he was, wandering in the field. And the man asked him, saying, "What are you seeking?"

16. So he said, "I am seeking my brothers. Please tell me where they are feeding their flocks.

17. And the man said, "They have departed from here, for I heard them say, 'Let us go to Dothan.'"

18. Now when they saw him afar off, even before he came near them, they conspired against him to kill him.

19. Then they said to one another, "Look, this dreamer is coming!"

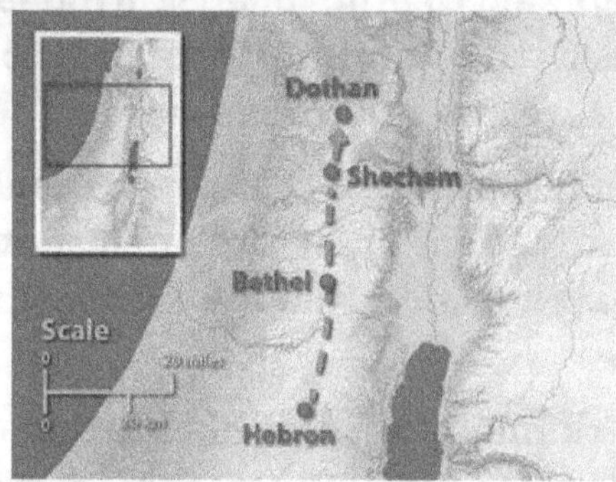

Bing.com maps

After a crisp morning walk to observe the feeding of the animals and to check out the new baby animals we arrive back at our camp in Hebron. Joseph is not far away walking among the livestock. Joseph's brothers, all eleven, approach him and draw our attention. We are not close enough to hear clearly so Master walks with us to be nearer. The ground around the pens is hard and damp and the animals are loud. The tension in the air is thick. The brothers are circling Joseph and we are uneasy. However, Master assures us this is not the time to be concerned.

It seems the brothers have come to confirm that they understand the dream Joseph shared with them earlier. They ask if Joseph really believes he will reign over them, have 'dominion' over them. He replies that yes, he believes God gave him this dream. The brothers laugh at him as they turn and leave Joseph to his dreams. They are whispering under their breath as they walk away but we cannot understand what they are saying.

We are not told how much time passes before Joseph has

another dream, but our scripture tells us that he does. Master walks with us to the family gathering place in front of Jacob's home where, at Jacob's request, Joseph and his eleven brothers are gathered. This area is green with vibrant grass and trees. There are benches and a fire pit for family gatherings and meals. There is an altar for their sacrifices in a separate area, but where they sit now is circled around the unlit fire pit. Their current conversation is about the animals. They believe they need to move them to a better grazing area. They obviously have freedom to graze wherever they please, and they agree to take the flocks north to Shechem about ninety miles.

You grab my arm as Joseph rises from his log to speak to his brothers about his second dream. I breathe a quiet "Oh No" as he begins to speak. You respond by asking if he does not realize how angry this makes them. While Joseph is speaking, Israel hears them talking and comes out to join them. Rachel is right behind him with little Benjamin close behind her. As we look on in disbelief, Joseph explains that this most recent dream involves eleven stars and the sun and moon. Waving his arm across the air he tells them that the eleven stars and the sun and moon bowed down to him as he dramatically places his hand on his chest. At the mention of eleven stars the brothers look down shaking their heads. I assume they are weary of this talk. The sun and moon intrigues them though so they stay to listen looking at each other impatiently. You and I notice that the telling of this dream is different from the first and now Israel is hearing that he and Rachel will bow down also. Israel asks Joseph if he expects his parents to bow down also. Joseph just nods his head in the affirmative. Israel is silent as he looks to Rachel whose expression is disbelief. I watch Joseph because in some way I feel sorry for him, knowing that Yahweh wants Joseph to tell his family these things. There are no more grand gestures from Joseph. What I do see is that he does not understand why his family is not excited that Yahweh has spoken to him. The brothers are fed up, they rise united and walk away. As they leave, Reuben yells back to their father that they are taking the flocks to Shechem to find fresh pastureland.

We leave Joseph standing before Israel and Rachel and walk with Master back to our shelter. You ask Master if the first dream was talking of earthly things, because the wheat was mentioned, and the second was talking of heavenly because of the sun moon and stars. He is please with your observation and assures us that we will go into great depth with this as we journey through His word. He mentions that He finds joy in our learning as He leaves us to walk back to our shelter alone.

There are still a few hours of daylight, so we decide to continue working at some finishing touches on our shelter. We are hopeful that we may be here longer than the last place. Our roof is covered with long but skinny sticks tightly woven together then covered with clay to keep the rain out. You have designed a way for our roof to open to see the stars at night and to allow air to circulate. It is magnificent!

A few days later, as we are fashioning the device to open and close the 'skylight,' we hear Israel talking with Joseph just in front of our shelter. He is asking Joseph to go alone to check on his brothers and the flocks. This is no small thing as they are now nearly 90 miles from here. Joseph agrees to go. We sit on the dirt outside our shelter and watch as Joseph gathers the supplies he will need, along with a camel and a couple goats. While he is packing the rack for the back of the camel, Master approaches us and asks if we would like to follow him. He need not ask twice, and we drop what we are doing to join Joseph on his journey. Then, cautiously you stop, turn to face Him, and ask Master if He is coming also. We have learned that we do not want to go on journeys without him. With a pleased smile He assures us He will travel with us. He gestures that we have time to clean up our things here before we go.

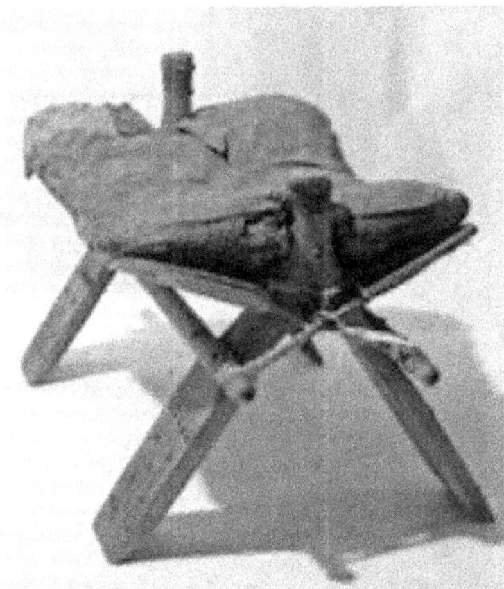

Bing.com Ancient Camel Saddle

The road to Shechem is familiar to us, we traveled it with Abraham and with Jacob in the past. We enjoy seeing familiar places and even remember places where we filled our water skins or learned a precious precept from our Master.

Some days later we arrive in Shechem, but Joseph's brothers and their large flocks are nowhere to be seen. We follow Joseph as he goes down one path then another, turns around and goes down the same path again. It would be comical if we were not tired from walking all day. He has searched every direction out of this city and his brothers are not here. We look to Master questioning what this is all about. Surely a flock this large should not be hard to find! Finally, a man approaches Joseph and asks him what he is looking for. We are relieved to hear him say that the men and their flocks have moved north about twenty more miles to a place called Dothan.

The name Dothan is new to us and we ask Master if we have passed this way and do not remember. He shares with we have not been here before but that this hilly area will appear later in our journey when the tribal lands are divided between the Children of Israel. Dothan will lie on the border between the land of Issachar and Manasseh. He adds that the name Dothan means 'two wells'.

Before we see Joseph's brothers in the distance, Master instructs us that they have already seen us coming. Adding that the brothers are conspiring against Joseph and they plan to kill him in this place.

What?

You and I have been enjoying this journey with the memories and the scenery. Now Master reveals that we have come here to see Joseph's brothers attempt to kill him. We know our scripture enough to know that they will not succeed. Still, we are concerned by what type of reception Joseph will face when he arrives at their camp. I ask Master to stay close by as we walk into this is uncomfortable scene.

Speaking of our concern, we observe that Joseph is pleased to have found his brothers and is walking faster toward them. We want to tell him to slow down but are not able. Master reaches His hand out, palm down, signaling to us that He can handle this.

JOSEPH CAST AWAY

Genesis 37: 20-27

20. "Come therefore, let us now kill him and cast him into some pit; and we shall say, 'Some wild beast has devoured him.' We shall see what will become of his dreams!"

21. But Reuben heard it, and he delivered him out of their hands, and said, "Let us not kill him."

22. And Reuben said to them, "Shed no blood, but cast him into this pit which is in the wilderness, and do not lay a hand on him"—that he might deliver him out of their hands, and bring him back to his father.

23. So it came to pass, when Joseph had come to his brothers, that they stripped Joseph of his tunic, and the tunic of many colors that was on him.

24. Then they took him and cast him into a pit. And the pit was empty; there was no water in it.

25. And they sat down to eat a meal. Then they lifted their eyes and looked, and there was a company of Ishmaelites, coming from Golead with their camels, bearing spices, balm, and myrrh, on their way to carry them down to Egypt.

26. So Judah said to his brothers, "What profit is there if we kill our brother and conceal his blood?

27. "Come and let us sell him to the Ishmaelites, and let not our hand be upon him, for he is our brother and our flesh." And his brothers listened.

As we walk toward the sons of Israel, Master shares with us what is in their hearts. He reminds us that Reuben has lost his position as the firstborn. However, however his brothers still regard him as leader, and he will be held ultimately responsible if anything happens to anyone of his brothers or the flock. The Spirit of God guides us to make a mental note of his maturity in judgment of this situation. I ask if the other brothers would kill Joseph if Reuben does not stop them. Master assures us they will.

Master takes us to **verse 22** and shows us that Reuben will allow the brothers to toss Joseph into the pit or dry well. Reuben plans to return later and take him out and see that Joseph gets back to his father.

When Joseph arrives, the brothers are standing waiting for him. They waste no time in taking Joseph's coat from him. They do not harm him, but at Reuben's request they toss him in a dry pit in the wilderness. We are reminded that this place is called two wells. Is it possible this is a well that these boys' ancestors dug which did not produce water or has possibly dried up? Either way this pit is deep and impossible to get out of without help. Joseph is frightened but he is ok, probably more ok than if he were in the camp with his brothers. You suggest that if Joseph were in camp, "He might say something that would make things worse for himself". I cannot stop myself from going to the edge of the pit to look in on Joseph. He is obviously scared, silent, and unsure of what his brothers are planning to do with him. In contrast to Reuben's actions, Joseph appears very immature and confused.

Forgetting about Joseph, the brothers are enjoying their meal of flatbread, nuts, berries, and wine when they hear bells and singing. They appear to know where the sound in coming from, but we do not. One of the brothers runs into the camp from the north and declares there is a company of Ishmaelites approaching. As they come closer, we note the dust around them. They are traveling four abreast as these companies do for protection. Master informs us that their camels have bells on their harnesses and the men sing to maintain rhythm in movement and calm among themselves and the animals. We are aware these are dangerous areas they are traveling. The lead man in the company announces them, yelling that they are traveling from Gilead and bearing spices, balm, and myrrh. They say they are going south to Egypt. Their desire is to rest nearby for the night. Master explains that the goods they carry will be used for incense and perfume, flavorings for food or tea, and possibly healing and embalming.

Leaning close to Master you ask Him to remind us who the Ishmaelites (also called Midianites) are. His response is a little comical as He asks you who Ishmael was. A bit embarrassed you say, "Oh yes, I remember, he is the brother of Isaac. These people are the descendants of Ishmael and Hagar. Abraham sent them away into the desert after the birth of Isaac."

Using this as an opportunity to remind us of what we have learned, Master guides us to remember what type of people the descendants of Ishmael are. At His prompting we venture that they live in camps in the desert of northern Arabia. I say that they are nomads and merchants and He assure us that they are, that is why they announce what they are carrying. They live off the sale of these goods. Before leaving this quick reminder, Master adds that, later in history, those who follow Mohammed's example will claim descent from Ishmael.

As the company trickles into a reasonably flat dusty place just outside the brother's camp, Judah suggests that they sell Joseph to the Ishmaelites. He sees this as a way for them to profit from Joseph's disappearance. Then they can truthfully claim innocence of his whereabouts. You remind us that Judah is Jacob's fourth son by Leah. Master cautions us to remember that Judah will soon appear again in our scriptures and we will pursue him further then. His brothers respect him enough now to take his counsel, and this respect will grow.

FACING PAST SINS

Genesis 37:28-36

28. Then Midianite traders passed by; so the brothers pulled Joseph up and lifted him out of the pit and sold him to the Ishmaelites for twenty shekels of silver. And they took Joseph to Egypt.

29. Then Reuben returned to the pit, and indeed Joseph was not in the pit; and he tore his clothes.

30. And he returned to his brothers and said, "The lad is no more, and I, where shall I go?"

31. So they took Joseph's tunic, killed a kid of the goats, ad dipped the tunic in the blood.

32. Then they sent the tunic of many colors, and they brought it to their father and said, "We have found this. Do you know whether it is your son's tunic or not?"

33. And he recognized it and said, "It is my son's tunic. A wild beast has devoured him. Without doubt Joseph is torn to pieces."

34. Then Jacob tore his clothes, put sackcloth on his waist, and mourned for his son many days.

35. And all his sons and all his daughters arose to comfort him; but he refused to be comforted, and he said, "For I shall go down into the grave to my son in the morning." Thus his father wept for him.

36. Now the Midianites had sold him in Egypt to Potiphar, an officer of Pharaoh and captain of the guard.

It is early in the morning when the sounds of a bustling

band of Ishmaelites awakens us as they prepare to leave headed toward Egypt. As we are getting dressed you mention that it is interesting that they speak the same tongue as Joseph's brothers. The Spirit of God shares with us that the Ishmaelites pride themselves on speaking the native tongues of almost all the surrounding area peoples. As we exit our shelter, we find Master waiting for us as He always does. It is such a comforting thing to see Him first every day. You ask if He has been here with us all night and we are not surprised to hear that He has. He adds that He is everywhere. This brings a chuckle as we walk to the stream to wash ourselves before joining Master for a breakfast of fresh mangos, pineapple, and flat bread. This morning He has prepared a welcome rosemary tea as the air is a bit cooler than the previous mornings. His care for us is so purposeful!

Before He can begin to share with us about these verses you ask Him why the terms Ishmaelites and Midianites have been interchanged in these verses. Are they really the same people or is there some underlying difference? As always, He desires we understand so He agrees to teach us again what He has taught us before:

Patiently He reminds us that Ishmael is the son of Abraham by Hagar, who was sent away into the desert. His descendants are nomads. The name Ishmaelites is often used in a wider sense meaning 'nomadic tribes of Northern Arabia'.

Midian is a son of Abraham by Keturah whom he married after the death of Sarah. The term Midianite refers to the land that they roam east of Jordan and the Dead Sea, then southward through the Akabah and eastern parts of the peninsula of Sinai. These two tribes are relatives and are all headed to Egypt, so they travel together for safety. The two tribes have become unrecognizable one from the other as a result of intermarrying, working together and living together.

Master adds one more thing to this understanding. He tells us that some throughout history will call this name discrepancy a bible error. It is not. It makes perfect sense when we will stop long enough to search out the reasons behind the differences. He whispers in our souls that He appreciates you asking the question and your desire to search out the reasons.

Our attention is drawn back to the people around us when we observe that a deal is agreed upon and we watch helplessly as the brothers pull Joseph up out of the pit and sell him for twenty shekels of silver. As quickly as the exchange is made, they are gone with Joseph. Almost in panic, you and I scan the area for Reuben but he is nowhere to be seen. The emotions I believe Joseph must be feeling overtake me as I plead with Master to not let this happen. Joseph will be sold again as a slave wherever the Ishmaelites decide to sell him. and Jacob is unlikely to ever see his son again. We ask Master why He is not intervening. He encourages us to stay with Him. There is a plan unfolding that will amaze us. At this moment I cannot imagine how anything good could possibly come out of this. Master looks my way as He knows how my heart is pulling at my faith. With His look I find I can again trust Him, let go of the circumstances and allow His will to weave this plan before us. My soul reveals again that in Him is peace and comfort. I try to refocus on His blessings around me rather than fearful feelings. I praise Him as I observe the magnificent creation around us and tell Him out loud that, "I trust You."

Seeing the caravan leaving, Reuben returns to the camp and immediately walks to the pit where Joseph had been thrown. He must suspect that the brothers removed Joseph from the pit and have sold him to the caravan. His first reaction is anger, then he builds the scenario in his mind. It does not take long before he figures out what the brothers have done. His reaction is violent and sudden as he begins to tear his clothes.

Shocked at Reuben, I ask Master what this reaction of tearing his cloths means and He explains that it is an outward expression of inward anguish. He adds that some will also put ashes on their heads. Another common expression would be to put on a garment of sackcloth. You venture to explain that sackcloth is a rough cloth made of camel's hair, goat hair, hemp, cotton, or flax. He adds to our understanding that the people of Ishmael are people of passionate emotions and that even in our day they will be seen tearing their clothing in great anguish or grief. We look at each other, then to Master, wondering if we should join Reuben in his grieving and the Spirit of God responds in our hearts that we had just this moment chosen to trust Master with Joseph's life and these circumstances. Before we can speak a word of this to Master, you whisper, "Amen."

We follow Reuben toward his brothers to inquire of Joseph, He knows he is responsible for Joseph's safety. Reuben appears afraid for his own safety when his father Jacob discovers Joseph is gone. At seeing Reuben in his sackcloth, the brothers fear the anger coming their way and tell Reuben of their scheme. While they are telling Reuben of their actions, they are in the process of dipping Joseph's tunic in the blood of a goat they have slaughtered. They intend to take it to Jacob and tell him that they found it. Then they plan to let Jacob draw his own conclusions.

Reuben does not respond but walks quietly back to his shelter alone.

The brothers continue with their scheme, chatting and conniving as they prepare to deliver the tunic of many colors back to their father.

Early the next morning all is readied in silence as we, along with the brothers, begin our journey back to Canaan. The nervousness of the group is in the air and on their faces. We cannot help but share their concern and yet, they are practicing every word and action that will come. Reuben is in the front of the group with the brothers scattered about the flocks as they travel. He has nothing to say as he carries Joseph's tunic over his arm to present it to his father. We would not have guessed that Reuben would join in his brothers lies but he has, and we find ourselves disappointed.

We walk in silence in the sparse plants of this area. The sky is clear blue, and the air is crisp. A good day for a walk with Master and still minds are not able to move from picturing Joseph and what must be happening to him. Is he in a cage? Is he being fed, what about water? Is he afraid? Master knows our fears and assures us that Yahweh is with him, he is going to be ok. I lean over and whisper in your ear, "OK is not enough for me." You nod in agreement as we both hope Master is not aware of our hearts at this moment.

When we arrive at the camp of Jacob, we see him in the distance not yet aware that we are near. The brothers hold back allowing Reuben to go first to greet their father. With no words from Reuben one of the brothers jumps to the front to offers to Jacob; **"We have found this. Do you know whether it is your son's tunic or not?"** This feels cruel to us, but we are not surprised. As soon as he says the words he steps back and almost trips over Reuben who is looking at his as though he is thinking that this was a cruel way to state the lie also. Jacob is still sitting on his wooden bench and has only looked up at his boys. He greets them with a welcoming, "Shalom" and they respond in kind. They are all staring at Jacob wondering if he will respond.

Jacob does recognize Joseph's coat and he concludes exactly what his sons hoped he would. We look to Reuben hoping he will be truthful with his father, hoping that Jacob could maybe rescue Joseph, but Reuben is silent. His head hanging low in shame and, though there is silence in the air for an ample amount of time, Reuben does not speak.

Jacob's mourning is great, and he expresses it in much the same way Reuben did, but Jacob determines in his heart that he will continue this mourning all the rest of his days. This choice is sad, and we decide that at the first opportunity we will talk with Master about Jacob's choice to carry this mourning out like this. All those around him try to console him and yet he refuses. Life in the camp of Jacob is not only sad, it feels as torn apart as his cloths are.

When we can sit with Master, he reminds us of when Jacob and Esau were young. Jacob and his mother Rebekah deceived their father with the skin of a goat. Now, Jacob himself is being deceived with the blood of a goat. This is in a remarkably similar manner as he deceived his father. Master leads us to **Galatians 6:7 "Be ye not deceived; God is not mocked; for whatsoever a man soweth, that shall he also reap".**

Oh Master, I am sure that Jacob believed that incident was so far in his past that you had forgotten it even though Jacob has not. "What is Jacob to do, Master?"

He is sitting with us outside our shelter as we visit about Jacob and his grief. I get my wrap as the cool air has made me shiver. I consider that maybe it is not the air but the tension in the camp that is cold. There is no breeze, only the still air causing goose bumps to rise on my arms as my heart breaks for this father. He shares with us that Jacob is learning to have faith, but he is not able to allow Yahweh to have His way with his heart yet. I ask if Jacob were to confess the wrong that he and his mother did to his father Isaac, would losing Joseph be easier for him? His answer is challenging, as He explains the truth that we need to confess everything we can remember that we have done against God. I sit back in my seat with my back solid against the log behind me. My mind whirls with memories as I I wonder if I have brought everything before my Master. My mind says, "Does he remember those things." My heart says, "Of course He does. These things stand between me being able to have complete faith in Him. They also stand in the way of me letting go of mourning the loss of my relationship with Him over past 'baggage in my heart'. Tears begin to well up in my eyes. I look to His face and know what I must do. I have a choice to allow these things from my past to change me for the rest of my life, or, I can lay them before Him as quickly as He brings them to my conscious mind and learn to trust him. One by one He draws from the depths of me the things I have held for an unknown reason. Each one He guides me to lay at His feet, allowing Him to pick them up as He tucks them securely in His robe.

I feel reluctance,

> then submission,

>> then freedom,

>>> followed by resolve to never reclaim those memories apart from the light of His knowing.

I am no different than Jacob!

As we are preparing to retire for the night Master informs us that Joseph has been sold to Potiphar, an officer of Pharaoh in Egypt.

He is ok.

Yahweh will protect him.

I lay my head down for the night; unfortunately, I do not confess all the sins the Spirit of God is lying on my heart. I fall asleep feeling shameful and worrying about facing my Master in the morning. Tears roll on my pillow as my stubborn self feels dirty and torn and I wonder if Jacob is feeling this same tonight.

As I drift off to sleep the Spirit of God whispers in my soul the similarities between Jacob and Jesus. Chart from Schofield Study Bible

	Jacob	Jesus
1. Object of a father's love	Genesis 37:3	Matthew 3:17; John 3:35; John 5:20
2. Their brothers hated them	Genesis 37:4	John 15:25
3. Their brothers rejected their superior claims	Genesis 37:8	Matthew 21:37-39 John 15:15:24-25

4. Their brothers conspired   *Genesis 37:18*   *Matthew 26:3-4*

      against them to kill them

5. In intent and purpose,   *Genesis 37:24*   *Matthew 27:35-37*

      their brothers killed them

6. Became a blessing among   *Genesis 41:1-45*   *Acts 15:14*

      The Gentiles, gained a bride   *Ephesians 5:25-32*

7. Reconciled with their   *Genesis 45:1-15*   *Romans 11:1*

      Brothers and exalted them   *Deuteronomy 30:1-10*

My sleep is restless as my mind continues to search for past sins I have not offered before my Master. The Spirit of God remains with me as He draws me to a time long ago in my grade school years. A new boy arrived at our class just as a new semester was starting. He was obviously poorer than the rest of us and it was soon evident to me and others that he was not safe at his home. He needed us, his classmates, more than we understood. I had many opportunities to draw him into our tight farming community groups. However, I made the horrific choice to join in the bullying of this innocent boy. He was with us only a few months as he appeared one day at school so beaten that the police were called. He asked me that morning if I was his friend and I ignored him. When the police came, they took James and his sister away and we never saw any of them again. Later in the safety of my bedroom I prayed for him, for his family. The teachers offered no explanation. I had opportunity and chose to not allow him the one thing he needed most, a friend. In fact, that is all he needed from any of us. As an adult I still think of him and what a kind word might have meant to him, a simple acknowledgment that he existed and was of value, a harsh word not said. I have long ago asked forgiveness for the wrong I did toward James. Today I realize I must place James and my relationship with him before my Master. I must allow Master to heal the hurt in my heart over this sin and not allow it to haunt my days any longer. When I have opportunity, I share this aching deep in my soul with both you and Master. I choose to lay it before Him and allow Him to heal that spot in my being.

Yes, I am not unlike Jacob.

You ask Master if it is necessary to repent of the sins of innocence or childhood. He lovingly shares with us that if the Spirit of God brings it to our memory then it must be addressed. There is such a thing as a sin of innocence when we do not know we are sinning, so, we must learn to allow the Spirit of God to speak and we must listen and act.

JUDAH

Genesis 38:1-5

1. It came to pass at that time that Judah departed from his brothers, and visited a certain Adullamite whose name was Hirah.

2. And Judah saw there a daughter of a certain Canaanite whose name was Shua, and he married her and went in to her.

3. So she conceived and bore a son, and he called his name Er.

4. She conceived again and bore a son, and she called his name Onan.

5. And she conceived yet again and bore a son, and called his name Shelah. He was at Chezib when she bore him.

> Master joins us just after our morning meal and invites us to walk with Him.

Excitedly we gather our water skins and a wrap, as we start walking you rush back to grab a few dried figs boiled in grape molasses and a slab of cheese whapped in two pieces of flax which we tuck in our pockets for later.

You have caught up with us just in time to hear Master sharing about Judah going to Adullam to visit his friend. This is the city in the low country between the hill country of Judah and the sea. It sits about thirteen miles SW of Bethlehem.

Google search, Images Abdulla Genesis 38

This is about all we will know of this friend Hirah who lives in Adullam, except that we will hear of this place again in David's time. It is a rugged place, uninviting unless you are running from something or someone. You ask Master if Judah is running away. To this He offers no answer but does share that we will follow Judah and he is not far ahead of us.

We find it interesting that Judah flees Canaan only to find a Canaanite woman in Adullam. You offer that perhaps he is drawn to the familiar things in his life. Her father's name is Shuah (or Shua) and our scripture tells us that Judah 'took' Shuah's daughter, meaning that he seized her for his wife, not necessarily by her will. Her father's name means 'prosperity'. This marriage will be the beginning of a long line of sinful events in the life of Judah.

Preparing to approach another genealogy, we do so with a different attitude this time, hopeful of finding our Master's love for these people. Especially because we see from the genealogy chart Master has brought us that Judah carries the scarlet thread through his descendants. Lovingly, Master places His powerful, gentle hand on the chart before us and asks us if we are ready. We both reply that we are and urge Him to proceed.

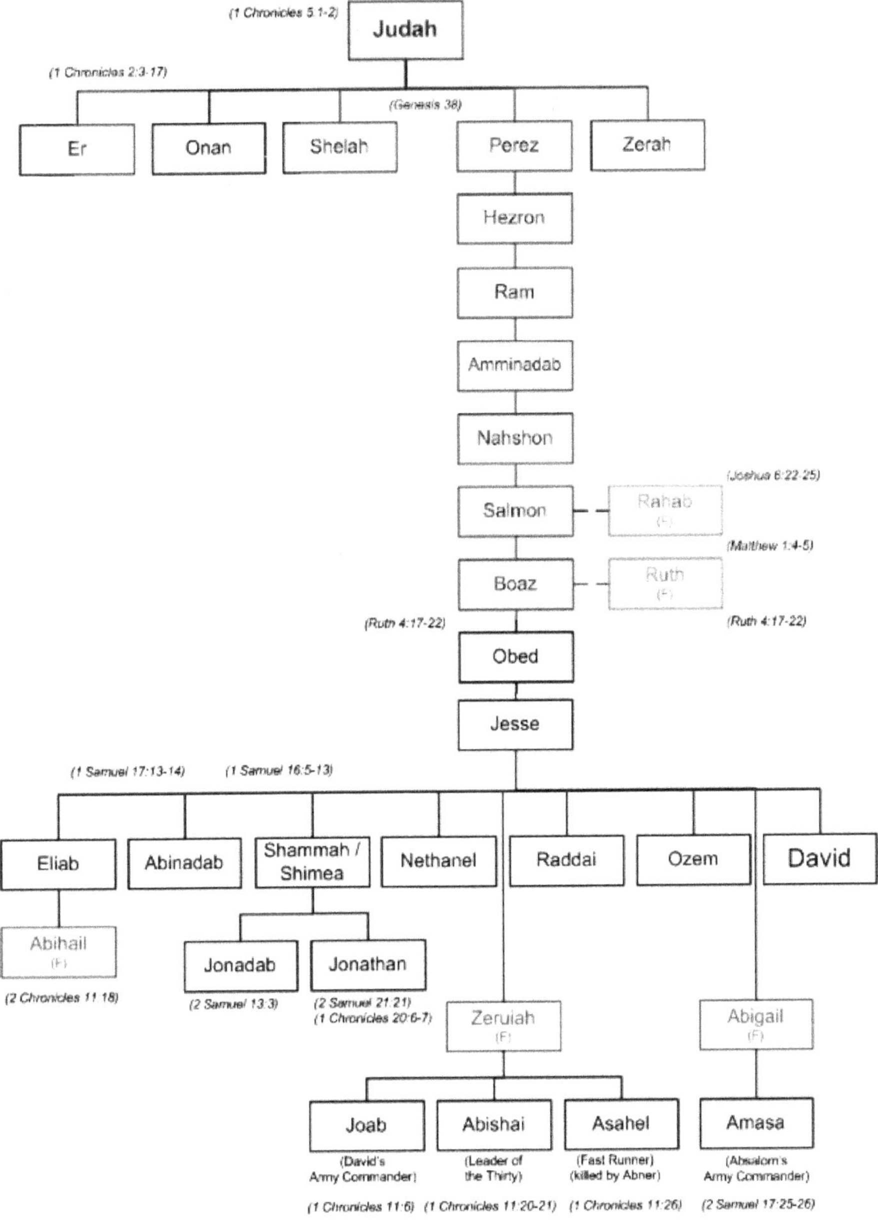

Scripture tells us that the first son born to Judah's wife

is named Er meaning 'watchful'. Master assures us that we will learn much more about this boy in just a few verses from now.

Her second son is named Onan, meaning 'strong' and again He asks us to be

patient as the scriptures will very soon reveal these men.

Judah's wife bore him another son and they named him Shelah meaning

'sprout,' he will be the father of the Shelanite people who we will see when Moses numbers the generation of men able to go to war as recorded in **Numbers 26:2 "Take a census of all the congregation of the children of Israel from twenty years old and above, by their father' houses, all who are able to go to war in Israel."**

The place where Shelah is born is called Chezib and the best guess we will have in our day is that it is possibly the place called Tell el-Beida, south-west of Adullam. Master adds that it will also be called Chozeba in **1 Chronicles 4:22.**

Again, Master asks for our patience as He unfolds what is happening before us.

We are learning to be still and listen. Learning to not get too concerned at the questions running in our heads and wait for His instruction.

SHAMEFUL SINS

Genesis 38:6-14

6. Then Judah took a wife for Er his firstborn, and her name was Tamar.

7. But Er, Judah's firstborn, and wicked in the sight of the LORD, and the LORD killed him.

8. And Judah said to Onan, "Go in to your brother's wife and marry her,

and raise up an heir to your brother."

9. But Onan knew that the heir would not be his; and it came to pass, when he went in to his brother's wife, that he emitted on the ground, lest he should give an heir to his brother

10. And the thing which he did displeased the LORD; therefore He killed him also.

11. Then Judah said to Tamar his daughter-in-law, "Remain a widow in your father's house till my son Shelah is grown." For he said, "Lest he also die like his brothers." And Tamar went and dwelt in her father's house.

12. Now in the process of time the daughter of Shua, Judah's wife, died; and Judah was comforted, and went up to his sheep-shearers at Timnah, he and his friend Hirah the Adullamite.

13. And it was told Tamar, saying "Look your father-in-law is going up to Timnah to sheer his sheep."

14. So she took off her widow's garments, covered herself with a veil and wrapped herself, and sat in an open place which was on the way to Timnah; for she saw the Shelah was grown, and she was not given to him as a wife.

We are excited when we find a small clearing where we can sit overlooking the valley. The grass is dry and uncomfortable to sit on, the rocks are jagged beneath our feet so surely not comfortable. However, the conversation is exciting, and we dive into this scripture ready to hear more about this man whom Yahweh has chosen to carry the scarlet thread.

The very first verse encourages us because we recognize the name Tamar whom Judah has chosen as a wife for his son Er. Then the sad truth happens as Master informs us that Er is such a wicked man that **"the LORD killed him."**

What?

These are strong words and Master can see the shock of our faces. He explains that the word 'wicked' in this verse includes the whole spectrum of evil, morally, and ethically. Er is literally, evil in his whole being. I believe I cannot even imagine what this looks like, but He says that I can. My life has been desensitized to this type of person and I just do not notice them. This is heartbreaking to me and the only response I can give is that I am sorry my heart is so hardened. He also adds that Er is evil in the sight of the LORD and there is no redemption possible, there is no other court to appeal to higher that Yahweh. There is not reason to allow that person to continue in their evil ways. So, God killed him. Before you can ask Master explains that the word 'kill' means to slaughter, slay, or offer as a sacrifice. Your expression changes as you consider this meaning as it is so different than holy sacrifices we have talked of before. You stare at Master waiting for a further explanation but when none comes you lower your eyes, knowing that Master loved Er anyway, and you breathe a soft, "I am sorry I demanded a response from You.

Together we sit in silence at the shock of this scene as Master reminds us that God killed all the people outside Noah's ark also. He cannot tolerate wickedness! He is a just God and He must protect His righteousness and those who might seek Him.

With that reminder Master continues to tell us about Onan, Er's younger brother. Judah instructed Onan to **"go in to"** Er's widow to bare an heir for Er. Our scripture tells us that Onan knew that the child would not be his but would be an heir to his dead brother. You ask if Judah is asking Onan to marry Tamar and Master explains to us that the custom of the day is that if a man dies childless his brother is to take care of his wife and the children. Then any children born by his brother's wife will be considered the children of the first husband, and there-fore will inherit his possessions.

You suggest that this custom explains why Onan 'emitting on the ground' displeases the LORD.

1. Onan is refusing the custom to carry on the family line.

2. Onan's act is selfish as he wants that inheritance for his own children.

3. Onan is disobedient to his father.

4. Onan is refusing to care for Tamar who at this point, has no one to care for her. She is by custom his responsibility now.

Unfortunately, because of his selfishness and disobedi-ence, Yahweh kills

him also.

We notice Judah and Tamar sitting in the family gather-ing place outside Judah's tent. The conversation is obviously serious and Master shares with us that Judah is sending Tamar back to her father's house until Judah's last son Shelah is grown enough to be her husband. Patiently, Master sits with us as you and I talk about our feelings on this event. We are saddened for Tamar. Her heart must be breaking as Judah is her family now and she is being sent away. We know that in this culture it is shameful to be returned to your father. He agrees that, Tamar is saddened but will obey and return to her father's home to wait for Shelah to mature. We are not told how old Shelah is, this may be years away. You inquire if Judah cannot afford to keep her here. Neither Master nor our scriptures answer this question but we both know that Judah has been taught to look out for his own ways before others. Does Judah not see her as the hope for the family line? Does he not see the scarlet thread through his family genealogy? Is he not aware he is the thread?

Master we need your guidance in these things.

Lovingly Master acknowledges our frustration as He encourages us to continue with Him. He assures us that Judah is aware of her situation and his desire is to care for her. He asks us to continue with Him even though this seems harsh now.

We agree, still hoping for a more comfortable resolve.

Master points out that Judah is instructing Tamar, his daughter-in-law to **"remain a widow in her father's house till Shelah is grown."** Judah adds that he is concerned that Shelah will also grow to be the kind of man his brothers were.

You ask Master if the evil runs so deep in this family that Judah is concerned Shelah will be as 'wicked' as his brothers. His answer unsettles us even more as He informs us that sin in this family runs generations back. Fathers in this family have not been godly fathers or even good fathers. This is a vivid picture of **Exodus 34:6-7 And the LORD passed before him and proclaimed, "The LORD, the LORD God, merciful and gracious, longsuffering, and abounding in goodness and truth, keeping mercy for thousands, forgiving iniquity and transgression and sin, by no means clearing the guilty, visiting the iniquity of the fathers upon the children and the children' children to the third and the fourth generation."** And to be sure we understand He takes us to **Deuteronomy 5:8-10 "You shall not make for yourselves a carved image – any likeness of anything that is in heaven above, or that is in the earth beneath, or that is in the water under the earth; you shall not bow down to them nor serve them. For I, the LORD your God, am a jealous God, visiting the iniquity of the fathers upon the children to the**

third and fourth generations of those who hate me, but show-ing mercy to thousands, to those who love me and keep My commandments.

Wow!

These are strong words!

With that you and I awkwardly shift ourselves on the coarse dry grass and jagged small rocks. After jostling for a moment, we settle onto our knees and sit back on our heels facing our Master. He moves closer to us as we bow our heads before Him. My words cannot escape my soul fast enough. Oh, Master search me, find all that is within me that is an idol or sin that I accept as 'normal' in my life! Especially the things from my childhood that were part of my growing up, those things that I may have been taught were ok before You or even 'necessary evils'. Father, I desire the mercy you declare in **Deuteronomy 5:10**. Master my desire is to love you with the kind of love that keeps your commandments and seeks to know them. I desire to be pleasing in your sight. I remain silent before Him, on my knees until His touch thrills my soul and warms my entire being. The Spirit of God assures me that He will do as I have requested. We will deal with the idols hidden in me. He adds that we will do it throughout this journey with Him, one at a time.

I am held in His mercy!

Master suggests that we walk a bit to change positions. He has found a staff for each of us to make the walking easier and has now located a path to walk down into the valley. This appears to be an animal path, perhaps a shepherd. It strikes me that if this is a shepherd's path, how appropriate it is for you and me.

We walk steadying ourselves with our staffs as Master reminds us that Judah is telling Tamar to remain a widow in her father's house until Shelah is grown. This is a promise that Judah will not be allowed to forget. A widow at this time is considered under God's special care. They wear special clothing to set themselves apart. These garments were usually dark clothing and always provide a head covering. They are required to stay in the corners and out of the way, so that men might not notice them and be tempted or bring them harm. The Hebrew people are commanded to treat them with special consideration or risk punishment from God.

Master has found a small clearing where the dry grasses are laying down and we lay our wraps down to sit on. This is much more comfortable. As Master joins us on the ground, we share the meal of dates boiled in molasses which we brought along with a brick of cheese. We have kept our water skins filled and we praise our LORD for His provision. We are surprised as Master shares with us that some time has passed as we have been walking and Judah's wife has died. You remind us her name was Shua. Master adds that Judah's time of mourning has passed, and he is going to the camp of his friend Hirah the Adullamite to help with shearing the sheep.

Master adds that we are going to follow Judah to Timnah, not far from where we are now. We will start our journey as soon as we have finished our meal.

We again eagerly finish our meal, gather our belonging and are ready to follow our Master (shepherd) wherever He leads us.

As we are walking, Master shares with us that Tamar has heard Judah will be coming by her home on his way to his friend's home in Timnah. He tells us that she has been waiting for opportunity to talk with Judah to hear of her prospective bridegroom, Shelah. She decides to remove her clothing of mourning, cover her head with a lightweight veil and dress as a woman no longer in mourning. She has positioned herself in the open, where a widow would not sit. Soon we are traveling with Judah and Shelah and see Tamar on the side of the road ahead of us. Tamar sees Shelah also. Master points out that Tamar is confused at seeing Shelah because he is grown, and she has not been called to be his wife.

TRICKERY AGAIN

Genesis 38:15-23

15. When Judah saw her, he thought she was a harlot, because she had covered her face.

16. Then he turned to her by the way, and said, "Please let me come in to you"; for he did not know that she was his daughter-in-law. So she said, "What will you give me that you may come in to me?"

17. And he said, "I will send a young goat from the flock." So she said, "Will you give me a pledge till you send it?"

18. Then he said, "What pledge shall I give you?" So she said, "Your signet and cord, and your staff that is in your hand." Then he gave them to her, and went in to her, and she conceived by him.

19. So she arose and went away, and laid aside her veil and put on the garments of her widowhood.

20. And Judah sent the young goat by the hand of his friend the Adullamite, to receive his pledge from the woman's hand, but he did not find her.

21. Then he asked the men of that place, saying, "Where is the harlot who was openly by the roadside?" And they said, "There was no harlot in this place."

22. So he returned to Judah and said, "I cannot find her. Also, the men of the place said there was no harlot in this place."

23. Then Judah said, "Let her take them for herself, lest we be shamed; for I sent this young goat and you have not found her."

We stand a short distance away and are amazed that

Judah obviously believes Tamar is a harlot. You remind me of **verse 15** of this passage and whisper to me that there is deceit on both of their parts because she has covered her face. We listen in shock as Judah asks if he may come into her. Our scripture tells us that he does not know she is his daughter-in-law. The question of payment arises as it must in all such arrangements, and they agree on a young goat from Judah's flock. However, Tamar asks for more. She asks for his signet, and cord. In shock we stand holding hands as Judah agrees. And the agreement is made.

You state that this is such a dark scene in the life of both people. Has Judah learned nothing of being a godly man? There is no reaction from Shelah suggesting this may be a normal occurrence. Has Tamar seen Judah's lack of morals and is using it to her own advantage?

We ask Master about these objects of surety which Tamar ask Judah for, the signet and the cord. He is pleased that we ask and instructs us that.

1. The signet is the same as a signature. It is a ring or a cylinder that a man keeps with him all times which they can press into a soft substance, when it hardens becomes a permanent mark of his signature. The practice is to use this to seal a legal transaction and purchases. These signets are made of stone or wood and are sometimes hung from the neck or waist by a cord. Signets may be rings cylinders or cones, but all were used as a representation of identity. We know that Judah's is on a cord as Tamar asks for the **"cord also."** Master adds to our understanding that thousands of signets will be found in archeological digs throughout time.

Google search, Images Judah's signet ring

2. Master also shares with us that by requesting the cord that holds the signet she is requesting his lineage. Judah does not take this request seriously because he thinks she is just harlot. He blows off the request while giving her the cord also.

3. When she requests Judah's staff, she is requesting rights to his livelihood and Judah freely hands that to her also.

Really?

You ask Master if Judah is in such mourning that he is not paying attention to what she is asking. We both know it has been several years since his sons died. You also mention that Shelah is standing right here, why does he not step in on his father's behalf or why is he not questioning this exchange?

In surprise we watch as Judah also offers Tamar a young goat from his flock which will be delivered later by his friend Hirah. This is common payment for the services of a harlot. Goats were easy for the harlot to trade for things they need and do not require very much care by their owner. They are commonly allowed to roam free and are not offensive to those living in the area. Before we can ask, Master shares that because the goat is to be delivered later Tamar asks Judah for another item of surety, his staff.

Judah soon appears back on the road with Shelah and

Master points out that Tamar has put aside her harlot's veil and is back in the garments of a woman in mourning.

Hirah does return with the goat for Tamar but she is nowhere to be found even when he asks many people, no one knows of her. Judah's reaction to this puzzle us because he does not retrieve the signet with cord or the staff from her. He seems almost uncaring as he says that she may keep them instead of his taking on the shame of pursuing them from her. Perhaps he intends to stop and visit her again and will retrieve his belongings at that time. Or perhaps he believes a harlot will not pursue her rights before a court and that he can purchase new items. We are not told so we do not know why he is reacting this way.

You voice that Judah seems to be showing a great deal of pride in not perusing her, but Master encourages us to look also to Tamar and her motives and actions. He encourages us, as He often does, to wait on Him as this story of Judah and Tamar is not over. Master assures us that all we have just witnessed is common among the Canaanite people. This with other similar customs is the reason He is going to move His chosen people out of this influence. We know from previous reading that He is moving them to Egypt. Even though we know where he is going, the shock shows on our faces as He continues teaching us.

He adds that in our day there will be no Canaanites He will have removed them from the earth. This statement piques out interest to follow these people to see what happens to them.

Our reaction has changed from not understanding to shock as Master continues to lead us. We are able, with the Spirit of God's help, to see a glimpse of God's view of the sin in this place and are beginning to understand why a just God cannot tolerate this behavior. You mention that you cannot see how he tolerates the actions of people in our day. In response He reminds us that we live in the time of grace. He is still a just God, who has made a covenant to not destroy man until the end of time.

He cannot go against His own word.

TWINS

Genesis 38:24-30

24. And it came to pass, about three months after, that Judah was told, saying, "Tamar your daughter-in-law has played the harlot; furthermore she is with child by harlotry." So Judah said, "Bring her out and let her be burned!"

25. When she was brought out, she sent to her father-in-law saying, by the man to whom these belong, I am with child. And she said, "Please determine whose these are – the signet and cord, and staff."

26. So Judah acknowledged them and said, "She has been more righteous than I, because I did not give her to Shelah my son." And he never knew her again.

27. Now it came to pass, at the time for giving birth, that behold, twins were in her womb.

28. And so it was, when she was giving birth, that one put out his hand; and the midwife took a scarlet thread and bound it on his hand, saying, "This one came out first."

29. Then it happened, as he drew back his hand, that his brother came out unexpectedly; and she said, "How did you break through? This breach be upon you!" Therefore his name was called Perez.

30. Afterward his brother came out who had the scarlet thread on his hand. And his name was called Zerah.

We are on a bench in front of a small merchant shop in the town where

Tamar and her father Shelah live. Our scripture tells us it has been three months since we followed Judah and Shelah to the community of his friend Hirah. Judah and his son Shelah were there to assist in shearing the sheep. We were present when Judah met unknowingly with Tamar and as she played the harlot, she conceived with what we now know are twins.

Today you and I are sitting beside the stream not far from our shelter. We are fishing for our noon meal when Master approaches. We have spent much time talking about Judah and the shock we feel that we relied on the stories we have heard of these 'godly men and women' and of the scarlet thread. We had not taken the time to look word for word at scripture to really understand them.

We have had months to search and examine the verses over and over and now realize these are just regular people. This is what people look like who are not constantly seeking God's guidance. Master now sits beside us, and He lifts a fishing stick inquiring what we are thinking.

Well!

1. You tell Him we were disgusted at the attitudes toward others in Jacob's life.

2. We were disappointed at such a man of stature as Judah to act so prideful and careless.

3. The manipulation on the part of Tamar left us wondering at her character also.

4. There have been so many things in the past three months that left us unsettled.

And then you bring us the scripture today and it is all coming clearer. I ask Master, "Why have you left us to ponder these things all these months". Bobbing His fishing stick, He shares with us that people sometimes need time to roll things around in their minds. Perhaps like trying on different ideas. They need to look at different angles and what truths they thought they understood that may not be valid. Then they need time to choose if they are willing to change what they had known as truth in the past.

At His last statement I look up from the water I have been staring at to see Him smiling at me. I know that He is answering my request to show me the things in my life that I accept as truth. Those things that I assumed were ok before Him that are not. I am amazed as I realize the grace and patience at which He is going to teach me these things. I now know, I will hold no fear at His revealing the idols and untruths I carry.

Eager to understand the scriptures He brought us today you ask if we may go on. Master is ready and excited to continue with us, so we look to verse 24. He sees our shock at hearing that Judah is ready to have Tamar burned for playing the harlot and for becoming pregnant. He reminds us that the way Judah sent her back to her father did not break her ties with the family of Judah as in a divorce. She is still part of Judah's family and is acting in desperation at this point. Master guides us to understand that there are several scriptures about having sexual relations with those of near kinship. These are always considered 'wicked' and require being burned to death.

Master explains to us that when Tamar is brought out to face Judah, she is in a court setting at the city gate. We understand judges are here as well as Judah, Tamar has around her own waist the signet with its cord, and in her hand the staff Judah had given her as a promise to pay. She asks the judge to examine the items and determine whose they are as she explains that they belong to the father of her unborn child. I am surprised when, before the judge even takes them Judah steps forward to claims the items and admits that he has done wrong by Tamar.

This is the first humility we have seen in Judah and we are pleased at his response. He admits that he did not do what he had promised in not calling her back to the home of Judah to become the wife of Shelah. You ask Master if Judah will now take her back to his home and He assures us that he will, but he will never have relations with her again. He encourages us to see that Yahweh is calling Judah to consider the customs and actions of the Canaanite people. Judah has a choice to make and we anxious to see how he handles this choice. At this point in our scripture we do not know what will become of her in Judah's household. But Master assures us that we will hear of her twin sons.

Our hearts are heavy as we know the emotions of being confronted publicly with a sin. Judah is not comfortable, and we wish he would choose to follow Yahweh. We want Judah to make things right between himself, the court, Tamar. And God. Yet, we understand how hard a task this is.

The time has come for the birth of the twin boys. We are present with Master as He desires, we understand the importance of the firstborn son. The first hand that appears from the womb is bound with a scarlet thread. But, to everyone's surprise the hand s drawn back. As the birth progresses this first baby to be delivered is not the one with the scarlet thread and Judah names him Perez, meaning 'breach'. Master whispers that Perez will become the father of the Parzite people. It is interesting that the midwife makes a point that she is not taking responsibility for which child is wearing the scarlet thread.

You mention that we have already learned that the firstborn's inheritance is a big deal. Then you add that this is an interesting event and we will need to pay close attention to keep these babies straight in our minds.

After the first child is born the baby with the scarlet thread is delivered and Judah names him Zerah, meaning 'rising'. Looking to Master, we are informed that this child will become the father of the Zarhite people also called the Zarahites. Master shares that we will see this family again at the Valley of Anchor in **Joshua 7:16-26.** Zerah's son Achan and his entire family will be stoned and burned by the Children of Israel after they disobey God's command concerning the spoils of war.

I love how Master baits our interest in the coming scriptures. I cannot wait to get to Joshua!

Master shares that He understands it is hard for us to see these men, whom we have considered great in history, as ordinary people. But He also tells us of His desire is for us to learn from their lives and know that they are not our example to be patterned after.

He is!

JOSEPH IS IN EGYPT

Genesis 39:1-12

1. Now Joseph had been taken down to Egypt. And Potiphar, an officer of Pharaoh, captain of the guard, an Egyptian, brought him from the Ishmaelites who had taken him down there.

2. The LORD was with Joseph, and he was a successful man; and he was in the house of his master the Egyptian.

3. And his master saw that the LORD was with him and that the LORD had all he did to prosper in his hand.

4. So Joseph found favor in his sight and served him. Then he made him overseer of his house, and all that he had he put under his authority.

5. So it was, from the time that he had made him overseer of his house and all that he had, that the LORD blessed the Egyptian's house for Joseph's sake; and the blessing of the LORD was on all that he had in the house and in the field.

6. Thus he left all that he had in Joseph's hand, and he did not know what he had except for the bread he ate. Now Joseph was handsome in form and appearance.

7. And it came to pass after these things that his master's wife cast longing eyes on Joseph, and she said, "Lie with me."

8. But he refused and said to his master's wife, "Look my master does not know what is with me in the house, and he has committed all that he has to my hand.

9. "There is no one greater in this house than I, nor has he kept back anything from me but you, because you are his wife. How then can I do this great wickedness, and sin against God?"

10. So it was as she spoke to Joseph day by day, that he did not heed her, to lie with her or to be with her.

11. But it happened about this time, when Joseph went into the house to do his work, and none of the men of the house were inside,

12. that she caught him by his garment, saying, "Lie with me." But he left his garment in her hand, and fled and ran outside.

Master greets us outside our shelter near the home of Judah and invites us to

join Him as He travels to Egypt to see Joseph. Our first reaction is to pause as we remember when Abram went to Egypt and Master refused to go with him. At that time, He offered our sandals if we chose to follow Abram, but He would not join us. Thankfully, we chose to not follow where He would not accompany us.

However, this time Master is offering to take us. This makes all the difference and we begin immediately discussing how badly we wanted to see Egypt when Abram went with Sarah. We have heard such amazing things of this place and people. Master tells us of the fine fabrics, the fanfare, and the royalty. He talks of the variety of foods and drinks and animals, but we can see He is most excited for us to witness His plan for Joseph unfold in this place. As we walk, Master instructs more on the Nile River. He teaches us that there is almost no rain that falls in the land there, only about eight inches in an entire year. It is not enough rain to sustain life on just that alone. He adds that without the Nile River there would be no Egypt, the yearly flooding of the Nile River deposits layers of silt over the whole valley, creating a rich soil that has made Egypt prosper with vast quantities of food to export all over the Mediterranean world.

He adds to our understanding of the main highway of Egypt as barges and boats float north with the current and the light wind is enough to carry sailing boats south also. Along the banks of the River the clay is perfect for making brick for homes, pottery, and dishes. The soil there also grows papyrus reeds used to make sheets for writing materials, and flax for linen clothing.

You ask Master how large this area is where we will be crossing, and He says that it can be compared to the state of Maryland in the United States. He adds that we will cross more than one river, all flowing from the southern plains to the Mediterranean Sea.

We surely are excited!

There you go again, dancing in circles around us as we walk.

I mention that I have been wondering how Joseph is doing there, remembering the heartbreaking departure from his brothers not so long ago.

We gather our belongings as Master informs us that we will be with Him in Egypt for a time as we observe Yahweh move through Joseph's life. You mention that you are anxious to see if the movies you have seen run true to the story and Master agrees that it will be interesting to compare.

We are increasingly aware that the little bits of vegetation we have been used to is disappearing the closer to what, is our day, is called the Sinai Peninsula. We remember camping here with Master, waiting for Abram and Sarah to return from Egypt. Today that event seems so long ago.

Having passed the Sinai Peninsula, we can see in the near distance the Nile River and we are experiencing great deal of sand and sandstone hills. Today I am thankful the wind is not blowing as this would be a miserable place to be in the wind. Beautifully, the river is wide this time of year and we look to Master asking how we are to cross. He assures us there are boats that will ferry us across.

Arriving at the bank of the first tributary of the Nile River, we climb into a small boat with the bottom carved out of wood. It is a simple boat much like we have seen Indians used in our U.S. history books. The bottom feels too rounded and unstable as we climb in one by one, steadying each other as we cautiously step to a seating place on the bottom of the boat. There is a rope that runs through a hole in each end of the tiny boat; I suppose to keep us straight in our crossing. This rope spans the river and there are men at each end whose job it is to pull the rope to ferry us across. As we move slowly across, we see larger boats just like this one upriver from us, they are carrying larger items and more people. Desiring to hide in my heart the memory of this moment, I lean over the side of the boat to touch the water with my fingertips. I hear my voice exclaim, "I am touching the Nile River!" Master smiles at the thrill of our experiencing His masterful creation. He splashes water on us and the joy of experiencing this with Him is beyond speaking. We experience this same event a few more times as we must cross more than one tributary on our journey to Egypt.

We arrive on the outskirts of a city and stop in awe at the vastness of the scene. So many people, how will we ever find Joseph? Then of course we remember Master knows exactly where he is.

We stay close to Master, as the farther we get into the city the people are everywhere. The noise of the bustling around us is a combination of laughter, shouting, playing children and construction of new projects. It is overwhelming and you ask if we can seek a side place where we can re-gather ourselves. Master, understanding the great change from what we have experienced before in His word, guides us to a place where we can fill our water skins afresh and sit in a patch of green grass. As we sit, I run my hand across the green, healthy grass beneath me and marvel that someone has carefully nurtured this area, probably for an animal to graze later. The exhaustion of the day's journey begs me to lie on the grass and look to the calmness of the clouds floating quietly in the sky above.

You and Master continue talking as I lay there and allow

my mind to escape to calmer places. However, it is not long before Master encourages us to press on as we want to locate Joseph before the day passes. We will also need to find ourselves lodging before dark.

We find the home of Potiphar and Master indicates the plaque on the large sandstone pillars next to the steps leading up to the building. As we pass the pillars, I run my hand across the carved words of identification remembering the wells we experienced with the names carved in the stone lids.

Entering through the open doorway we step onto polished stone which is cool to our feet. There is sweet incense in the air that floats with the breeze among the stone walls. Embroidered linens are hung in seemingly unlikely places that dance with the light breezes and I assume that they help keep the air circulating. Very few people are about in the building and even our bare feet make a sound as we walk.

Walking the hallways with high ceilings, Master tells us of Potiphar and the fact that this is his name and not a title; it means 'whom Re has given'. True to whom I have come to know, you immediately ask who Re is and Master shares with us that Re is one of the many gods of the Egyptian people. He is believed to be a child of the sun god. Later in our journey we will witness Joseph marry the daughter of the priest in a faction of the god Re, called On. Reminding us of what we have already learned, Master speaks of **Genesis 41:45 And Pharaoh called Joseph's name Zaphnath-Paaneah. And he gave him as a wife Asenath, the daughter of Poti-Pherah priest of On. So Joseph went out over all the land of Egypt.**

We are in the home of Potiphar and Master is helping us by setting the groundwork for these later lessons.

Continuing to explain, Master tells us that the title "Pharaoh" is the name for the supreme government official. He instructs that this title for this office can be traced back to the beginning of the Egyptian kingdom. The title "Pharaoh" is usually attached to the front of the pharaoh's personal name. Then, without telling us the present pharaoh's name, we move on.

He instructs us that Potiphar is a 'captain of the guard' and that he is an Egyptian. The literal meaning of the title is 'chief of the slaughterers' so we may assume Potiphar is chief of the cooks. That would explain why he had encountered the Ishmaelites who were coming to Egypt carrying spices and herbs. When Potiphar purchased the spices and herbs, he also purchased Joseph for his own household.

Master leads us into a further understanding of God's word as He shares

With us that nonbelievers may.

1. Strip us of outward appearances but they can never take our wisdom and grace.

2. They may take away family and believing friends, but they cannot take away God's presence from us.

3. They may rob our freedoms and confine us in dungeons, but they cannot take away our communion with God.

With these truths He also reminds us that, Satan has been on Joseph's heels his entire life. You interject that you can see the interference and conflict in Joseph's family, and Joseph's need for acceptance from all of them. Shifting in my sitting position I suggest that we can see the need for acceptance in all the brothers too.

We find this sad need, perhaps a weakness in mankind that Satan plays on, but it certainly is universal. You voice the question of what life would be like if we could focus only on what Master thinks of us and not concern ourselves of what others think. With that comment, my mind flies into thoughts of the things I seek that are not always pleasing to my Master. I look to Him acknowledging that He is once again gently guiding me to find those things in my life.

Again, I am in awe of who He is.

Drawing my attention back to the present event, Master points out that Satan is approaching Joseph with a greater temptation; that of being accepted by Potaphar's wife which would assuredly grant him greater status. We agree that a any male would have been greatly tempted in this trial. Master gathers our attention to point out the strength of Joseph's faith in Yahweh.

1. Joseph is considering who he is before God and who is tempting him.

2. Joseph identifies the sin for what it is. He declares it as sin and flees.

3. Joseph identifies who is tempting him and determines to leave, no conversation, no thought of 'what if'.

You whisper that Joseph has more faith and stability in his life with Yahweh that you do. With joy, Master agrees that Joseph is being blessed in the house of Potiphar. Also, He reminds us that there is a special protection and blessing on Joseph for Yahweh's purposes.

He reminds us that Joseph is a seventeen-year-old fine-looking young man and a prize slave. The truth does not escape Potiphar that, with the addition of Joseph to his household, blessings have come to the home. Master also shares that it seems that it would be great if things were to stay so blessed for Joseph, but we must remember this is Egypt, the symbol of worldly living in this day. Joseph, the man of God is going to experience temptation, troubles, and trials in Egypt. He also instructs us that the scripture describes Joseph as 'successful', meaning he is gaining a good reputation from those he encounters. Master adds to our understanding the truth that a good reputation is the natural result when we purpose to walk with God.

You ask if Joseph's father Jacob has taught him something of the God of their fathers that he did not teach Joseph's older brothers. Master assures us that we will see the truth of this in Joseph's life. He also cautions us that Yahweh is working His plan in the life of Joseph. You ask if Yahweh is protecting Joseph and caring for him because of the role Yahweh has called him to. He answers with another truth that surprises us as He explains that people are prepared by the Spirit of God to receive and fulfill the call of God on their lives. However, this preparation does not do away with man's choice to follow God. Joseph could choose to not follow Yahweh's call. The key is that he was born for this. Yahweh knew him before he was born and knew he would 'choose' to follow the God of his fathers. To guide us to stable ground for this new truth He takes us to **Esther 4:14 "For if you remain completely silent at this time, relief and deliverance will arise for the Jews from another place, but you and your father's house will perish. Yet who knows whether you have come to the kingdom for such a time as this?"** We remember the story of Mordecai and Esther and you ask Master to confirm if this is what Mordecai said to Esther when he was encouraging her to stay and serve her God even in the palace of King Ahasuerus. I add, even when it may cost her and Mordecai their lives. He nods approval that we remember the event in Esther's life. Adding to this picture, He impresses the question if we know what He has called us to. I am sure of my response to this as I offer that, presently I am called to this study while leading my family to salvation and in their walk with Him. You add; "and remaining in His presence spiritually to not risk making Him look bad." Our Master sits silently across the table from us then He reaches for our hands. He lifts my fingers into His warm welcoming hand, and He squeezes approvingly. My heart swells with peace that flows from Him as my mind stumbles at the things He might ask of me. Even as we sit in this precious moment tears well up in my repentant eyes as I investigate His, He knows my weaknesses. I am sorrowful that the thought of reservation raced into my mind even as I held His hand. My weakness to these thoughts is too evident as the Spirit of God draws my heart back to Joseph and the fact that his mind is no stronger than mine.

Master, "Oh how I need you!"

It is fun for us to see that Potiphar has noticed the influence of LORD on Joseph's life. You ask if it is 'Yahweh' that Potiphar sees in Joseph and Master assures that it is. It is exciting to think that possibly because of Joseph's family line or his ways Potiphar sees Yahweh in him, especially when Potiphar is aware of so many gods in his own culture. He could easily have attributed this success to any of these other gods but, he saw the influence of Yahweh!

Master tells us that Potiphar gained so much respect for Joseph that he caused him, a foreigner, to rule over his entire household. With this I also remember that the Pharaoh is a Kyksos King. I remember that we learned about this pharaoh earlier in our study and that he was accepting of many different peoples.

Master gathers our hands in His, drawing our hearts to remember with Him. He takes us back to Laban and his acknowledgment of Jacob's blessing in **Genesis 30:27 And Laban said to him, "Please stay, if I have found favor in your eyes, for I have learned by experience that the LORD has blessed me for your sake."** You respond by asking if our lives are a blessing in the world because He is with us. The smile on His face is bigger than usual at our small bit of realization and He responds that our lives are a vessel of His blessing. It is none of who we are. Then to enlarge this thought He takes us to **2 Samuel 6:11 The ark of the LORD remained in the house of Obed-Edom the Gittite three months. And the LORD blessed Obed-Edom and all his household.** The understanding that the object of His presence, even a nonliving object, would bring blessings is overwhelming! The ark is an amazing presence, but then so is my bible, a cross on a hill above a city declaring Him, a church on a corner or my head bowed at a public eating place. Wow! Our heads are spinning with the opportunities and the power. Then as the realization of what our own country is doing in our day, by removing these godly representations causes shame and horror to in hearts. Cautiously, you ask about Master's statement that it is not the result of who we ourselves are. He cautions back to both of us that this is a true statement, a humbling statement. He suggests we look around at the people in Egypt who are without the Spirit of God's guidance or presence. What type of people are they in their basic nature? Humbled by this understanding I acknowledge the truth of the scripture in **Romans 7:23 But I see another law in my members, warring against the law of my mind, and bringing me into captivity to the law of sin which is in my members. O wretched man that I am! Who will deliver me from this body of death? I thank God-through Jesus Christ our Lord! So then, with the mind I myself serve the law of God, but with the flesh the law of sin.** Sitting straighter in your seat you try to clarify what we are learning and ask, "Without God's influence in my life, I cannot do godly things?" Master responds with the truth that we can do **good** things, but not **godly** things. Then He adds that the good things are those things which are acceptable and good in the eyes of mankind. He asks us to consider that the word 'good' carries many meanings and at the end of the discussion – only God is 'good'.

Drawing us back to our scriptures, Master continues by showing us that others have noticed the difference and the blessing that have come on the home of Potiphar. Potiphar's wife is noticing, and she is intrigued by him. To her, Joseph is a seventeen-year-old handsome man who brings prosperity. Her response is to ask him to lay with her for an unknown reason other than that is an acceptable response in this present day. Part of the custom of lying with someone of such reputation is the same that we have seen before in our scripture, perhaps she might bare a son as fine and blessed as Joseph.

Joseph knows that to lie with her would be against the God of his fathers and that this same knowledge says that if he does this, he is to be put to death. This is the best life Joseph has experienced and he knows better than anyone that Yahweh is with him. I whisper, "Please Joseph, don't mess this up." The Spirit of God whispers **Proverbs 1:10 My son, if sinners entice you, do not consent.** At this moment I am sure that the Spirit of God grasps my plea for Joseph and carried it to the throne of God. This thought thrills me as I have never felt this before. He took my weak plea, filled it with God's word and carried it to God Himself.

I am in awe!

Our scriptures tell us that she is not satisfied with his refusal and continues to pursue him. We are standing in her private quarters when she calls for Joseph and lies in wait until the entire household is empty. I reach for your hand as she has cornered him to press this sin on him. Shock grabs me when she grasps his clothing urging him to lie with her. Quietly, graciously he removes his garment, turns, and runs from her presence. In celebration of his strength, and maybe some temptation, you and I give each other a high five.

"Victory belongs to the LORD", you shout.

FALSE ACCUSATIONS

Genesis 39:13-23

13. And so it was, when she saw that he had left his garment in her hand and fled outside,

14. that she called to the men of her house and spoke to them, saying, "See, he has brought in to us a Hebrew to mock us. He came in to me to lie with me, and I cried out with a loud voice.

15. "And it happened, when he heard that I lifted my voice and cried out, that he left his garment with me, and fled and went outside."

16. So she kept his garment with her until his master came home.

17. Then she spoke to him with words like these, saying, "The Hebrew servant whom you brought to us came in to me to mock me;

18. "so it happened, as I lifted my voice and cried out, that he left his garment with me and fled outside."

19. So it was, when his master heard the words which his wife spoke to him, saying, "Your servant did to me after this manner," that his anger was aroused.

20. Then Joseph's master took him and put him into the prison, a place where the king's prisoners were confined. And he was there in the prison.

21. But the LORD was with Joseph and showed him mercy, and He gave him favor in the sight of the keeper of the prison.

22. And the keeper of the prison committed to Joseph's hand all the prisoners who were in the prison; whatever they did there,

it was his doing.

23. The keeper of the prison did not look into anything that was under Joseph's authority, because the LORD was with him; and whatever he did, the LORD made it prosper.

We are amazed that we are standing where we are today, in Potiphar's wife's private quarters. This woman, 'Potiphar's wife, whom we really know nothing about except that she seems to be a lonely woman desiring attention from whatever source. We watch her humiliation as Joseph wisely refuses her advances. In fact, he leaves her presence so quickly that he leaves his tunic behind, with it secure in her hand.

She is screaming her frustration and complaint so loudly that it echoes through the stone walls. Deafening! You mention that our scriptures just stated that she and Joseph are alone in the palace today, yet running to her aid are a few men. She immediately sends them to find Joseph as he runs away. They kneel on one knee, lay their hand across their chest in understanding, and then turn to pursue Joseph. She remains, in her room crying, I assume in embarrassment, and reclining on her lounge with Joseph's robe still in her hand. Quietly you and I back out of her presence and walk with Master, silently back toward the courtyard in Potiphar's home.

Later this same day we are standing with Master when Potiphar arrives home. He is angered at the events of the day and seems to not quite understand, but to keep peace in his home he commands that Joseph be arrested. Master whispers to us that Potiphar desires to understand better what has happened, he is controlling the present situation to keep his wife happy. Normally, he would have had Joseph put to death immediately.

This is the first mention of prison in our scriptures and you ask Master what type of prison Joseph is going to. He tells us that prison, in this case, is called a 'round house'. This prison is probably a famous round tower or dungeon where prisoners accused of an official crime are housed. Master adds that life in this 'round house' prison is not desirable but He restates for us the scripture that **"The LORD was with Joseph and showed him mercy, and He gave him favor in the sight of the keeper of the prison."** He also reminds us that Yahweh has now opened the door for Joseph's honor to be revealed. Joseph is far away from any friend or family, so he has no one to help him but his LORD, which is more than enough.

At the next verse you and I find ourselves just outside the prison where Joseph is housed. The walls are all stone and noisy with the echo of every movement of the few prisoners and the moving about of the guards. The smell is rank and the floor cold on our bare feet. Master looks on Joseph with compassion and He appears to minister to Joseph's soul right where He stands. The chains on Joseph's ankles are causing sores as this young servant of Yahweh leans against a wall mouthing a prayer for mercy.

Master, encourages us as He shares with us that the keeper of the prison will very soon commit to Joseph's care all the prisoners in this prison. You ask Him what that means, and He is more than happy to share with us the meaning. He explains that the 'keeper' is trusted to handle all the affairs of the prison. Master looks at us with the truth that a godly man will do what is right before God regardless of the circumstance. Joseph is about to experience a nod from heaven, declaring him 'righteous'.

Thrilled, you step forward and touch the rock wall us as you remember the definition Master had given us of 'righteousness'. He taught us that righteousness is when we go through a trial without sin. To do this we rely on our Master as He alone is righteous and will give us the strength to do so. Master desires that we understand that righteousness is who He is and what He covers us with when we belong to Him.

I whisper, "This is a big deal for Joseph!"

Excited, Master takes us to **Daniel 1:8-9 But Daniel purposed in his heart that he would not defile himself with the portion of the king's delicacies, nor with the wine which he drank; therefore he requested of the chief of the eunuchs that he might not defile himself. Now God had brought Daniel into the favor and goodwill of the chief of the eunuchs.** Reminding us that He will do this same thing for those who decide they will not compromise on their commitment to God.

Before we leave the prison cell of Joseph Master shares His desire to tell us more of the phrase in **verse 22 'whatever they did there, it was his doing'.** He explains that Joseph is taking responsibility for whatever is happening in this prison. Personal responsibility. Joseph is standing in their place to take their punishments or praise, whatever the case, whomever the source. You say, "This is an example of what Jesus did for you and me on Calvary and what He does today before God's throne!

FORGOTTEN IN PRISON

Genesis 40:1-4

1. It came to pass after these things that the butler and the baker of the king of Egypt offended their lord, the king of Egypt.

2. And Pharaoh was angry with his two officers, the chief butler and the chief baker.

3. So he put them in custody in the house of the captain of the guard, in the prison, the place where Joseph was confined.

4. And the captain of the guard charged Joseph with them, and he served them; so they were in custody for a while.

It is early morning when Master asks us to walk with Him to the round house prison where Joseph is being held. The sun is rising and has not yet warmed the stone floors or walls of the house of the captain of the guard. Dancing off the polished stone walls the sun seems playful in the crisp morning air causing excitement in our steps as we are anxious to see how Joseph is doing.

As we walk, Master shares with us that He desires to draw more similarities between Joseph and Jesus, and we will stop just outside the prison door to talk of these things. It interests us that this is a strange place to make these comparisons, but we choose to trust Him and follow Him to a stone bench where moments earlier a guard was resting. Master begins to list comparisons as He draws a clean flax parchment from His tunic to share with us. He tells us that these comparison lists will be common in our time and they will often be referred to as a "type and shadow of Jesus Christ". We recognize the title and feel comfortable thinking we will grasp this lesson quickly.

	Joseph	Jesus
1.	Sent to his brothers	Sent to the lost sheep of Israel
2.	Hated by his brothers without cause	"They hated me without cause."
3.	Sold by his brothers	Sold by one of His own.
4.	Sold for 20 pieces of silver.	Sold for 30 pieces of silver.
5.	Brothers plotted to kill him.	His own plotted to kill Him.
6.	Brothers put him in the pit.	His own put Him on the cross.
7.	Joseph was raised from pit.	Jesus was raised from the dead.
8.	Joseph obeyed his father.	Jesus pleased His Father.
9.	Joseph sent to seek his brothers	Jesus sent to seek the lost.
10.	Joseph mocked by brothers.	Jesus mocked by His own.
11.	Brothers refused to accept Joseph	His own refused to accept Him.
12.	Brothers agreed to kill Joseph	His own agreed to kill Him.
13.	Joseph's coat covered in blood	His own gambled for His robe.
14.	Joseph was sold into Egypt	Jesus ascended to heaven
15.	Joseph was tempted by the world	Jesus was 40 days tempted by Satan.
16.	Joseph became his brother's savior	Jesus is savior to His own.
17.	Joseph delivered to Gentiles	Jesus delivered to Gentile leaders.

18. Potiphar sentenced Joseph even   Pilot punished Jesus even when he

When he was suspicious of charges   did not believe accusations.

19. Joseph found favor in eyes of jailer   Jesus found favor in eyes of executioner

20. Joseph was numbered with criminals   Jesus crucified between thieves.

While we see the comparisons between Jesus and Joseph we continue to wonder at this setting and the comparison. However, our Master has brought us here and we trust Him. We are open to His guidance. After a short time of our minds rolling in the list He presented, He asks us for any comment on what we see. We have no comment but feel certain there must be something He wants us to see so we look at the list again.

Lifting our chins to face Him, He tells us that the term's 'type' and 'shadow' are simple comparisons. "What?" you exclaim. He drops his hand from our chins and asks us if we remember the purpose for which we were created. Oh, this must be a trick question, so we do not answer. Soon He reminds us that we were created for fellowship with Him. "Of course, fellowship," He created us to have fellowship with Him. Guiding us gently, Master continues by explaining to us that descriptions of who He is are far beyond what we can understand so we use comparisons to help us remember and understand. We nod in agreement, still waiting for the whole picture.

Leaning forward on one elbow, He tells us that His desire is to share every moment of our lives with us. He is omnipresent, meaning that He not only can be but is, everywhere, all the time. Laying His hand on my knee, He says that He desires to share all the moments of my life with me. My soul thrills at this thought as I had never considered that we could be this close, all the time. Looking directly at me, He instructs me that anything that is a 'type' or a 'shadow' of Him is not Him but is a simple comparison. He stresses the importance of this truth as we do not want to be in the position of worshiping these men and women whom God uses for His glory. With that comment, you suggest that possibly this is why we have believed these were godly men without searching their lives for God's influence on them.

He emphatically declares that nothing worldly is like Him.

You state that Joseph is a picture of Jesus and therefore we call him a type. He asks if we think that the prosperity of Joseph is because Joseph is here or because God is here. You respond that our scripture says that the people prospered because Joseph is here. Master takes us back to the scripture and reads again; **Genesis 39:3 And the master saw that <u>the LORD was with him</u> and that the LORD made all he did to prosper in his hand.** Master adds that three times in Chapter 39 we are told that the LORD is with Joseph. Joseph is a willing vessel for God to use; therefore, the LORD can flow through him to bless those around him. Joseph is not a reflection, type, shadow, or anything else of God.

He was open and willing for God to use him.

You move restlessly on the bench as you tell Master that you want to be used in this manner. Pleased with your response He assures us that all He asks is that we are emptying ourselves and allow Him to flow through us. He adds that we are about to watch Joseph do exactly what we are talking about. This piques our interest as we hear footsteps coming on the stone floor. I whisper to you, "let us revisit the idea of 'empty ourselves' when we are alone with Master again."

It is only moments before Joseph approaches the gate to the cell where the chief butler and chief baker of the king of Egypt (Pharaoh) are being held. Joseph approaches them with joy in the new day set before them. A knowing smile crosses our faces as Master is pleased. He reminds us that the dungeon is a different place since Joseph (the open vessel) is here.

He informs us that these two men are in prison because they offended the king of Egypt in some manner. He adds that, it is not hard to do. Sometimes the offense is merely a whim or a show of authority on the part of the king. After all, the Pharaoh (king) is believed to be a god.

You ask Master what the role of the butler is, and He is happy to share with us that literally he is the cupbearer or drink giver. He adds that this trusted servant's entire responsibility is to serve the wine or drink at the kings table. He is a valuable, trusted man whom the king depends on to be certain that the drink is not poisoned or tampered with in any manner.

You interject that obviously; something has gone wrong.

To help us relate Master reminds us that in our day we will set up agencies to perform this same act on our behalf. At that, you and I look to each other in acknowledgment of the wisdom of the butler cupbearer. Master adds to our understanding that butlers will be used by nearly every ruler throughout history. Continuing, He informs us that it is also required for the butler to taste the food before the ruler does in order to be certain of quality and security. The butler enjoys the esteem and confidence of his ruler and he is present at every event, always ready to care for any need that may arise.

I ask, "What is the role of the baker?" Master, knowing that would be our next question, is ready with an answer. He instructs us that there are several classes of bakers, from public bakers to the royal baker. This man is a royal baker.

He tells us of the king's ovens which are large stone jars made of clay standing about three feet high, with removable lids. The jar is heated with wood, grasses or dung and the bread dough flattened and placed on the outside of the jar to cook.

This chief baker is responsible for the quality of the breads as well as its presentation to the king.

We are not told how these two men offended the king even though we would like to know. Master encourages that the greater lesson is for us to see how God is moving in Joseph's life in this circumstance. He adds that the fact that both these men are in prison currently and Joseph is their keeper is not an accident.

God is in this!

DREAMS

Genesis 40:5-19

5. Then the butler and the baker of the king of Egypt, who were confined in the prison, had a dream, both of them, each man's dream in one night and each man's dream with its own interpretation.

6. And Joseph came in to them in the morning and looked at them, and saw that they were sad.

7. So he asked Pharaoh's officers who were with him in the custody of his lord's house, saying, "Why do you look so sad today?"

8. And they said to him, "We each have had a dream, and there is no interpreter of it." So Joseph said to them, "Do not interpretations belong to God? Tell them to me, please."

9. Then the chief butler told his dream to Joseph, and said to him, "Behold, in my dream a vine was before me,

10. "and in the vine were three branches; it was as though it budded, its blossoms shot forth, and its clusters brought forth ripe grapes.

11. Then Pharaoh's cup was in my hand; and I took the grapes and pressed them into Pharaoh's cup, and placed the cup in Pharaoh's hand."

12. And Joseph said to him, "This is the interpretation of it; The three branches are three days.

13. "Now within three days Pharaoh will lift up your head and restore you to your place, and you will put Pharaoh's cup in his hand according to the former manner, when you were his but-

ler.

14. "But remember me when it is well with you, and please show kindness to me; make mention of me to Pharaoh, and get me out of this house.

15. "For indeed I was stolen away from the land of the Hebrews; and also I have done nothing here that they should put me into the dungeon."

16. When the chief baker saw that the interpretation was good, he said to Joseph, "I also was in my dream, and there were three white baskets on my head.

17. "In the uppermost basket were all kinds of baked goods for Pharaoh, and the birds ate them out of the basket on my head."

18. So Joseph answered and said, "This is the interpretation of it: The three baskets are three days.

19. "Within three days Pharaoh will lift off your head from you and hang you on a tree; and the birds will eat your flesh from you."

We are standing outside the prison cell where the chief butler and the chief baker are held. Master points out that in one night both these men have dreams that have them visibly upset. Joseph has arrived to check on them and go through their morning routine. Noticing that they are not their normal selves, Joseph inquires to their well being. We remember that Joseph is responsible for every aspect of the prisoner's lives, including their mental state.

Master encourages to us to listen as Joseph gives God the glory for the interpretation of the dreams. As He recites **verse 8** again to us, He emphasizes the words **"Do not interpretations belong to God?"** We smile at the realization of this insight and nod in agreement. Then He continues by explaining that in the Old Testament God talks with people in dreams. You ask if the reason for the change in communication is because the Spirit of God is more active in the New Testament. He is pleased at your understanding but reminds us that the role of the Spirit of God changes after the death of Jesus. He reminds us that we will encounter King Nebuchadnezzar in the book of Daniel, he will have a dream that the godly man Daniel will interpret. That dream will have a huge prophecy impact on mankind. Daniel will also give all the glory to God for the interpretation.

Our minds are drawn back to this prison cell as we listen with great curiosity as each of these men relay their dreams to Joseph. Both of them are seeking answers to their meaning. You ask if Joseph had told them of his dreams because we wonder why they offer their own, or are they just making conversation. I wonder if Joseph also shared with these men that he had seen Yahweh in a dream. We hear him tell them that God interprets dreams when he suggests they share their dreams with him. Master assures us that they are asking Joseph to help them understand their dreams.

I cannot help but wonder what they thought of Joseph's dreams.

Or did they even care to hear?

With genuine concern Joseph listens to them. The chief butler goes first telling Joseph that he saw a vine with three branches. The vine was in the budding stage and he witnessed the blossoms open into clusters of ripe grapes. He shares that Pharaoh's cup was in his hand and he crushed the grapes with his hand, dripping the juice into Pharaoh's cup. He then placed the cup in Pharaoh's hand.

After only moments of thought, Joseph offers an interpretation. He starts with the vine and branches and says that the three branches are three days. He says that within the next three days Pharaoh will restore the chief butler to his place in the palace. He adds that life for the butler will return to his normal routine.

The butler has an obvious look of relief as Joseph pleads with him to remember who told him the meaning of his dream. He asks the butler to make mention of him to Pharaoh and help

Joseph get out of this prison. Pleading his case, he adds again his story of being sold and taken to a foreign land. Including that he is innocent of all charges!

The chief baker is almost unable to stand still waiting his turn for interpretation of his dream. He does not quite wait for Joseph to finish telling his story when he begins with the fact that his dream was about three white baskets on his head. He shares that the top basket held baked goods for Pharaoh and that birds ate of the breads. Joseph offers the interpretation quickly this time and directly. He tells the baker that within the next three days Pharaoh is going to behead him and hang him in a tree. Then, almost without emotion, he says he will be left there for the birds to eat his flesh. At that the baker drops his hands to his sides in silence, a definite look of shock on his face.

An audible gasp escapes both of us as we hear this. I whisper that I am shocked at Joseph's matter–of–fact interpretation. No sugar coating, no compassion, just the interpretation. We turn to Master and ask him why this is in our scripture? Horrified, is a calm way of stating how we are feeling. Master continues to remind us that God is at work and we must be patient.

Master walks beside us on our way back to our camp after the interpretations of the men's dreams. We walk mostly in silence with our minds full of questions that cannot be voiced. He knows our turmoil and yet He allows us to think on these things. He desires that we blindly trust Him and His ways, but it is hard when we cannot see the purpose in things.

When we arrive at our camp, we silently hug Master. Then finding the security of our sleeping mats, we retire for the night.

JOSEPH FORGOTTEN
IN PRISON

Genesis 40:20-23

20. Now it came to pass on the third day, which was Pharaoh's birthday that he made a feast for all his servants; and he lifted up the head of the chief butler and of the chief baker among his servants.

21. Then he restored the chief butler to his butlership again, and he placed the cup in Pharaoh's hand.

22. But he hanged the chief baker, as Joseph had interpreted to them.

23. Yet the chief butler did not remember Joseph, but forgot him.

During the following days we spend time with Master trying to understand the events we are witnessing, and He is gracious to hear but continues to encourage our patience.

I am puzzled at my own thoughts and why I have narrowed my thoughts so. He shares with me that I know Yahweh is with Joseph, and the butler seems to have not been affected by the events, so I choose to trust my Master, for now. Then He adds, that sometimes, the believer who appears to be fine is not. He asks me to remember that Joseph pled with the butler. Joseph has been alone since he left his father to find his brothers. In his present circumstance he cannot feel secure. Master urges me to pray for a believer in such circumstances, that they will be 'remembered'. Then He adds that Yahweh has great plans for Joseph that cannot be carried out from this dungeon.

He gives us a peek into the third day of these dreams. Pharaoh will be celebrating his birthday with a party and he is inviting all his servants and as the custom goes, he will have opportunity to grant pardon to any prisoner he wishes.

We know already the outcome of this party and are torn between joy for the cup bearer and our heavy hearts as we consider the baker hearing of the party. Knowing of this future even causes us to focus on the coming day's events and we have little communication with Master apart from this issue.

The third day arrives and Master shares with us that the butler has been released from the dungeon and returned to his regular duties. He knows our question but waits for us to ask, and for the Spirit of God to whisper in our hearts. He inquires if we are more anxious to hear about the baker being beheaded and hanged or anxious to hear if the butler spoke to Pharaoh about Joseph. Ashamed, I admit that I had forgotten about Joseph's plea to the butler. I even forgot to praise Yahweh for His work in Joseph's life. I look at you and wonder if you are experiencing the same thing. We have gone about the last three days keeping ourselves busy and trying not to think of the beheading and hanging. We have talked of the dreams but not of Joseph. Honestly, we have not talked of Joseph's life in Yahweh's care at all. Master knows the thoughts going on in my heart, and the words the Spirit of God has spoken to me. He reaches for my hand and as he holds it, He rubs the top of my fingers. He tells me that the baker has been beheaded and is hanging in the tree. I look at Him surprised that He would think I want to hear this but then He adds that Yahweh has given an exact interpretation of the dream and it is important that I see that. Then He adds that the butler, to this moment, has not mentioned Joseph to Pharaoh.

I express that I feel deeply sorry for Joseph as the butler has not done as Joseph pled with him to do. I am sure Joseph is discouraged. Master replies that Yahweh has more plans for Joseph and keeping him in prison until the right time is a safe place for him, even though it is uncomfortable. Master points out again the character Joseph is displaying as he is faithful in every relationship of his life.

He was faithful to Potiphar

He is faithful to the keeper of the prison.

He is faithful to God, always giving Him the glory.

Soon we will see him being faithful to Pharaoh

He will be faithful to his own brothers.

You ask what it means to be 'faithful.' "We see Joseph's actions, but in our lives what does faithful mean?" Master explains that there is a difference in being faithful to Him and being faithful to those around us. There are those our LORD desires our lives to bless and we know that if we are not faithful to Him this cannot happen. Then He adds that 'dependable' is a good description of faithful. Looking at both of us He asks if others can depend on us to stand with them. Can they depend on us to pray when they ask us to, or come when they need us? Maybe just to hear them when they need to speak, or silently sit with them when life is overwhelming. He asks if we have someone human, we can <u>always</u> depend on.

Wow!

Then He asks if our faith in our LORD causes us to be 'kind,' even in trials?

Joseph is kind even to the captors in Potipher's prison. We look forward to seeing Joseph's kindness to his brothers. Still looking at us He asks if we are kind without considering our own circumstances.

Wow!

We have witnessed Joseph being 'humble' in every circumstance. Master reminds us of when he approached his brothers in the plain of Dothan, where they were shepherding their flocks. He approached them in humility, not concerned of what they might do to him. In the home of Potiphar, he has been a faithful servant. In every circumstance Joseph has given God all the glory for everything. This time Master does not say anything but looks at us and we know what He is asking.

Wow!

You and I look at each other with guilt in our hearts and yet, in Master's eyes there is no condemnation. He assures us that no matter our circumstances, we can always have faith that God is working in our lives. He is refining, purifying, growing, correcting, nurturing. He is drawing us closer to Him. Then He adds that it is <u>always</u> for our good.

With tears in my eyes, I acknowledge that I forgot to praise Yahweh for Joseph. I hear my own words repeat, **"Yet the chief butler did not remember Joseph, but forgot him."** I look at you remembering what Master has just said and yet desiring that things were different for Joseph. Master seeing my miss-understanding takes us to **Isaiah 49:15 "Can a woman forget her nursing child, And not have compassion on the son of her womb? Surely they may forget, yet I will not forget you.** At these words, my tear-filled eyes empty themselves down my cheeks. Feeling as though I did not hear anything Master just shared with us, I know I already took my eyes off my LORD and placed them on the circumstances before me. Master, "Please help my unbelief. My desire is to be faithful to you even when I struggle being faithful to all else." He touches my cheek, wiping away my tears; gently he holds my tears in His able hand and covers them with His other hand.

And I understand.

PHARAOH'S DREAMS

Genesis 41:1-13

1. Then it came to pass, at the end of two full years, that Pharaoh had a dream; and behold, he stood by the river.

2. Suddenly there came up out of the river seven cows, fine looking and fat; and they fed in the meadow.

3. Then behold, seven other cows came up after them out of the river, ugly and gaunt, and stood by the other cows on the bank of the river.

4. And the ugly and gaunt cows ate up the seven fine looking and fat cows. So Pharaoh awoke.

5. He slept and dreamed a second time; and suddenly seven heads of grain came up on one stalk, plump and good.

6. Then behold, seven thin heads, blighted by the east wind, sprang up after them.

7. And the seven thin heads devoured the seven plump and full heads. So Pharaoh awoke, and indeed, it was a dream.

8. Now it came to pass in the morning that his spirit was troubled, and he sent and called for the magicians of Egypt and all its wise men. And Pharaoh told them his dreams, but there was no one who could interpret them for Pharaoh.

9. Then the chief butler spoke to Pharaoh, saying; "I remember my faults this day.

10. "When Pharaoh was angry with his servants, and put me in custody in the house of the captain of the guard, both me and the chief baker,

11. "we each had a dream in one night, he and I. Each of us

dreamed according to the interpretation of his own dream.

12. "Now there was a young Hebrew man with us there, a servant of the captain of the guard. And we told him, and he interpreted our dreams for us; to each man he interpreted according to his own dream.

13. "And it came to pass, just as he interpreted for us, so it happened. He restored me to my office, and he hanged him."

It has been two years since Joseph requested that the butler not forget him. Master has, in this time, introduced us to the wonders of Egypt that we feared we would never see. The Nile River winds its way through the entire area. Some manmade waterways direct the river through the palace and the living areas of the people. Master teaches us that this river runs approximately four thousand miles through this land. He explains that we are in the area of Egypt that is rich with good soil, but to the south is a far different land of sand and famine.

He teaches us of many gods that the people worship. They have become carved idols from every medium possible. We see evidence of that everywhere. We see the idols of Osiris and Isis who later will be well known for their influence on Greece and Rome. There is Ra (Re) a sun god. Horis is another sun god who is believed to be the son of Osiris and Isis. The god 'Set' is the rival of Osiris and Isis and Horis. The last one He taught us of is Amon-Re who will later become the god of Memphis and Ptah. He tells us we will learn more of Amon-Re later, the god of craftsman and creativity. There are many more gods, more than we care to pursue. Divination is used on every corner it seems, with all sorts of mysterious acts. It makes me uncomfortable when we pass by them. We camp outside the city as the noise of festivities is constant, interspersed with the cries of hard task masters over their slaves.

The Egyptian people have a class of servants called the priesthood with specific rights. They are involved primarily with embalming and preparations for moving from this life to the next. He instructs that these 'priests'; are called magicians and practice in natural and miraculous phenomena, meaning mostly witchcraft.

Master reminds us that most of the people of Egypt are descendants of Ham, Noah's son. However, there is a huge variety of nationalities here and every tongue is spoken. We hear a new language almost every day.

Exciting!

Master shows us vast herds of cattle and fields of grain. There are horses, llamas, and oxen. All types of domesticated animals as well as wild tigers, lions, monkeys, and on and on. The animals fascinate me, and I love the time we get to spend watching them.

The Egyptians are the first to shave "creatively" you suggest. They not only shave their faces but their heads and some shave their entire bodies. There are many taxes on the people which change with the attitude of the tax collector or the taxpayer, or some form of agreement. Gold is abundant! The sun daily enjoys dancing off the sides of buildings, chariots, and the jewelry of individuals themselves. The people of this land are masters at working with metal and everywhere is a display of gold and silver, all sorts of metal and precious stonework. The food is abundant, and everyone is satisfied. One day you and I try to think of a food we know of that is not found here in some form, there is none. We see markets overflowing with fish, cucumbers, leeks, onions, garlic to name only a few.

One day, Master took us to see far reaching fields for brick making. The bricks made are transported far distances, but most of them go to the building of this area and the pyramids of the gods. It seems that every person of influence must build something to leave here when they die.

There are magnificent animals like we never imagined. The horses are bigger and more muscular than the ones we know. Lions walk leisurely through the palaces, tethered only by a chain held by a servant. They are also in the wild, but we did not see them. We see all manner of animal life seemingly unthreatened by the men living among them. Snakes are exceptionally large and threatening, they are worshiped as well as used to control unsuspecting people.

This truly is an amazing place, yet, the people do not know our God. Their possessions are many and their life abundant, yet they do not have the security of our God and the eternity He offers. It feels like their desire is to ignore the fact that the God of Abraham, Isaac, and Jacob exists.

On this day you and I arise to find Master sitting on a large rock we have moved close to our dwelling. We use this rock for everything from drying our cloths to cooking bread when the day is extremely hot, and to sit when it is not. He has prepared our morning meal from the abundance of Egypt and we thrill at the sight. You ask Him if we are going to see more of Egypt today and we are pleased when He tells us we are going to return to our scriptures. In fact, today we are going to Pharaoh's court which we have not seen inside before. We are excited as we eat our meal, wash in the stream by our dwelling, and dress appropriately for the day. I laugh as I mention that we are acting like Pharaoh will know we are there. You reply that we will know.

As we walk toward the palace, we inquire of Joseph and if we might see him. Master informs us that we will, and it will be thrilling to watch. He says that Pharaoh has had two dreams and we are going to witness as God uses Joseph to interpret them for him.

Listening to Master recite the scriptures for us we are fascinated by Pharaoh's dreams. You mention that it makes no sense to you that there is meaning in these dreams. Master assures us that there is meaning that is important to the Gentile people and He reminds us of **Romans 5:3 And not only that, but we also glory in tribulation, knowing that tribulation produces perseverance; and perseverance, character; and char-**

acter, hope. And He adds that Joseph is maturing well. These dreams, while a guide for the men of Egypt, are more meaningful for the trust Joseph is gaining in Yahweh.

Apparently, Pharaoh had a dream some time ago that still bothers him. He has no one to tell him the meaning. This has him irritated especially since his magicians and wise men cannot help. They are usually his 'go to' people when he has something troubling him. You ask about who these magicians are, and Master explains that they are a group of priests who 'understand and can interpret sacred writings.' To do this they use knowledge of art and sciences as well as divination and sorcery. When magicians could not interpret Pharaoh's dreams, he called for his wise men who also could not interpret them. Master reminds us that King Nebuchadnezzar will also call for magicians to interpret his dreams before he asks Daniel to help him in **Daniel 2:2 Then the king gave the command to call the magicians, the astrologers, the sorcerers, and the Chaldeans to tell the king his dreams. So they came and stood before the king**.

Soon we are entering Pharaoh's court. The marble walls are adorned with gold figures that glisten in the sun streaming through small slits that act as windows. The hallways are flanked by huge statues of strange man like figures with heads of animals of different types. We remember Master's explanation of the gods of Egypt and assume these are tributes to those gods. You lean close to me and whisper, "creepy". We enter the grand hall and find ourselves a place to observe on one side. This is a space for those who are coming to talk with Pharaoh.

The chief butler is near when he remembers Joseph and his interpretation, when he himself had a dream. We listen as the chief butler tells Pharaoh his own experience with Joseph and suggests that Joseph may be able to interpret the dreams.

THE BUTLER REMEMBERS

Genesis 41:14-32

14. Then Pharaoh sent and called Joseph, and they brought him quickly out of the dungeon; and he shaved, changed his clothing, and came to Pharaoh.

15. And Pharaoh said to Joseph, "I have had a dream, and there is no one who can interpret it. But I have heard it said of you that you can understand a dream, to interpret it."

16. So Joseph answered Pharaoh, saying, "It is not in me; God will give Pharaoh an answer of peace."

17. Then Pharaoh said to Joseph: "Behold, in my dream I stood on the bank of the river.

18. "Suddenly seven cows came up out of the river, fine looking and fat; and they fed in the meadow.

19. "Then behold, seven other cows came up after them, poor and very ugly and gaunt, such ugliness as I have never seen in all the land of Egypt.

20. "And the gaunt and ugly cows ate up the first seven, the fat cows.

21. "When they had eaten them up, no one would have known that they had eaten them, for many were just as ugly as at the beginning. So I awoke.

22. "Also I saw in my dream, and suddenly seven heads came up on one stalk, full and good.

23. "Then behold, seven heads, withered, thin, and blighted by

the east wind, sprang up after them.

24. "And the thin heads devoured the seven good heads. So I told this to the magicians, but there was no one who could explain it to me.

25. Then Joseph said to Pharaoh, "The dreams of Pharaoh are one: God has shown Pharaoh what He is about to do:

26. The seven good cows are seven years, and the seven good heads are seven years; the dreams are one.

27, "And the seven thin and ugly cows which came up after them are seven years, and the seven empty heads blighted by the east wind are seven years of famine.

28. "This is the thing which I have spoken to Pharaoh. God has shown Pharaoh what He is about to do.

29. "Indeed seven years of great plenty will come throughout all the land of Egypt;

30. "but after the seven years of famine will arise, and all the plenty will be forgotten in the land of Egypt; and the famine will deplete the land.

31. "So the plenty will not be known in the land because of the famine following, for it will be very severe.

32. "And the dream was repeated to Pharaoh twice because the thing is established by God, and God will shortly bring it to pass.

We are observing from the sideline of this awe-inspiring hall of Pharaoh's throne room. At the suggestion from the butler. Pharaoh decides that since he has no one else to help he will call Joseph from the dungeon to test if he can interpret his dreams. I assume he considers that, if Joseph cannot do this, he will be great sport and entertainment for the day.

Only one man moves in the entire room as he runs to retrieve Joseph. The guards beside us are motionless, looking only at the throne where Pharaoh is seated. You notice that just a few men away from us is one man, who is less than motionless as he is desperately trying not to sneeze. You find it comical until the huge doors open to allow Joseph to enter. At his entering, there is enough of a commotion for the guard to rub his nose to stop his sneeze. At that, you and I enjoy the amusement of the moment.

You mention that Joseph looks good; healthy, clean shaven and dressed like an Egyptian. I agree, yet I am anxious to see him walk past us to see him closer. I suggest that he must be hopeful.

Joseph is prepared to be presented before Pharaoh. Master mentions to us that it is a big deal for Joseph to shave himself. You mention that we have not seen a Hebrew man shaven before and wonder if this is a problem for Joseph. We agree Joseph knows that this is a critical moment in his life. Master continues to explain that Egyptians are well known for their careful attention to personal cleanliness. In fact, they only allow a beard and hair to grow as a sign of mourning, which is the reverse of the custom of the Hebrew people. Master tells us that it is possible that Joseph has been kept shaven because cleanliness is so important in the Egyptian world. This is the least of Joseph's worries, so it is probably not a problem. Master also informs us that it is required to be clean shaven before approaching Pharaoh. Then Master adds that archeology will find that while pictures in hieroglyphics will show the Egyptian men with beards, we should know that most of these beards are not real but only attached for special occasions.

Interesting!

As Joseph enters the hall he is walking confidently and prepared for whatever is coming. We are reminded that "**whatever he did, the LORD made it prosper.**" Master repeats to us **verse 15** of this chapter being certain that we see that Joseph again gives God the glory for the interpretation of the dream. You ask, "Why does Joseph call the interpretation, an answer of <u>peace</u>?" In answer to your question Master takes us ahead in time to the days of Daniel when he is in the service of Nebuchadnezzar in **Daniel 2:28-29 "But there is a God in heaven who reveals secrets, and He has made known to King Nebuchadnezzar what will be in the latter days. Your dream, and the visions of your head upon your bed, were these: "As for you, O King, thoughts came to your mind while on the bed about what would come to pass after this; and He who reveals secrets has made known to you what will be.**

We are wondering what relationship this event has to do with your question about God's answer being one of peace. He knows our thoughts and reminds us that Pharaoh has been very agitated about these dreams and Joseph is telling him that knowing the answer from God will bring him peace. Still looking at Him, he knows we do not understand so He steps in front of us to get our full attention from distractions, and assures us that just having an answer, good or bad will calm his irritation of not knowing. "Oh, okay," you respond as we return our attention to the grand display before us. Pharaoh begins to speak, and you and I glance at each other with a shrug of our shoulders acknowledging that we were distracted.

Joseph begins by telling Pharaoh that both dreams have the same interpretation. Then he tells Pharaoh that the fact that it is repeated is of value, as that increases the importance of the events about to take place. I whisper, "The law of re-occurrence." You smile at me and nod agreement. Joseph assures Pharaoh that the dreams are a foretelling of what the God is about to do.

This has Pharaoh's attention as he leans forward on his throne laying his forearm across his knee to listen closely. He waves his hand toward the scribe sitting beside him to be sure that every word is being recorded. He even signals Joseph to step a little closer.

Joseph begins by stating that:

1. The seven good cows are seven good years.

The seven good heads of grain are seven good years.

2. The seven thin and ill-favored cows are also seven years.

The seven empty stalks of grain blasted with the east wind are seven years of famine.

Pharaoh is still leaning forward, waiting for more explanation, as Joseph offers that the next seven years will be plentiful for all the land of Egypt. Following the years of plenty will be seven years of famine which will consume the land. He adds that the famine will be so great that the people will forget the days of plenty and the conditions in of all of Egypt will be "severe." Master points out that the severity of this famine is described in **verse 19** as **"...poor and very ugly and gaunt, such ugliness as I have never seen in all the land of Egypt."**

Joseph draws back a step. We assume he is not certain how Pharaoh is receiving this interpretation. Joseph then adds that the dream is repeated in slightly different ways to help us understand that this event is appointed by God, and it will surely come to pass.

Master draws our attention and suggests we notice the graciousness of Yahweh as He grants seven years of plenty before the judgment. You ask if this is like the one hundred and twenty years before the flood when the people had time to repent. He assures us that it is just like that. Then He includes again that His desire is that none perish.

He surprises us as He assures us that our lives are not guaranteed a tomorrow and we do not know what type of day each will be. We must learn to rely on His word, seek to understand what it is telling us and heed His guidance. Then we must learn to save up for the hard times from the abundance of today. I ask if He is referring to storing up His word, food, relationships, memories, or money. Smiling at our attempt to be precise we understand He means all types of blessings, as we can rely on all these for strength in times of famine.

I look around this huge, gorgeous hall with its display of all the finest of everything Egypt has to offer. The Spirit of God whispers in my soul that all this can be gone in a moment. Then he reminds me of that one moment Joseph was approaching his brothers, wearing his beautiful coat, eager to tell them of the welfare of their father. The next moment he is stripped of his coat, rejected by his brothers and in a dry, lifeless pit alone.

I get it!

You reach over and touch my arm, pointing to a cheetah that is reclining in a small wooden cage toward the back of the hall. It is near the large doors Joseph came through only minutes before. You whisper that she is steadfastly looking at our Master. I ask if you think she knows who He is. You add that she has not taken her eyes off Him since the servants brought her in. I will surely ask Master about her later!

Yet another distraction.

JOSEPH'S ADVISE

Genesis 41:33-

33. "Now therefore, let Pharaoh select a discerning and wise man, and set him over the land of Egypt.

34 "Let Pharaoh do this, and let him appoint officers over the land, to collect one-fifth of the produce of the land of Egypt in the seven plentiful years.

35. "And let them gather all the food of those good years that are coming, and store up grain under the authority of Pharaoh, and let them keep food in the cities.

36. "Then that food shall be as a reserve for the land for the seven years of famine which shall be in the land of Egypt, that the land may not perish during the famine."

We are still in the throne room of the Pharaoh of Egypt where Joseph has interpreted two dreams that have been bothering the Pharaoh. Joseph not only came to Pharaoh with an interpretation from God, he came with advice on how to handle the interpretation. Joseph continues speaking to Pharaoh telling him that he needs to appoint a wise man over the land of Egypt to collect a portion of each crop to set aside for the years of famine. Joseph specifies one-fifth of the produce of the land to be set aside for the famine years.

We are learning that in scripture, when exact numbers, measurements and names are given, we need to slow down and seek understanding. The measure of one-fifth catches our attention and we look at Master for explanation. He shares that during the years of plenty there will be an excess in the people's crops, beyond what they can use. Joseph is suggesting that Pharaoh collect or purchase from the people these surpluses for the Pharaoh's grain houses. These will be stored for use during the time of famine. Before we can ask, Master instructs us that bible scholars will not agree whether this grain will be purchased or taken as a tax on the people. It is not uncommon for the government to seize portions of whatever they want from the people, but the words used in these verses indicate that this is an agreeable transaction as opposed to a forced one.

Pharaoh is pleased with Joseph's suggestion, nods his head, and waves his hand again to the scribe to be certain this is all being recorded word for word.

There is silence in the room as we wait for Pharaoh as he sits thinking on what he will do concerning the interpretation of his dreams and the suggested action. As we are waiting, I cannot contain myself and I ask Master if He has noticed the cheetah, who has yet to take her eyes off Him. She is now relaxed and resting her chin on her feet in front of her, but her eyes have not moved. He smiles at her than at me and expresses that she is magnificent! Then surprising me, He adds that she knows Him. "What?" I reply. Master winks at me and whispers for me to wait, sharing that He has something beyond amazing for us later today. Then He adds that a domesticated wild animal is common in a ruler's court as a symbol of power and a threat to any who might think to not comply with commands from the throne.

Whoa!

"Such a Man"

Genesis 41:38-44

38. And Pharaoh said to his servants, "Can we find such a one as this, a man in whom is the Spirit of God?"

39. Then Pharaoh said to Joseph, "Inasmuch as God has shown you all this, there is no one discerning and wise as you.

40. "You shall be over my house, and all my people shall be ruled according to your word; only in regard to the throne will I be greater than you."

41. And Pharaoh said to Joseph, "See, I have set you over all the land of Egypt."

42. Then Pharaoh took his signet ring off his hand and put it on Joseph's hand; and he clothed him in garments of fine linen and put a gold chain around his neck.

43. And he had him ride in the second chariot which he had; and they cried out before him, "Bow the knee!" So he set him over all the land of Egypt.

44. Pharaoh also said to Joseph, "I am Pharaoh, and without your consent no man may lift his hand or foot in all the land of Egypt."

Still we stand in the throne room of Pharaoh. You and I are in awe of the way God is moving Pharaoh through the words of Joseph. With anticipation, we listen as Pharaoh asks his servants if they know of a man who can take the responsibility of storing and the distributing food for the entire land. None of them speaks, which does not surprise us. However, we are surprised when Pharaoh adds that he is looking for a man **"In whom is the Spirit of God."** Without looking your way, I nod as I wonder if Pharaoh's heart is softening toward Yahweh.

Pharaoh does not stop there but speaks directly to Joseph and declares him the most discerning and wise man in the land. You ask me if he has forgotten Joseph is a Hebrew and has just this day come from the dungeon. I hear you but do not turn to agree but continue to watch this unfold.

We both startle as all the soldiers and servants in the hall come to attention. Pharaoh raises his scepter to declare his wishes. The sound reminds me of the stomp from heaven that we hear when God speaks to one of His own. The soldiers beside us have, in one unified stomp, tapped the butt of their spears on the marble floor. Those without spears stomped their foot. You and I take a sidestep closer to Master, as this display feels somewhat threatening. We have no desire to fall to our knees, no desire to worship. This feels very strange and somewhat 'wrong' to us. I glance over and the lioness has risen to her feet, keeping her eyes on our Master.

In our witness Pharaoh declares to Joseph that:

1. He is to have unquestionable rule over Pharaoh's house.

2. Joseph's word is Pharaoh's word.

3. Joseph has authority not only Pharaoh's house but all the land of Egypt.

Pharaoh reserved for himself ultimate control by stating that Joseph is to be <u>second</u> in command under him.

You and I are now holding hands. Pharaoh seals this legal declaration by removing his signet ring from his own hand and orders Joseph to approach him. As all present watch he places the ring on Joseph's middle finger. As quickly as the ring is on his hand, servants' approach with new Egyptian garments to place on Joseph. This new garment is white, made of fine linen not at all like the ones he arrived in. One servant steps in front of Joseph and without a word places a thick heavy gold 'chain' around his neck. All of this is happening so quickly, and our minds are racing with questions to be asked later.

Ask.com Ancient Egyptian neck chain

As Pharaoh rises from his throne, there is some commotion in the room as all prepare to exit the room to go to the chariot prepared for Joseph. The chariot is outside the front of the palace, at the foot of the stairs just behind Pharaoh's own chariot. We exit behind the last of the soldiers and with one last look at the cheetah on our way, we notice her still staring at Master. I touch the sleeve of His garment to get His attention.

She has lowered her front legs to the floor leaving her back legs in a standing position. Her head is down on her front feet as if she is stretching. Her eyes close and I ask Master what she is doing. He stops before her, bends down to touch her head as He replies that she is worshiping. Tears fill my eyes as I have never seen anything like this. You ask how He knew, and He replies that He knows her.

Making a comparison Master tells us that Pharaoh believes he is the master of this cheetah but in truth, she bows to her creator.

Master,

You are amazing!

We watch as Joseph's chariot pulls away from the palace behind Pharaoh's. Before them, servants are running, yelling "Bow the knee!" In response, everyone within hearing distance bows obediently as Pharaoh and Joseph ride by. Our scripture tells us that Pharaoh has declared to Joseph that, without Joseph's consent, no man will do anything in the land.

We are left on the marble steps outside the palace as Joseph rides away into his new position in Egypt. Master invites us to sit with Him on a raised area to the side of the steps where we can talk of what we have witnessed.

The first thing He mentions is that it is not a common thing, but there are times when servants are promoted to positions of importance. In explanation, He reminds us that there is such importance placed on dreams that someone who can interpret them is of great value. You suggest that this is a great way for God to use man's dreams. Master nods in agreement.

We remember the signet cylinder that Jacob unknowingly gave his daughter-in-law Tamar in **Genesis 38:18 Then he said, "What pledge shall I give you?" So she said, "Your signet and cord, and your staff that is in your hand." Then he gave them to her, and went in to her, and she conceived by him.** Master reminds us that we know this was a cylinder because he also gave her the cord it was attached to. In Joseph's case it is a ring that Pharaoh gave him. Both items are used for identification. The stamp from these is legal in any court.

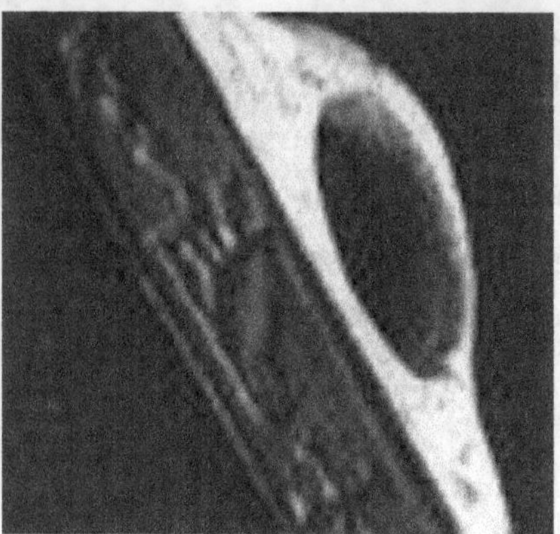

Ask.com. Ancient Egyptian Signet Ring

I wonder out loud what authority this ring gives Joseph, Master replies that he is like a prime minister of our day. This position places him as chief justice of the Egyptian courts, as well as controller of the reservoirs and food supplies. He will supervise industries and conservation programs and maintain a census of the cattle and herds. He will keep agricultural statistics including tax records and receipts. He will also keep the records of the census of the people of Egypt. He will remain in contact with Pharaoh constantly except when he is traveling far distances.

You ask about the chain around Joseph's neck and Master tells us that it is made of gold, heavy, and is the symbol of authority.

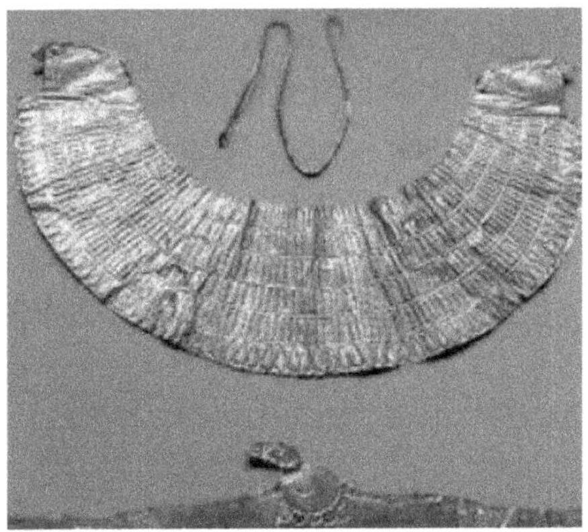

Ask.com Ancient Royal Egyptian Neck Chain

The sun is warm as we sit on the side of the steps outside Pharaoh's palace. I can hardly believe I am here! I remember when I so desired to see this place, and here I am. This place is utterly amazing! We sit for a few minutes taking in the activities around us and the warmth of the sun, then Master asks us if we will walk with Him. Without hesitation, we gather our water skins and we are ready to follow Him wherever He leads.

We next find ourselves in the fields around a huge circular structure where Master tells us all types of activities take place. This is a place of entertainment, judgment, declarations, and sporting events. He tells us that when man is seated on the benches inside you can hear clearly what is being said in the place where the people of importance speak to the people. Master tells us that this fact will baffle men of our day and they will spend a great deal of time studying to understand how this happens. He adds that it is the design of the building that fascinates mankind. However, He does not take us inside, but to the fields behind. There are tents scattered throughout the area and fenced areas where a huge variety of animals are cared for. So many men moving about doing what they do in connection with this place! Walking between the pens of animals, we are overwhelmed with awe as <u>every</u> animal in every pen acknowledges the presence of their creator. You exclaim the wonder of their reactions. Some bow their heads; others lift their heads to look His way. Most voice gentle sounds in His direction but a large male elephant trumpets his loudest praise, raising his trunk high in worship. The farther we walk among the animals, the more you and I cannot hold in our own praise. Our walking turns to dancing with our arms in the air, shouting that the King, The Creator of Heaven and Earth is present! I am laughing joyfully, totally in awe of my Master; acknowledging that, even though man ignores Him, His creation surely does not!

SEVEN YEARS LATER

Genesis 41:45-57

45. And Pharaoh called Joseph's name Zaphnath-Paaneah. And he gave him as a wife Asenath, the daughter of Poti-Pherah priest of On. So Joseph went out over all the land of Egypt.

46. Joseph was thirty years old when he stood before Pharaoh King of Egypt, and Joseph went out from the presence of Pharaoh, and went throughout all the land of Egypt.

47. Now in the seven plentiful years the ground brought forth abundantly.

48. So he gathered up all the food of the seven years which were in the land of Egypt, and laid up the food in the cities; he laid up in every city the food of the fields which surrounded them.

49. Joseph gathered very much grain, as the sand of the sea, until he stopped counting, for it was immeasurable.

We have found a nice log to sit on as we witness the marriage of Joseph to Asenath, daughter of Poti-pherah, priest of On. It surprises us when Pharaoh first changes Joseph's name to Zaphnath-Paaneah. I look at you and raise my hands palms up, questioning why he is doing this. When you offer no answer, I turn to Master who motions us to observe as He whispers that it is a Hebrew name meaning 'The revealer of secret things. I determine that I will ask this question again later when Master can openly explain.

However, Master does talk with us of Asenath. Her name means; 'belonging to and a worshipper of the god Neith, the Egyptian god of war. You marvel that this pagan princess will soon become the wife of Joseph and be joined forever with the nation of Israel! Then you add' "Not only that, she is joined to its covenant and it's destiny." We watch as the feasting for the marriage begins with more food, dancing, and performers in the area than we have ever seen.

Drawing our attention, Master asks us who the bride of the Messiah is. I respond confidently that it is the church. He continues teaching us that we can compare Asenath with the church as she is far removed from God until she is united with Joseph and the covenant he carries. Again, He asks us who the church is. You suggest it is those who once lived in chaos and darkness apart from God. Joy begins to fill our souls as we realize that through our joining with the Messiah, we are now part of the covenant Jehovah has placed on those who accept the sacrifice of the Redeemer as payment for our sinful lives.

Wow! That is the grace of God!

We are honored to be present when Joseph weds Asenath. Master states again that her father Poti-pherah is a priest near Cairo, Egypt. This is a place that in our day will be called Heliopolis. He adds that the name of this place means 'the city of the sun'. It is located to the south of where we are today and there is a temple to the sun god 'On'. Asenath's father is one of the learned priests who serve there. Taking us forward in time He says that during the time between the Old and New Testaments there will be a Jewish temple built on top of the heathen temple to a lioness-goddess. A Jewish priest will build it for the Jews to be used for worship and sacrifices. He adds that in our day this area will be called El-Matariye. We will be able to journey there and find many archeological diggings and many incredible findings, some from the time of Joseph.

The marriage is grand, and we enjoy ourselves a great deal now that we understand more of Asenath. We talk of how we are sure she does not realize the depth of her new commitment, and how lovely and royal she appears.

You ask if this is going to create problems for Joseph,

bringing evil into his home like this. Master assures us that any time we open our lives to an evil influence we put ourselves, and those we love, in danger. Then He reminds us of our conversations earlier about being married to an unbeliever and the strife that brings to the relationship. In short, this relationship is not going to help Joseph any.

I ask if it is unusual for a Hebrew to marry an Egyptian and Master shares with us that it is not uncommon. While the Hebrew people are sojourning in Egypt, we know that they will intermarry often because we read in **Exodus 12:38 A mixed multitude went up with them also, and flocks and herds – a great deal of livestock.** You ask about when the Children of Israel, while wandering in the wilderness, build a calf to worship. The answer is that certainly the influence will be there. Master also impresses on us that a 'mixed multitude' as spoken of in this verse means a mixed race.

Egyptian weddings are social events with a series of activities: feasting, dancing, and a lot of music. He tells us that Asenath will move into Joseph's home and her chief role will be to provide Joseph a male heir. She will rule the household and especially oversee raising any children they have.

It is not long before the marriage ceremony is ended and Joseph (Zaphnath-Paaneah) settles with Ashnath in their own residence within the palace compound. Their home is elaborate, and we are anxious to walk the halls, feel the walls and floors, and experience their life in Egypt. As we observe these things Master shares with us that Joseph has been in Egypt for thirteen years now, as he is thirty years old. Joseph is spending his time laying up grain in the cities for distribution when the famine arrives.

It is clear to us that, under Joseph's guidance, Egypt will provide abundantly for the entire known world.

Before we leave this chapter of Genesis Master guides us to the scriptures that tell us Joseph is now thirty years old. We know that he has been in Egypt for thirteen years. Two of those years he spent in prison after he interpreted the dreams of the butler and the baker. We are not told how long he had been in the house of Potiphar. You do your math quickly and say that we know he was seventeen when he arrived in Egypt and now, he is thirty. He has been here thirteen years.

JOSEPH'S TWO SONS

Genesis 41:50-57

50. And to Joseph were born two sons before the years of famine came, whom Asenath, the daughter of Poti-Pherah priest of On, bore to him.

51. Joseph called the name of the firstborn Manasseh: "For God has made me forget all my toil and all my father's house."

52. And the name of the second he called Ephraim; "For God has caused me to be fruitful in the land of my affliction."

53. Then the seven years of plenty which were in the land of Egypt ended,

54. And the seven years of famine began to come, as Joseph had said. The famine was in all lands, but in all the land of Egypt there was bread.

55. So when all the land of Egypt was famished, the people cried to Pharaoh for bread. Then Pharaoh said to all the Egyptians, "Go to Joseph; whatever he says to you, do."

56. The famine was over all the face of the earth, and Joseph opened all the storehouses and sold to the Egyptians. And the famine became severe in the land of Egypt.

57. So all countries came to Joseph in Egypt to buy grain, because the famine was severe in all lands.

Some time has passed and Joseph and Asenath are settled. We are walking with Master toward our camp when the wind begins to blow causing the air to become thick with sand. Wrapping our heads with our scarves we walk close beside Him. He continues talking with us, teaching, instructing, sharing; this time is so precious.

You ask Master why Pharaoh is so easily trusting Joseph, a Hebrew. He instructs us again that some through the years will believe that Pharaoh was one of the Hyksos kings. These men are Bedouins from the Arabian Desert. They are a nomadic group that for a time have taken over the throne of Egypt. This makes Joseph, in nationality, closer to Pharaoh than the Egyptian people. These Hyksos kings find it hard to find Egyptians who will be faithful to them. Joseph has surely proven himself faithful. Master adds that later the Hyksos kings will be expelled from Egypt and an Egyptian Pharaoh will take the throne as we read in **Exodus 1:8 Now there arose a new king over Egypt, who did not know Joseph.** Before we leave this idea, I ask Master what Hyksos means. He is pleased that I ask and explains that these are a Western Semitic people who rule an empire consisting of Syria and Palestine. They are called the shepherd kings by the Egyptian people. They invented the horse drawn chariot which enabled them to conquer Egypt. He tells us that later Joseph's family will dwell in Goshen, near the Hyksos capital. Their ethnic heritage will determine that they are a Canaanite, Amorite people.

Holding up your hand you ask us to wait as you question what the word, 'gentile' means. The conversation continues as He explains that the word is used in a variety of ways. It can mean; 'people', 'heathen', 'nation'. Seeing our confusion, He instructs us that generally it means anyone who is not an Israelite. "So, anyone who is not a descendant of Jacob?" you ask. Nodding He agrees that for now this is a clear enough definition.

During the years of plenty Ashnath has given Joseph two sons. Joseph called the first son 'Manasseh'. Master points out that the scripture tells us the meaning of his name, **"For God has made me forget all my toil and all my father's house."** And she also bore for Joseph 'Ephraim' meaning **"For God has caused me to be fruitful in the land of my affliction."**

At this point in scripture this is all we know of these boys, but the names are familiar to us, so I assume we are not finish with their story. You mention that the names of these boys display the heartache in Joseph for his father and brothers. Master nods in agreement and tells us that in years ahead these boys will be publicly adopted into the tribe of Jacob and become heads of two tribes of Israel. **Genesis 48:5-6 And now your two sons, Ephraim and Manasseh, who were born to you in the land of Egypt before I came to you in Egypt, are mine; as Reuben and Simeon, they shall be mine. "Your offspring whom you beget after them shall be yours; they will be called by the name of their brothers in their inheritance."** You ask how this can be as we know there will be only twelve tribes and Joseph already has eleven brothers, then when we include Benjamin and now there are thirteen sons of Jacob (Israel). Master smiles at us through the dust in the air and expresses that the mysteries of studying His word keeps us coming back for more. With that, He promises that when it is time we will understand.

As we near our shelter, Master shares that the seven years of plenty have passed and we are beginning the time of famine. We look at each other shocked at the time He has brought us through, and you comment that it was quite a dust storm.

Master stresses that the famine is great everywhere, but Egypt has bread. Joseph is now thirty-seven years old and He wants us to remember this fact for our next chapter of Genesis. We each make a mental note of Joseph's age as we listen for Master's next instruction.

I ask if Joseph is the only one with grain and bread for all the people. Master suggests that, just like Jesus being the Bread of Life, Joseph is providing the only bread in the known world.

He explains to us that the storage places for the grain are specifically for grain that has already had the chaff removed. The storages vary in size and shape. Some are multi roomed buildings, some are above ground silos, and some are holes in the ground that have stairs carved into the sides for walking down into them. These later storages are often walled with rocks or a type of plaster.

Our scripture tells us that the people are 'famished,' meaning that they are in serious need of food. Pharaoh turns the issue over to Joseph and he opens all the storehouses he had been filling and sells the grain to the people of Egypt. Even with this provision the famine is 'severe'. The severity of the famine is so great that <u>all</u> the people, including other nations, are coming to buy grain from Joseph.

Master takes us back in our scriptures to.

Genesis 27:28 Therefore may God give you

Of the dew of heaven,

Of the fatness of the earth,

And plenty of grain and wine.

We remember that this is part of Isaac's blessing to his son Jacob when Isaac was being deceived. Isaac thought then that he was blessing Esau. Joseph is Jacob's son along with Reuben, Simeon, Levi, Judah, Dan, Nephtali, Gad, (sister Dinah), Asher, Isschar, Zebulun, and Benjamin. Master reminds us that Joseph is a brother of Judah whom He tells us will carry the scarlet thread to the messiah. I ask why the scarlet thread will go through a son of Jacob who is not of Rachel, but I receive no answer at this time. I will remember to ask again.

I bow before my Master and praise Him for this time in the court of Pharaoh. I tell Him I feel honored to be witnessing Joseph prospering in His care. I ask Him to forgive me for the times I complain that His blessings for me are not enough. I often want more than what He sees I need. I ask Him to forgive me for my impatience. I kneel before Him and offer all that I am to serve Him, even to the point that my soul might be 'famished' for the desire for Him to fill me with Himself.

JOSEPH'S BROTHERS

Genesis 42:1-23

1. When Jacob saw that there was grain in Egypt, Jacob said to his sons, "why do you look at one another?"

2. And he said, "Indeed I have heard that there is grain in Egypt; go down to that place and buy for us there, that we may live and not die."

3. So Joseph's ten brothers went down to by grain in Egypt.

4. But Jacob did not send Joseph's brother Benjamin with his brothers, for he said, "Lest some calamity befall him."

5. And the sons of Israel went to buy grain among those who journeyed, for the famine was in the land of Canaan.

6. Now Joseph was governor over the land; and it was he who sold to all the people of the land. And Joseph's brothers came and bowed down before him with their faces to the earth.

7. Joseph saw his brothers and recognized them, but he acted as a stranger to them and spoke roughly to them. Then he said to them, "Where do you come from?" And they said, "From the land of Canaan to buy food."

8. So Joseph recognized his brothers, but they did not recognize him.

9. Then Joseph remembered the dreams which he had dreamed about them, and said to them, "You are spies! You have come to see the nakedness of the land!"

10. And they said to him, "No, my lord, but your servants have come to buy food.

11. "We are all one man's sons; we are honest men; your ser-

vants are not spies."

12. But he said to them, "No, but you have come to see the nakedness of the land."

13. And they said, "Your servants are twelve brothers, the sons of one man in the land of Canaan; and in fact, the youngest is with our father today, and one is no more."

14. But Joseph said to them, "It is as I spoke to you saying, "You are spies."

15. "In this manner you shall be tested: by the life of Pharaoh, you shall not leave this place unless your youngest brother comes here.

16. "Send one of you, and let him bring your brother; and you shall be kept in prison, that your words may be tested to see whether there is any truth in you; or else, by the life of Pharaoh, surely you are spies."

17. So he put them all together in prison three days.

18. Then Joseph said to them the third day, "Do this and live, for I fear God:

19. If you are honest men, let one of your brothers be confined to your prison house; but you, go and carry grain for the famine of your houses.

20. "And bring your youngest brother to me; so your words will be verified, and you shall not die." And they did so.

21. Then they said to one another, "We are truly guilty concerning our brother, for we saw the anguish of his soul when he pleaded with us, and we would not hear; therefore this distress has come upon us."

22. And Reuben answered them, saying, "Did I not speak to you, saying, 'Do not sin against the boy'; and you would not listen? Therefore behold, his blood is now required of us."

23. But they did not know that Joseph understood them, for he spoke to them through an interpreter.

The air is so dry when we awaken that our tongues feel attached to the roof of our mouths. The ground outside our shelter is dust and any grasses left are brown and starved for moisture, as we are. We are pleased that the Pharaoh of Egypt has released the grain for the people and the assurance of Yahweh's provision is evident in the hope of the people we see passing by on their way to the granaries. Master joins us as we watch the people, mostly women with empty vessels going toward the promised grain and ones with full vessels returning. He brings us freshwater skins to nourish our parched throats. After your first swallow you breathe a relieved sigh, "Ah, living water!"

You mention to us that you saw Joseph pass by last evening on his way to the granary and he impressed you that he was so upbeat and optimistically chatting with his companion. I suggest that possibly he has had grain all along since he is the keeper of the grain. But Master corrects me by stating that Joseph trusts Yahweh, he believes what Yahweh has told him. This is where a positive, optimistic attitude comes from. This is joy and peace in the face of trials.

Master shares with us that Jacob has sent his ten sons to Egypt to obtain grain for their families. You ask how Jacob knows of the grain in Egypt and why he believes, when it is nowhere else. Master instructs us that this is faith when we hear something and believe it enough to act on it. Not only in desperation of starvation but in need. He takes us to **Acts 16:30-31 And he brought them out and said, "Sirs, what must I do to be saved?" So they said, "Believe on the Lord Jesus Christ, and you will be saved, you and your household."** At the stating of these verses He challenges us to consider what we 'believe about Him'.

My first response it to say that I believe everything about Him but then stop myself to consider the second part of this definition; 'Believe enough to act upon'. You look at me and our eyes meet considering the 'acting' part of this. I am forced to ponder what I believe about my God that I am presently acting on. Then you question, "What about belief looks like joy and peace and patience in this world of unbelief?"

We both look to our Master and He is watching us reason through these ideas. He knows we struggle with unbelief as all mankind does. He also knows that we desire to trust Him more. You speak for both of us when you ask Him for more of His grace as we purpose to grow our 'action' belief.

Drawing us back to our scripture, Master shows us that Jacob believed what he heard of Egypt having grain and in faith sent ten of his sons to Egypt to save his families lives. You mention that Jacob knows of the dangers in Egypt. You also mention that Jacob holds back his son Benjamin. You point out that the scripture says that Jacob is afraid something might happen to his sons and he cannot deal with losing Benjamin also. Master reminds us that Benjamin is Rachel's son, the only son of Rachel that Jacob has left. You ask if this fear ruins the faith that Jacob is acting on. Master is quick to assure us that faith is a learning and growing thing. We grow in faith as we experience God's faithfulness. Jacob is learning to trust again after losing Joseph years ago.

The excitement is clear as He states for us again **verse 5** of this chapter. **And the sons of Israel went to buy grain among those who journeyed, for the famine was in the land of Canaan.** I notice that Jacob is suddenly called Israel in this verse and I ask why. Thrilled that I noticed, He shares with us that it is important we understand the children of Israel are going to Egypt. You respond with anticipation saying, "Okay?" Without further explanation, Master leads us on with the promise of an exciting revelation coming quickly. He encourages us to be patient.

We are privileged to journey with the sons of Israel and our Master as He points out again for us what Joseph's title is in Egypt, Governor over the land. We are just outside the granary when they arrive with containers ready to be filled. We watch as they get in line with all the others, waiting their turn. The process is well organized and proceeding peacefully under Joseph's direction. When Joseph gazes over the line of people he sees his brothers and the smile of excitement mixed with apprehension shows bold on his face until he remembers his Egyptian position and regains his sober look. You notice he is moving toward them slowly, possibly looking for Benjamin among them. As he passes the people in line, they lower their faces and back away a couple steps in respect of his clothing that sets him apart as an Egyptian of the ruling class. We notice that when these people reach the front of the line they bow before Joseph as a scribe records where the people are from and how many people, they are collecting grain for.

It is not long until the 'sons of Israel' reach the front of the line where Joseph stands, and they also fall on their faces before him. You laugh out loud with joy as we witness Joseph's childhood dream fulfilled right in front of us in this moment. **Genesis 37:7 There we were, binding sheaves in the field. Then behold, my sheaf arose and also stood upright; and indeed your sheaves stood all around and bowed down to my sheaf.** We are surprised that Joseph's brothers do not recognize him, but we remember that this clean shaven, thirty-year-old, confident man of authority standing before then is quite different from the seventeen-year-old they had seen last.

We listen to Joseph speaking to them more roughly than he has spoken to the others who have come through the line. There are questions asked and more apparent suspicion. You suggest that perhaps Joseph wants them a bit uncomfortable. When Joseph accuses them of being spies, we both put our hands over our mouths in shock. This is very confrontational and can mean death to all ten of these men and they know it.

As they bow lower in submission, they plead with Joseph while telling him that they are brothers. Then they add the remaining point of the dream by declaring themselves Joseph's 'servants. You grab my arm as Joseph challenges them, accusing his brothers a second time of being spies and forcing them a second time to declare who they are. This time they admit that, in truth, they are of twelve brothers and they are from Canaan. They add that their youngest brother is at home with their father. You comment that in this Joseph has learned that Benjamin and his father still live and have not moved from Canaan. I suggest that these have probably been burning questions in Joseph's heart for many years. Master points out to us that the scripture also tells us they said, **"…the youngest is this day with our father, and one is not"**. This statement tells us that they believe Joseph is dead.

Joseph accuses them a third time of being spies and follows with stating that he is going to allow them to prove their claims. He is allowing them to present their younger brother as proof of what they say. You remind us that Benjamin is his full brother while these are his half brothers. Joseph wants to see Benjamin.

Curiosity gets the best of you and you ask Master why Joseph is accusing them of being 'spies. He explains to us that the border between Canaan and Egypt is the most vulnerable border in Egypt and the threat of invasion is worsened by the famine. The threat is intensified by the fact that the rest of the world now knows that Egypt has been able to store up grain to sustain life during this time.

We are surprised when Joseph throws them in jail because we would think he would send them immediately to get Benjamin. The fear on their faces is evident as they walk away with guards on either side of them. I ask Master why Joseph is being so harsh, and he encourages me to continue in our scriptures. Yahweh is doing a mighty work in this scene.

I feel frustrated at Joseph's constant testing of his brothers and seek Master's explanation. He assures me again that I must be patient to see Yahweh's plan unfold. He assures me I will understand.

We wait three days at our camp until Master encourages us to come with Him as Joseph is going to the jail to speak with his brothers. We find them in a small mud brick building with a few other men. They are seated on the ground but not chained as they would be in prison. This holding place or jail is not far from the granary and seems to be used as a place to check into those who might be trying to obtain grain untruthfully.

Master guides our understanding as we hear the statement of Joseph as he says to them, **"…This do, and live; for I fear God."** This statement interests us as we wonder if he is trying to give them a clue to who he is. Is he declaring his belief in the God of Abraham, Isaac, and Jacob to comfort his brothers in their fear? Or, is Joseph simply declaring His God as he always gives God the glory in every situation?

Immediately, Joseph proposes a way for them to prove their innocence. They are to leave one of the brothers with Joseph, bound in prison, while the others take grain home and bring back their younger brother when they come to gather the one in prison. Master reminds us that these are grown men with families at home. Some of these men are fifty years old. They remember their father's reaction when they came home without Joseph years ago and they are afraid to come home again without one of the men. But Joseph's motive is to see Benjamin and he will put his brothers through this to make that happen.

Placing His finger on **verse 21** Master points out that Joseph's previous communication with his brothers has been in Egyptian with an interpreter, even though he could understand them. But in this verse the brothers are talking '…**one to another**' in their Hebrew tongue assuming Joseph cannot understand them. The scripture records their confession of guilt concerning their brother Joseph as he stands before them witnessing their confession.

As they continue talking '…**one to another**' Reuben reminds them that he told them not to harm him and they did not listen. I wonder if this pleased Joseph's heart knowing that his oldest brother tried to save him. Master stresses that these men feel that God is taking vengeance on them for the way they treated Joseph.

Turning to face Master, I ask Him if sins from so long ago, even sins that we played along with but did not instigate, are held against us in His eyes. To my surprise and dismay, He replies that they are sins that affect our lives and the lives of those around us so the answer must be that they are to be dealt with before God.

I am in horror as my mind reels with my past. I know there are times I went along with ungodly stuff that I have not addressed with Him. I know I was silent when I should have spoken up. There are sins that were set in motion even though I was not the one who carried them out. A bit fearful I declare, "Oh Master, bring these to my heart so I can present them at your feet. I do not want these things between you and me!" Then remembering the things we have learned in the life of Jacob in this chapter, I ask Him to strengthen my faith as I am fearful of what He might bring to my mind.

He wants me to trust Him to forgive me.

SIMEON LEFT BEHIND

Genesis 42:24-38

24. And he turned himself away from them and wept. Then he returned to them again, and talked with them. And he took Simeon from them and bound him before their eyes.

25. Then Joseph gave a command to fill their sacks with grain, to restore every man's money to his sack, and to give them provisions for the journey. Thus he did for them.

26. So they loaded their donkeys with the grain and departed from there.

27. But as one of them opened his sack to give his donkey feed at the encampment, he saw his money' and there it was, in the mouth of his sack.

28. So he said to his brother, "My money has been restored, and there it is, in my sack!" Then their hearts failed them and they were afraid, saying to one another, "What is this that God has done to us?"

29. Then they went to Jacob their father in the land of Canaan and told him all that had happened to them saying:

30. "The man who is lord of the land spoke roughly to us, and took us for spies of the country.

31. "But we said to him, 'We are honest men; we are not spies.'

32. 'We are twelve brothers, sons of our father; one is no more, and the youngest is with our father this day in the land of Canaan.'

33. "Then the man, the lord of the country, said to us, 'By this I will know that you are honest men: Leave one of your brothers

here with me, take food for the famine of your households, and be gone.

34. And bring your youngest brother to me; so I shall know that you are not spies, but that you are honest men. I will grant your brother to you, and you may trade in the land.'"

35. Then it happened as they emptied their sacks, that surprisingly each man's bundle of money was in his sack; and when they and their father saw the bundles of money they were afraid.

36. And Jacob their father said to them, "You have bereaved me: Joseph is no more, Simeon is no more, and you want to take Benjamin. All these things are against me."

37. Then Reuben spoke to his father saying, "Kill my two sons if I do not bring him back to you; put him in my hands, and I will bring him back to you."

38. But he said, "My son shall not go down with you, for his brother is dead, and he is left alone. If any calamity should befall him along the way in which you go, then you would bring down my gray hair with sorrow to the grave."

We are still in the jail where Joseph has placed his brothers. The floors are hard from long years of use and the air reeks of sweating, dirty prisoners. There are sounds of chains in the shadows, however Joseph's brothers are not chained at this time. We hear whispers of prisoners wondering why the Governor would be here and yet the brothers do not seem to have thought of that.

It appears that, while Joseph stepped away, the brothers agreed that Simeon be the brother to stay in Egypt while the rest deliver the grain and gather Benjamin to bring back to Joseph as ransom for Simeon. I am surprised when Joseph puts chains on Simeon and releases his brothers. I ask Master if the chains are necessary. I guess I am feeling a bit protective of these brothers now in their vulnerable state. He assures me that it is necessary and encourages me to wait on Him again. I also ask if there is a reason they selected Simeon, Jacob's second son by Leah, to stay behind. He leads me to tradition as an explanation. According to Josephus, an ancient historian, Simeon is the most harsh spirited of the brothers. You and I look at each other and wonder what that means while we agree that it is the best explanation we are going to get so; we will leave it at that.

There is a cooling breeze and our feet stir up the dust as we follow the nine brothers being escorted from the jail to the granary. Joseph is already there when they arrive and he has commanded; **"fill their sacks be filled with grain, to restore every man's money to his sack, and to give them provisions for the journey."**

This command is not known by the brothers because they do not question the money or the extra provisions. At the time however, you and I did hear the statement and are left looking at Master as they load their donkey's and ride off toward Canaan. As soon as they are away, you ask Master what Joseph is doing and again He lovingly encourages us to wait on Him. He also encourages us to hurry as we are going back to Canaan with them. We snatch up our water skins and hurry to not fall behind.

He hands us some nuts for our pocket, and we follow the brothers. I love this journey because we get to cross the Nile River again. I find such wonder in this River as it brings life to the land. It is less adventurous with less water flowing, but none the less I find opportunity to reach my hand down to touch the magic of it. As I do so, you toss me a knowing smile. You ask Master about the sacks the brothers are carrying, and He is pleased to share with us. He teaches us that these bags are usually used by shepherds and travelers to carry their personal supplies. It normally holds enough supplies for a day or two, but these sacks are much larger and made of animal skins. I notice that the men carry them across their shoulders or attached to the backs of their donkeys.

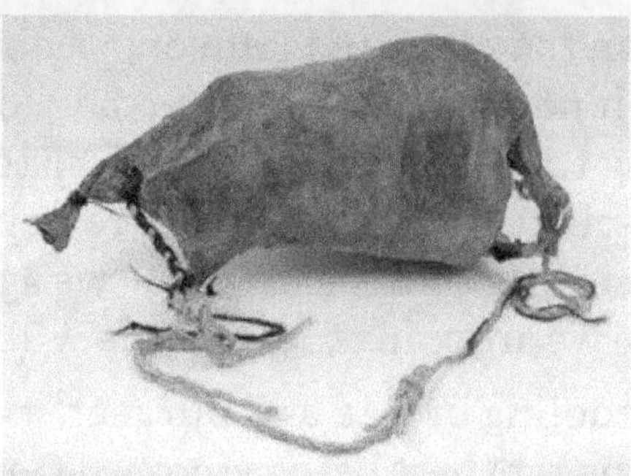

Bing.com Ancient animal skin bags

We settle for the night close to where we had camped with Master when Abram came to Egypt so long ago. We remember well waiting for his return and the anticipation of our Master as he watched for Abram.

As the brothers are settling, one of the brothers opens his sack and quickly closes it in shock. Slowly he approaches his brothers to tell them that his money is in his sack of grain. The fear that grips them is indescribable. One of them begins rolling up his bed to prepare to leave as others drop what they are doing to pace about in fear. When they compose themselves, they determine to arise at first light and take the situation to their father. I am sure they are afraid to go back to Egypt for fear they will be accused of stealing the money. As we observe, you point out that they blame Elohim, the Supreme God, for this blunder. Master indicates with a smile that He is responsible for this timing and discovery. He shares with us that this entire encounter is not being missed by the brothers as they see it as a result of how they treated Joseph and Jacob so many years ago.

Early the next morning, the nervous brothers do not take long to gather their belongings along with the purchased grain and lead their donkeys north toward their father's wisdom and protection. There is not much conversation along the journey as these men are traveling in fear and deep intent. You and I are walking briskly to keep up and, as Master has requested, we are looking to Him for understanding.

I am excited to be back at the camp of Jacob as I look

around for familiar things. There still stands our shelter with the bench in front of it. The memories of that bench warm my soul and, as I look past it, I notice the corral where Joseph's brothers surrounded him to hear his dream. That was just before they left to take the flocks north for better grazing. Near where Jacob's tent still stands is the circle where the family meets. The last time I sat there the boys were making plans to move the flocks. It was not long after, that Joseph followed them. They sold him into slavery, only a short time later. You walk over to our shelter and sit quietly on the bench and express your thanks to Master for how far He has brought us on this journey.

The boys talking to Jacob interrupt our reminiscing and we move close to listen. They are with Jacob, telling him of the events that transpired in Egypt and seeking his wisdom. One of the brothers remembering the words Joseph spoke to them is reciting them again. **Verse 34 And bring your youngest brother to me; so I shall know that you are not spies, but that you are honest men. I will grant your brother to you, and you may trade in the land."** Even as the words leave his mouth, he is not sure how Jacob is going to receive the request. You lean over to me and say, "This is a very frightening and difficult time for these brothers." I smile and agree, this is tough. I whisper back that I wish Jacob, had the verse in **Romans 8:28 "And we know that all things work together for good to those who love god, to those who are the called according to His purpose."** Leaving the bulk of the gain on their donkeys, one by one the brothers are opening their sacks to present them to their father. One by one they realize that their money is also in their sacks. Now, not only the brothers but Jacob is fearful. Jacob, picking one of the bundles of money, sees that the amount of money is more than was required. I wonder if he considers that the extra money was for the journey.

Jacob is really scared now. He lashes out at his sons as he reminds them that he has lost Joseph. Now Simeon did not return to him!

Reuben, Jacob's oldest son steps forward to explain the demand from the Governor of Egypt concerning Simeon and Benjamin. He vows that he will be responsible for Benjamin and if for some unknown reason he returns without Benjamin, Jacob may kill Reuben's two sons. Unfortunately, Jacob is having none of this plan and refuses to allow Benjamin to return to Egypt with the brothers.

Master leads us to understand that even when we have the kind of faith that Jacob presented when he sent his son's to Egypt to buy grain, it is subject to wavering when we don't understand what is happening in our circumstances. He adds that fear is a good indicator of when our faith is wavering. In fact, Jacob is afraid that if he loses Benjamin, he will lose hope and die.

He asks us to consider that it is a very difficult thing for man to lose hope. Master asks us to consider in our own lives what we might not be able to continue living without. Is it the death of a loved one or perhaps the loss of our home or our job? Then as we saw it coming, He asks us if we trust Him this much. We are fully aware He is asking us were our security lies.

I am forced to consider, and I do not know.

My heart desires this degree of faith.

My intent is to trust Him in every circumstance.

I pray that He does not ask me to face these hard things alone.

I know now that I am placing conditions on what I can trust Him with and realize that without His strength, I cannot.

Fear grips me as I ask Master to teach me to trust Him this much. You look at me surprised and I tell you that I mean it. The Spirit of God whispers in our souls that we cheat ourselves out of the seeing the blessings of His provision when fear overwhelms our faith.

I want to experience this level of peace. Master reaches for my hand and assures me that we will grow in this desire and I determine.

I am in!

RETURN TO EGYPT

Genesis 43:1-15

1. Now the famine was severe in the land.

2. And it came to pass, when they had eaten up the grain which they had brought from Egypt, that their father said to them, "Go back, buy us a little food."

3. But Judah spoke to him, saying, "The man solemnly warned us, saying, "You shall not see my face unless your brother is with you."

4. "If you send our brother with us, we will go down and buy you food." "But if you will not send him we will not go down; for the man said to us, 'You shall not see my face unless your brother is with you.'"

6. And Israel said, "Why did you deal so wrongfully with me as to tell the man whether you had still another brother?"

7. But they said, "The man asked us pointedly about ourselves and our family saying, 'Is your father still alive? Have you another brother? And we told him according to these words. Could we possibly have known that he would say, "Bring your brother down'?"

8. Then Judah said to Israel his father, "Send the lad with me, and we will arise and go, that we may live and not die, both we and you and also our little ones.

9. "I myself will be surety for him; from my hand you shall require him. If I do not bring him back to you and set him before you, then let me bear the blame forever.

10. "For if we had not lingered, surely by now we would have

returned this second time."

11. And their father Israel said to them, "If it must be so, then do this: Take some of the best fruits of the land in your vessels and carry down a present for the man – a little balm and a little honey, spices and myrrh, pistachio nuts and almonds.

12. "Take double money in your hand, and take back in your hand the money that was returned in the mouth of your sacks; perhaps it was an oversight.

13. "Take your brother also, and arise, go back to the man.

14. "And may God Almighty give you mercy before the man, that he may release your other brother and Benjamin. If I am bereaved, I am bereaved!"

15. So the men took that present and Benjamin, and they took double money in their hand, and arose and went down to Egypt; and they stood before Joseph.

We have remained in Canaan in the camp of Jacob for some time. We are not certain how much time has passed but the harvest is upon us and there are meager supplies of fruit and nuts available for food. However, the grain is nearly gone, and the famine continues in the land.

Master shares that bread is a basic food for the people of this day. In fact, the word for bread is often translated 'food or meal'.

Jacob has agonized over the decision to send Benjamin to Egypt with his brothers. However, this morning it seems Jacob has determined it is time to make the decision. We are sitting with Master when we hear his young servant boy calling for Jacob's sons to join him at the family meeting area near his home. By the time we have gathered our wraps and readied ourselves the sons are sitting on log benches in a circle. Master has brought you and I near and we position ourselves on a log right in the circle with the brothers. We can hear easily and see all their faces and body language as they discuss what is about to transpire. As Jacob approaches them, I touch your knee and say, "Look, he still favors his hip!" With a knowing smile we listen as he addresses his sons. I notice that there is a place left empty which appears to have not been used for some time. I ask Master why no one sits there, and He explains that custom of the day states that this is Joseph's seat. In respect for those gone without having opportunity to bury them a sitting place is left vacant in the hope that they might return.

Jacob's heart is obviously heavy, as he carries his sadness on his bent shoulders. Fear has etched deep lines in his forehead. All the brothers know what the meeting is about as Jacob proceeds to tells them to **go** again, buy us a little food."

Judah leans forward on his bench to remind Jacob that 'the man' had told them if they return without Benjamin, they will not have an audience with him. There would then not be a release for Simeon. Judah is noticeably aware that they <u>must</u> take Benjamin with them.

As we listen to Judah, I am reminded that he is the brother that convinced the others not to harm Joseph but to instead sell him to the travelers. Master takes us back to **Genesis 37:26-27 So Judah said to his brothers, "What profit is there if we kill our brother and conceal his blood? "Come and let us sell him to the Ishmaelites, and let not our hand be upon him, for he is our brother and our flesh." And his brothers listened.** You mention that Judah is a negotiator. You also remind me that he is the fourth son of Leah and Jacob and his name means 'Yahweh be praised'. I half giggle at you in amazement at the details you remember.

Master shares with us that in the next few chapters we will see Judah rise to a leadership position among the brothers. He adds that a rivalry will also arise between him and his brothers that will later lead to the division of the kingdom of Israel. We are thrilled when Master shares with us that through Judah's son Perez, the 'scarlet thread' will follow through to King David and on to Jesus Christ. It is fun to sit face to face with this man and watch his interaction with his father and brothers, knowing what lies in his future. I lean closer to Master and thank Him for this amazing opportunity.

I am still in awe at the way Master can open His word to me and cause me to feel and understand these things through the Spirit of God.

You confirm with Master that when the scripture says, 'the man' it is talking about Joseph. He agrees but reminds us that the brothers do not recognize him.

When **verse 6** of this chapter calls Jacob, 'Israel' you snap your head in Master's direction as He had told us He would explain why the bouncing back and forth between Jacob and Israel. There is still no answer, but His smile tells us that the answer is about to unfold for us. The Spirit of God does answer in my soul telling me that things are about to become exciting in our journey. I cannot help but smile. Looking back on this journey I feel every moment has been exciting.

Life Changing!

How can it possibly just be getting exciting now?

Israel is frustrated with his sons and questions why they told 'the man' about Benjamin. Judah however explains that they told 'the man' the truth when he asked the question. Israel is struggling with fear as Judah offers to be the guarantee for Benjamin's return just as Reuben had done when the brothers first returned from Egypt. However, some time has passed and the camp of Jacob needs grain again. Judah has a decision to make.

Judah is continuing to plead his case when he adds that if they had returned to Egypt when Reuben suggested, they would have settled with 'the man' in Egypt and returned to Canaan with Simeon already. The sons of Israel know they must go and that there is only one way they can do it.

It appears they intend to stay in this circle until Israel decides to let them take Benjamin.

Finally, Israel, staring at Benjamin with tears welling up in his tired eyes, wringing his hands around the staff he now carries with him always, agrees to allow Benjamin to go to Egypt with his brothers. The relief is evident in the men as they relax their posture and sigh in agreement. However, Israel is not at ease, his gaze on Benjamin is solid and his shoulders carry the weight of his fears.

You notice that the scripture tells us that the only thing they seem to be lacking in their diet is grain. Israel suggests the men take honey, nuts, and spices as a gift to 'the man' and double the money for the grain in case they need to return it from the last trip. Israel is resigned that this is the only way to resolve this issue and regain his son Simeon. He offers a blessing on his sons. **May God Almighty give you mercy before the man, that he may release your other brother and Benjamin.**

Rising from the circle, the agreement is made that they will leave for Egypt in a short time. They gather their donkeys as before, the gifts for 'the man' and advise Benjamin to prepare himself. Israel watches tearfully as they leave the camp heading southeast.

You and I walk past Israel and I notice the tears streaking his worn face. His eyes are fearful, and his left hand is holding his chest from heaving. On his left he grips his staff which appears to be holding him erect.

The days are few and we arrive back in Egypt

Before you can ask, Master explains that "God Almighty" in **verse 14** is 'El' the God of all. And, He reminds us that El is who met with Jacob when He changed his name to Israel in **Genesis 35:11 Also God said to him: "I am God Almighty. Be fruitful and multiply; a nation and a company of nations shall proceed from you, and kings shall come from your body.** Wow, I am excited to see if in these verses where Jacob's name 'Israel' is used will stick. Right now, I do not understand why it has taken so long for that to happen.

IN JOSEPH'S HOME?

Genesis 43:16-22

16. When Joseph saw Benjamin with them, he said to the steward of his house, "Take these men to my home, and slaughter an animal and make ready; for these men will dine with me at noon."

17. Then the man did as Joseph ordered, and the man brought the men into Joseph's house.

18. Now the men were afraid because they were brought into Joseph's house; and they said, "It is because of the money, which was returned in our sacks the first time, that we are brought in, so that he may make a case against us and seize us, to take us as slaves with our donkeys."

19. When they drew near to the steward of Joseph's house, they talked with him at the door of the house,

20. and said, "O sir, we indeed came down the first time to buy food;

21. "but it happened, when we came to the encampment, that we opened our sacks, and there, each man's money was in the mouth of his sack, our money in full weight; so we have brought it back in our hand.

22. "And we have brought down other money in our hands to buy food. We do not know who put our money in our sacks."

Together we stand with Master and Joseph's eleven brothers including Benjamin in the presence of Joseph. This is quite a sight, these brothers all together. The brothers bow appropriately before Joseph and offer their gifts. They introduce

Benjamin as their youngest brother. I smile at you pleased for the healing in Joseph's heart, in fact the healing that is about to take place in this entire family.

It is hard to watch the panic Joseph's brothers are feeling as they find themselves inside the stone walls surrounding Joseph's home. They are seated on the ground with their donkeys laden with the gifts for Joseph. I look to Benjamin who has seldom left his father's side and he has scooted close enough to Judah that they are touching. Benjamin appears to be awe struck more than fearful and maybe does not comprehend the weight of responsibility Judah finds himself in.

While we wait for Joseph, Master explains to us that animals for meals are killed only when they are going to be prepared immediately. They have no way to preserve the animal, so it is immediately butchered, and all the meat is prepared for consumption. We observe that this butchering is done in a courtyard outside Joseph's home and then the meat is taken to the baker. He explains that there are shops that kill poultry and fish, smaller animals but less demand for the larger animals causes them to be butchered at one's residence. As we watch this event unfold before us, Master reminds us of **Genesis 18:7 And Abraham ran to the herd, took a tender and good calf, gave it to a young man, and he hastened to prepare it.** You raise your hand as if you were in a classroom and exclaim, "I remember that, it is when the three heavenly visitors came to Abraham to tell him that Sarah was going to have a son." I respond with recognition, "Yes, this is when she laughed at the thought of a son in her old age and the Lord confronted Abraham about her laughing."

Master draws our attention back to these brothers sitting in the dirt in the courtyard of Joseph's home waiting for whatever is about to happen to them. We are not told which brother is speaking for the group, but we are told that they begin trying to explain that they have brought the money back to Egypt, having come this time intending to buy more grain. I understand their panic as I remember the harshness with which Joseph dealt with them their last time in Egypt. We are certain these brothers have not forgotten selling Joseph into slavery and wondering if now they are headed in that same direction. They are feeling very guilty and Master enlightens us by stating that they are guilty, and guilt changes things.

It changes joy into misery.

I wonder at the understanding that this lunch with Joseph could be a joyful time in a 'rich ruler's' home. It could be a marvelous wonder of a different culture and a time of reuniting with Simeon, but guilt has ruined all that. I do not like watching them squirm for what seems like hours as the preparations of the lunch meal take place. But here we are, watching the silence intermingled with short comments of other sins that have gone un-confessed and comments of speculation, all while the guard of Joseph's home stands silent against the wall by the doorway.

DO NOT BE AFRAID

Genesis 43:23-

23. But he said, "Peace be with you, do not be afraid. Your God and the God of your father has given you treasure in your sacks; I had your money." Then he brought Simeon out to them.

24. So the man brought the men into Joseph's house and gave them water, and they washed their feet; and he gave their donkeys feed.

25. Then they made the present ready for Joseph's coming at noon, for they heard that they would eat bread there.

The dread in the brothers' hearts becomes so great that they proceed to explain their side of the story to the guard. After some time, the guard speaks to them telling them; **"Peace be with you, do not be afraid. Your God and the God of your father has given you treasure in your sacks; I had your money."**

This unexpected response causes the brothers to huddle a bit closer, fear will not leave them. To tell them not to be afraid at this point seems useless. Then the guard speaks again telling them that their God has acted. Not only does he mention their God but also the God of their father. When he states that their God has presented them with a treasure (a blessing) you and I look at each other surprised that he would speak this way. He looks like an Egyptian and we assume he has no understanding of these brothers' God. Then the guard adds that He remembers taking their payment for the grain they purchased earlier.

Wow!

Now they are confused!

But, as the guard speaks, he waves outside the door and ushers in Simeon, rejoining him with his brothers. Benjamin is the first to rise to meet him and embraces the brother he had feared not seeing again. As soon as they are all standing the guard motions the men to follow him into an inner room in Joseph's home where he gives them water to wash their feet. They grab the presents they have for Joseph and follow the guard inside. As they do so they hear the guard give the order that their donkeys be cared for.

I do not think they realize at first that they are going to share the noon meal with Joseph or at least that was not the focus of their thoughts. They seem surprised when they find themselves in a dining hall with exquisite furniture encircling an ornate table. The table is has carving like nothing I have ever seen. The black wooden top shines with a mirror finish and the carvings on and around it is detailed and inlaid with gold. I am sure they tell a story.

Google
search; Ancient Egyptian Furniture

Joseph's chair is elaborate and sturdy, I am certain it is nothing like what these men have ever seen, Benjamin begins walking toward it to touch it until Reuben reaches out touching his shoulder and stop him.

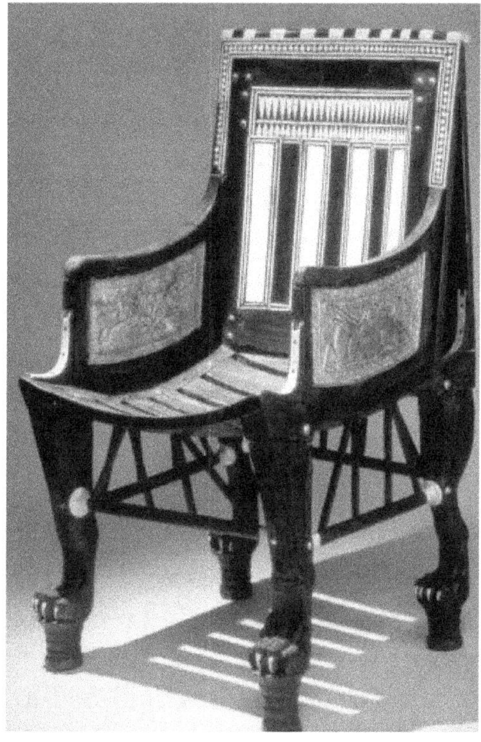

Google search; Ancient Egyptian Furniture

The rest of the chairs around the table all obviously match the table in their grandeur. The leather seats have been died with fascinating detail and the legs are carved to match the table they surround.

Without speaking the men stand around the room waiting Joseph's arrival. Each man is holding a present for 'the man'. I imagine they are all nervous about how he will be received and if his gift is enough. Reuben takes one final look at the gifts, adjusting some of them so they display well and whispers encouragement to his brothers that you and I do not hear.

Master reminds us that the master of the home must be seated first. Then according to age, the rest will be seated after him. Custom will put the oldest on his right and around until Benjamin is directly to Joseph's left. However, that is not how this seating arrangement will happen as Joseph is now living according to Egyptian customs.

The fear in these men is obvious as their silence is deafening. I lean close to Master and whisper that it occurs to me how much they have discussed their sins concerning Joseph and yet they do not recognize him. You add that they have discussed their sins with each other but fail to bring those sins before the God of their father in repentance. Turning to face me, Master asks me to consider how often in my own life I share concerns for my relationship with God among my fellow believers. I even ask them to pray for me. You add that we even put our requests out on prayer chains and to prayer groups and yet, we do not take those concerns to our God.

Guilty.

Master asks us how often we approach God and pray for ourselves. I have no response because I recognize that I usually only pray for myself when I want something from Him. I do however know that I confess my sin before Him. Still, is He the first place I go?

Our attention is drawn back to the dining room as we hear footsteps echoing in the hallway just outside the door. The men stand a bit closer to each other now.

A FAMILY MEAL

Genesis 43:26-34

26. And when Joseph came home, they brought him the present which was in their hand into the house and bowed down before him to the earth.

27. Then he asked them about their well-being, and said, "Is your father well, the old man of whom you spoke? Is he still alive?"

28. And they answered, "Your servant our father is in good health; he is still alive." And they bowed their heads down and prostrated themselves.

29. Then he lifted his eyes and saw his brother Benjamin, his mother's son, and said, "Is this your younger brother of whom you spoke to me?" And he said, "God be gracious to you, my son."

30. Now his heart yearned for his brother; so Joseph made haste and sought somewhere to weep. And he went into his chamber and wept there.

31. Then he washed his face and came out; and he restrained himself, and said, "Serve the bread."

32. So they set him a place by himself, and them by themselves, and the Egyptians who ate with him by themselves; because the Egyptians could not eat food with the Hebrews, for that is an abomination to the Egyptians.

33. And they sat before him, the firstborn according to his birthright and the youngest according to his youth; and the men looked in astonishment at one another.

34. Then he took servings to them from before him, but Benjamin's serving was five times as much as any of theirs. So they drank and were merry with him.

This royal Egyptian enters the room with authority and what we know is vulnerability. He is now right in front of his brothers standing almost at attention when all eleven of them fall to their faces in reverence before him. They maintain the gifts in their hands even as they are not as carefully held as before. You and I smile at each other as we remember again the dreams Joseph had as a young man.

Joseph is about to ask about their father, Jacob when they rise a bit and readjust themselves. Even while he inquires about Jacob, Joseph waves a servant to gather the gifts. Quickly the gifts disappear from the room as if they had never been there. Joseph is speaking while looking at each of his brothers intently studying them. Then, as soon as they assure Joseph that their father, his father, is alive and well they fall to their faces a third time before him. It is exciting to watch these dreams being fulfilled right here, now, while we watch.

Seeing his brothers face down on the stone floor before him and I am certain he is remembering his childhood dreams also. My mind is racing with what else is on his mind when I notice he has located Benjamin among the men and his gaze is fixed on his youngest brother. Benjamin is the only man among these men before him who is Joseph's full brother. The rest of these men are half brothers by Jacobs other wife Leah and his concubines. Joseph's voice is strained as he confirms this man is Benjamin the younger brother whom they had mentioned during their last visit with Joseph. Being assured that this is Benjamin, Joseph is nearly overcome with emotion and rushes out of the room. Our scripture tells us that Joseph went to his own private room where he could weep openly without interruption. You mention that we did not expect this reaction from Joseph who always seems so in control, confident and secure. And yet, here he is overcome with joy and possibly even the wonder of

Yahweh and His blessings.

When Joseph regains his composure, he washes his face and returns to the dining area where his brothers have again positioned themselves against the wall, silent. Joseph enters the room and simply declares he is ready to eat. The men locate themselves around the table and Joseph is seated at his own table in the same room but not with his brothers. You whisper that you are certain Joseph would like to be seated with his brothers and I agree. However, according to custom, an Egyptian cannot sit with a Hebrew because they are lesser people, dirty and will defile the status of an Egyptian. You ask Master why Joseph is sitting alone at a table, not with his brothers nor with the Egyptians. Wait, who are the Egyptians eating in this room? Our scripture does not tell us but possibly Joseph's family. The guards nor the servants would have eaten with them.

You mention that Joseph's brothers are arranged in birth order around their table and wonder if they placed themselves that way or if a servant instructed them where to sit. If a servant instructed them, how did he know their ages? Master assures us that a servant instructed them where to sit and Joseph had instructed that servant where to place the men. You wonder if the brothers noticed that the birth order was correct and questioned how he knew. Or, did the servant ask?

You and I marvel at the sight before us! Then we are shocked when Joseph rises to serve the meal to his brothers. I am certain my mouth is hanging open at the sight as he places the food before each brother. Then when he gets to Benjamin, WOW he loads his plate up with five times as much food. Really, five times as much!

Master hands you and I each a handful of grapes as we watch these men enjoy their meal together. They are joyful and 'merry' together.

I wish Jacob could see this.

JOSEPH SENDS HIS BROTHERS HOME

Genesis 44:1-15

1. And he commanded the steward of his house, saying, "Fill the men's sacks with food, as much as they can carry, and put each man's money in the mouth of his sack.

2. "Also put my cup, the silver cup, in the mouth of the sack of the youngest, and his grain money." So he did according to the word that Joseph had spoken.

3. As soon as the morning dawned, the men were sent away, they and their donkeys.

4. When they had gone out of the city, and were not yet far off, Joseph said to his steward, "Get up, follow the men; and when you overtake them, say to them, "Why have you repaid evil for good?

5. Is not this the one from which my lord drinks, and with which he indeed practices divination? You have done evil in so doing.'"

6. So he overtook them, and he spoke to them these same words.

7. And they said to him, "Why does my lord say these words? Far be it from us that your servants should do such a ting.

8. "Look, we brought back to you from the land of Canaan the money which we found in the mouth of our sacks. How then could we steal silver or gold from your lord's house?

9. "With whomever of your servants it is found, let him die, and

we also will be my lord's slaves."

10. And he said, "Now also let it be according to your words; he with whom it is found shall be my slave, and you shall be blameless."

11. Then each man speedily let down his sack to the ground and each opened his sack.

12. So he searched. He began with the oldest and left off with the youngest; and the cup was found in Benjamin's sack.

13. Then they tore their clothes, and each man loaded his donkey and returned to the city.

14. So Judah and his brothers came to Joseph's house, and he was still there; and they fell before him on the ground.

15. And Joseph said to them, "What deed is this you have done? Did you not know that such a man as I can certainly practice divination?"

We awaken the next morning to the sound of our Master preparing our table with fresh fruit and goat cheese. He has placed a fresh fish in the center of the table for us to share. I marvel at His care and His desire to nourish us every day both physically and spiritually. After washing ourselves in preparation of being in His presence we bow before Him quietly. Without speaking I express my love for Him and my wonder at who He is. With my hands open in my lap I offer myself to him in this day without knowing what the day holds. I desire to be a blessing to others, but I desire more to please Him. I hear my own voice thanking Him for the meal He has prepared and for all that this day presents.

Master leads us back to the court of Joseph and he is standing before his brothers but speaking to the servant at his side. This servant is the same one that was called a steward earlier and had led the brothers to Joseph's home before sharing a meal with him. He surely is a close confident of Joseph's as he is always close by.

Joseph commands his steward to **"Fill the men's sacks with food, as much as they can carry, and put each man's money in the mouth of his sack."** You and I are amazed that Joseph is doing the same test on his brothers as he did the last time they were here. I ask Master why he is doing this again as He reminds me of the following verse. **"Also put my cup, the silver cup, in the mouth of the sack of the youngest, and his grain money."** Now I really am confused, why would he set Benjamin up like this?

As we observe the steward does exactly as Joseph commands and even takes Joseph's personal cup from his table to place in the top of Benjamin's bag.

Turning to Master, I ask Him what the significance of this cup is because it is the difference this time in the brother's sacks. He explains that high officials all throughout the world of this day have their own personal cups. Usually so they can be certain no one has tampered with their drinks. In this case Joseph's is made of silver and ornately crafted. He adds that it is a sure thing that this steward kept a close watch on this cup.

You interject and ask about the divination reference to the cup. Master adds to our understanding that our scriptures use this reference to the cup but that there are no other scriptures indicating Joseph involved himself in this practice. However, He explains that when divination is used in these cups it is done with pure water being poured into the cup, then gold, silver or precious stones are thrown into the water. The cup is shaken slightly or swirled, and the fragments form a picture in the cup, the pictures are then read by trained men who practice the magic called 'hydromancy'.

Master assures us that the reference to the cup and the purpose of placing it in Benjamin's food bag is to test whether the older brothers will protect Benjamin. He reminds us that they did not protect Joseph when they sold him to the Ishmaelites years ago.

Master walks with us back to our shelter and suggests we prepare our things as we will be leaving in the morning with Joseph's brothers to travel back to Jacob their father. He shares with us that the brothers are relieved and confident as they settle for the night, prepared to leave at the first light of the morning.

We are prepared and with Master, we join the brothers as they are **"sent away from Egypt, they and their donkeys."** Master shares with us that the words 'sent away' simply mean that they were released by the Egyptian guard stating that everything is completed with their food supplies. Without looking back each brother gathers his own sack, laying it on the back of his donkey and walks quickly toward home. They have accomplished the purchase of more grain and have retrieved Simeon from the hands of the Egyptians. There is a cautious hurried step in their leaving.

Walking close beside the brothers we listen as they express their relief in the end of their journey to Egypt. Some of the brothers keep watch behind them as there is the ever-present memory of their last leaving when they were followed by Egyptian guards who accused them.

Master tells us that Joseph has commanded his steward to wait only a short time then pursue the brothers. He is instructed to accuse the brothers of stealing the silver cup that will be recovered from Benjamin's sack.

As we walk, the brothers are feeling more secure in their journey. I am certain they are anxious for tomorrow to come so they feel confident they are truly away from Egypt. Master reminds us that Joseph does have a prophetic gift given by Yahweh to interpret dreams. You exclaim, "Oh yes, remember the butcher and the baker and their dreams!" I add that he also interpreted the Pharaoh's dream as Yahweh revealed it to him. This remembering gives us comfort as we are a little hung up on why Joseph would set Benjamin up.

We, with the brothers had only just reached the first tributary of the Nile River when the Egyptian steward approached us. Nervousness gripped the brothers as they glanced between each other. Each man is standing beside his donkey facing the steward questioning why they would do such a thing as they had already returned the money that was found in their sack on the last trip. Their voices carry a hint of panic as they question how they could even have had access to steal Joseph's cup. Desperate and filled with fear the brothers refer to themselves as servants and state that if one of them has this cup he may be put to death. You whisper to me that they seem noticeably confident. To this groveling the steward lessons the sentence from death to stating that whoever has the cup will immediately become a servant of Egypt and the rest may go free.

Nervously, we watch as the sacks of the brothers are opened, and the money spills on the ground before the steward. He does not seem to even notice the money or the brothers glancing between each other in fear of what he must be thinking of them. Reuban is watching each sack and the money on the ground and I am certain he is considering how he will explain this to his father, if he ever sees him again. Each sack opened, each sack containing money, and in Benjamin's sack not only money but a silver ornate cup tumbles to the ground. Benjamin is panicked as he looks at Reuben in disbelief.

Without a sound the brothers begin to tear their clothing, mourning all they have lost in this moment of unbelief. Knowing they cannot let Benjamin be led alone back to Egypt they each silently load their donkeys with the food again and follow the Egyptian steward back to Egypt to face Joseph. We walk with Joseph's brothers in silence as fear is etched on each face. Arriving before Joseph the brothers, at Judah's leading, bow themselves before Joseph seeking mercy for Benjamin. Joseph addresses the men as the steward hands him the silver divination cup, questioning if they thought he would not know what was going on as he was able to **"practice divination."**

However, when the Hebrew brothers touch the cup it is now rendered unusable and therefore a severe crime in the Egyptian court punishable by death. Joseph is testing to see if the brothers will turn over their brother Benjamin to protect themselves. Master can see the shock on our faces as we cannot believe Joseph would set his brothers up like this, so He encourages us to continue to watch as Joseph's mercy is about to be revealed.

Master points out to us that again that the brothers are bowed before Joseph as he had seen in his dream so many years prior to this event. I am certain Joseph is remembering his dreams also and his soul is comforted in knowing his dreams are being fulfilled. I hear you whisper that Jacob has yet to bow before Joseph, so this is not entirely fulfilled.

I wonder if the brothers are remembering Joseph's dreams and making any connection between 'the man' and Joseph.

JUDAH STEPS UP

Genesis 44:16-34

16. Then Judah said, "What shall we say to my lord? What shall we speak? Or how shall we clear ourselves? God has found out the iniquity of your servants; here we are, my lord's slaves, both we and he also with whom the cup was found."

17. But he said, "Far be it from me that I should do so; the man in whose hand the cup was found, he shall be my slave. And as for you go up in peace to your father."

18. Then Judah came near to him and said: "O my lord, please let your servant speak a word in my lord's hearing, and do not let your anger burn against your servant; for you are even like Pharaoh.

19. "My lord asked his servants, saying, 'Have you a father or a brother?'

20. "And we said to my lord, 'We have a father, an old man, and a child of his old age, who is young; his brother is dead, and he alone is left of his mother's children, and his father loves him.'

21. Then you said to your servants. 'Bring him down to me, that I may set my eyes on him.'

22. "And we said to my lord, 'The lad cannot leave his father for if he should leave his father his father would die.'

23. "But you said to your servants, 'Unless your youngest brother comes down with you, you shall see my face no more.'

24. "So it was, when we went up to your servant my father, that we told him the words of my lord.

25. "And our father said, 'Go back and buy us a little food.'

26. "But we said, 'We cannot go down; if our youngest brother is not with us, then we may not see the man's face unless our youngest brother is with us.'

27. "Then your servant my father said to us, 'You know that my wife bore me two sons;

28. 'and the one went out from me, and I said, "Surely he is torn to pieces"; and I have not seen him since.

29. 'But if you take this one also from me, and calamity befalls him, you shall bring down my gray hair with sorrow to the grave.'

30. "Now therefore, when I come to your servant my father, and the lad is not with us, since his life is bound up in the lad's life,

31. "it will happen, when he sees that the lad is not with us, that he will die. So your servants will bring down the gray hair of your servant our father with sorrow to the grave.

32. "For your servant became surety for the lad to my father, saying, 'If I do not bring him back to you, then I shall bear the blame before my father forever.'

33. "Now therefore, please let your servant remain instead of the lad as a slave to my lord, and let the lad go up with his brothers.

34. "For how shall I go up to my father if the lad is not with me, lest perhaps I see the evil that would come upon my father?"

Master brings you and I near to where the brothers stand before Joseph. At first, they stare at him in silence, perhaps not knowing if it is ok to speak. I look to Master questioning what is about to transpire and when will Joseph stop this charade. This scene is uncomfortable. I feel like Joseph is setting his brothers up to torment them and I do not like this. Master impresses upon me that he is testing them, and this testing will bring them to confession and repentance. You ask, "Is testing different that tempting?" Master replies pleased at the opportunity to show us a new precept.

Temptation is to set up an opportunity to fail.

Testing is to set up opportunity to succeed!

And He left us with this precept with no further explanation. I will ponder it for a long time allowing the Spirit of God to nourish my soul with this understanding.

As Judah takes one step forward toward Joseph, you grab my arm to draw my attention. The Egyptian soldiers ready themselves as the tension in the room rises. After assessing the response in the room Judah asks Joseph for permission to speak then pleads for answers. Joseph waves his hand in a horizontal manner to tell the soldiers to stand down as Judah continues. He boldly yet respectfully asks Joseph what they can do to please him. Without looking to his brothers, Judah offers all the brothers as slaves along with Benjamin. Their heads snap toward Judah, but they do not say a word, they know this is the only way. They cannot go home without Benjamin. Master points out to us that Judah offered no excuse, made no denial, but simply plead with the mighty Egyptian for the life and freedom of Benjamin. He guides us to see the spirit of self sacrifice in contrast to Judah's spirit at the time Joseph was sold into slavery in **Genesis 37:26-27 So Judah said to his brothers, "What profit is there if we kill our brother and conceal his blood? "Come and let us sell him to the Ishmaelites, and let not our hand be upon him, for he is our brother and our flesh." And his brothers listened.**

Joseph tightens the screws one more time as he insists Benjamin is the only one he wants to remain as a servant. You ask if Joseph is testing to see if the brothers have treated Benjamin, the only other son of Rachel, as they treated him. The look on Joseph's face is stern and unwavering.

It is an incredible scene!

Judah, at first standing perfectly still, then begins to move dramatically and urgently as he pleads for Benjamin's freedom. I glance at you wondering if Joseph will tolerate

Judah's commotion, but then notice that Joseph is standing still, listening. Judah is confessing not only his sin but also his brother's sin before Joseph. Judah even acknowledges that God is judging them. He includes that they have caused both Benjamin and their father unspeakable grief. Joseph knows they did not steal the money or the silver cup but indeed they did sell their brother then withheld the truth from their father all these years. Leaning close you mention to Master that this is a different Judah than we know. He appears to have developed some values and relationship skills. Judah then, offers himself in Benjamin's place.

With a smile of approval on His face, Master shares with us that Judah has come a long way. He quietly reminds us that the Messiah will come through the line of Judah. I had forgotten that and am thrilled at what I am seeing in this man before us. He also reminds us that Reuben forfeited his double portion of Jacob's blessing because of his immorality. When he forfeited the blessing it was divided between Judah and Joseph as stated in **1 Chronicles 5:1-2 Now the sons of Reuben the firstborn of Israel – he was indeed the firstborn, but because he defiled his father's bed, his birthright was given to the sons of Joseph, the son of Israel, so that the genealogy is not listed according to the birthright; yet Judah prevailed over his brothers, and from him came a ruler, although the birthright was Josephs -.** Master promises us that when we get into **Genesis 45,** He will explain this further.

Before we leave this chapter of Genesis, Master points out that Jacob's security is in Benjamin instead of Yahweh. He asks us to ponder this idea and see where it takes us.

True to the fun Master that He is, He adds to our understanding that later in scripture we will see the relationship between Joseph and Benjamin remain. We agree this will be a fun thing to watch as we walk through our scriptures. Master motions us to find ourselves a place to sit as we continue to observe Joseph and his brothers, Master whispers with a tempting smile that Saul of Tarsus will be of the tribe of Benjamin.

What? Really!

I love this!

Master adds that we will get to know these men much better as we journey, and He includes that we are going to enjoy this.

JOSEPH REVEALED

Genesis 45:1-15

1. Then Joseph could not restrain himself before all those who stood by him, and he cried out, "Make everyone go out from me!" So no one stood with him while Joseph made himself known to his brothers.

2. And he wept aloud, and the Egyptians and the house of Pharaoh heard it.

3. Then Joseph said to his brothers, "I am Joseph; does my father still live?" But his brothers could not answer him, for they were dismayed in his presence.

4. And Joseph said to his brothers "Please come near to me." So they came near. Then he said; "I am Joseph your brother whom you sold into Egypt.

5. "But now, do not therefore he grieved or angry with yourselves because you sold me here; for God sent me before you to preserve life.

6. "For these two years the famine has been in the land, and there are still five years in which there will be neither plowing nor harvesting.

7. "And God sent me before you to preserve posterity for you in the earth and to save your lives by a great deliverance.

8. "So now it was not you who sent me here, but God; and He has made me a father to Pharaoh, and lord of all his house, and a ruler throughout all the land of Egypt.

9. "Hurry and go up to my father, and say to him, "Thus says your son Joseph: "God had made me lord of all Egypt; come

down to me, do not tarry.

10. "You shall dwell in the land of Goshen, and you shall be near to me, you and your children, your children's children, your flocks and your heardsmen, and all that you have.

11. "There I will provide for you lest you and your household, and all that you have, come to poverty; for there is still five years of famine." '

12. "And behold, your eyes and the eyes of my brother Benjamin see that it is my mouth that speaks to you.

13. "So you shall tell my father of all my glory in Egypt, and of all that you have seen, and you shall hurry and bring my father down here."

14. Then he fell on his brother Benjamin's neck and wept and Benjamin wept on his neck.

15. Moreover he kissed all his brothers and wept over them, and after that his brothers talked with him.

You and I are still seated in Joseph's residence observing the scene with Joseph and his brothers. The brothers do not yet know who Joseph is when he commands his Egyptian assistants to leave the room. It is an odd request because this means his interpreter also leaves the room. In obedience the soldiers bow and back out of the room as Joseph commanded. Joseph reaches up and removes his Egyptian head covering that sets him apart as Governor of Egypt. Tears begin to roll down his sun-tanned cheeks. It is not long until Joseph is weeping loud enough for those outside his home to hear him.

You remind me of earlier studies when we learned that the descendants of Isaac and Ishmael are passionate and expressive people and will be in our day also. They even appear excessive to those of other cultures. I remember **Genesis 16:12** when the angel of the LORD described to Hagar who her son Ishmael would be; **"He shall be a wild man;**

His hand shall be against every man,

And every man's hand against him.

And he shall dwell in the presence of all his brethren." I wonder out loud if this expressiveness adds to his trouble of fitting in.

Looking at Joseph's brothers, they appear confused and embarrassed for Joseph until he speaks in their own language stating that he is Joseph and inquires if his father still lives. Until this moment Joseph has been speaking to them through an interpreter. They stand frozen in fear as though Joseph has gone mad. They know the power he possesses. They also know it has been twenty-five years since they sold him, and he now has the authority to take revenge. As they stand, silent Joseph removes the gold chain from around his neck and reaches out his hand toward them requesting that they come to him.

You ask Master why Joseph is not angry or does not want revenge and He replies by taking us to the very next verse **Genesis 45:5 "But now, do not therefore be grieved or angry with yourselves because you sold me here; for God sent me before you to preserve life.**

Master suggests that if we could see the hand of God in our lives it would be easier to always give the glory to God. Joseph did not need to see God's hand; he has lived it.

Joseph was seventeen when he was sold into slavery

He was thirty when he stood before Pharaoh.

He has served Pharaoh seven years of plenty in the land.

Now there have been two years of famine in the land.

Joseph is not thirty-nine years old and he has seen well the hand of God in

his life.

We cannot help but smile as Joseph expresses his desire for his brothers to hurry and fetch his father, Jacob and bring him to Egypt. The brothers are still not saying anything, but they are sneaking glances at each other in disbelief.

I notice that, for reasons not told, Joseph is treating his older half brothers with kindness and his full-brother Benjamin, as a rich man. Master reminds us that when they shared the meal together in **Genesis 43:34 "Then he took serving to them before him, but Benjamin's serving was five times as much as any of theirs. So they drank and were merry with him."** Then Master adds that whatever the reason he is also now giving Benjamin five changes of clothing. You ask, "Why give clothing?" He enlightens us that clothing is often a gift given to kings and prophets for great deeds done. He encourages us to search this interesting fact by referring to; **2 Kings 5:5, 22-23; 2 Chronicles 9:24; Esther 6:8-9** and **Daniel 5:29**. We agree that we will search these verses before the day ends.

Master shares with us that the land of Goshen is the best part of Egypt and it is a place where they will be safe. He adds that through archeological digs it will be proven that the Kyksos people live there. The Kyksos people presently rule Egypt and have favored Joseph because they are sympathetic to the Hebrew people.

Benjamin is the first brother to move toward Joseph and their embrace is sweet and tearful. I reach for your hand hardly believing what I am witnessing. After Benjamin steps forward, the other brothers tearfully embrace Joseph also. It is not long until they are all sitting on the cool stone floor of Joseph's home, chatting and planning.

Hearing the weeping and laughter Pharaoh comes in the door of Joseph's home to find Joseph and his brothers sitting on the floor. We are cautious at first as are the eleven brothers until the Pharaoh expresses his delight and interest. Master explains that Pharaoh knows Joseph has been a blessing to Pharaoh's kingdom. He also is quite aware that, as a Kyksos ruler, he has had a hard time knowing who to trust beyond Joseph. This must be a good thing for him.

Pharaoh is so thrilled that he orders metal wheeled

wagons to be sent back with these brothers to get their families. Master interjects that the metal wheel is an invention that came with the Kyksos people and their chariots. These Hebrew men have probably never seen metal wheels. The wagons or carts they know are usually wooden and break easily, they are pulled by oxen. Then the most surprising statement from the Pharaoh as he tells the brothers that they will not need to bring their own possessions **"Do not be concerned about your goods, for the best of all the land of Egypt is yours."**

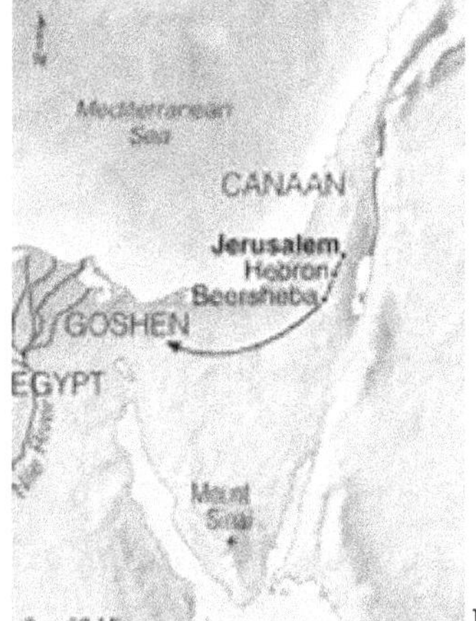

Bing.com

I ask Master to tell us about Goshen and He eagerly shares that this area is rich with pastureland for Jacob's sheep, it presently has few residents so there is plenty of room for the Hebrew people to expand. Master adds that sheepherders will irritate the cattle people of Egypt so they will be far enough away to not cause conflict. They will also be far enough away from the Egyptians to not be so easily influenced by their idolatry. And, the greatest benefit of all; they will be close to Joseph. Master takes us back to our map of Goshen and points out the city of "Rameses" located just to the east of the tributaries of the Nile River. He taps His finger on this city as He explains that the fact this city is in the middle of where the Hebrew people are going to settle is going to be a problem. He encourages us to watch for this.

Master is pleased to tell us, and we are excited to learn that, we are going with these men back to the land of Canaan to fetch Jacob and the families of the 'Children of Israel.' They are in such a hurry we barely are ready to go when they gather to leave. With them they are taking; wagons filled with provisions for the journey, ten donkeys, loaded with good things from Egypt, ten female donkeys loaded with grain and bread for Jacob. As we roll away, the men begin singing Hebrew praises to the God of their father Jacob. You mention that you remember Leah singing this as she cared for her family. They are exuberant in their joy to tell Jacob all about what has happened. I am sure each man is imagining how Jacob will receive the news that Joseph lives.

When we arrive in Canaan Jacob does not believe them. It takes more convincing than the brothers expected but Jacob does finally believe when he sees all the provisions loaded on the metal wheeled wagons.

In an old shaky voice Jacob says, **"It is enough, Joseph my son is still alive, I will go and see him before I die."** I cannot control myself and I reach for Master's hand as tears of renewed relationships roll down my face.

The Hebrew people gather for their move to Goshen in Egypt where they will assume the name and calling of 'The Children of Israel.' Their intention at this point is to dwell there until the famine is over. However, Jacob will live in Egypt until he dies and then return to Canaan to be buried next to his wife Leah.

Master encourages us to look again at Joseph and his life. For the last twenty-five years he has been estranged from his family and eventually being the hope to the world during this famine. He is dressed as an Egyptian official while they believed him dead, that is why they did not recognize him, and they dare not look him over too closely out of respect.

Then Master adds that for the past two thousand years

Messiah has been the Savior to the people of every nation while being estranged from his family, Israel. Joseph's brothers do not recognize their brother because of his clothing and his affiliation with the Egyptians. Even as the Hebrew people, do not recognize the Messiah for His affiliation with the Gentile people. They will one day recognize Him however, when they stand face to face with their Messiah. Master takes us to **Romans 11:25 For I do not desire, brethren, that you should be ignorant of this mystery, lest you should be wise in your own opinion, that blindness in part has happened to Israel until the fullness of the Gentiles has come in.** You ask Master if the 'fullness of the Gentiles' is during the 'church age'. You continue adding, from the time the disciples began teaching the good news to the Gentiles until Jesus the Messiah returns and reveals Himself to the people of the world. He agrees that it is and that during that time the Israelite people will be blinded by God from knowing who Jesus is. This time allows the Gentile people to have opportunity to become part of the body of believers who will inherit the same salvation and inheritance that the Israelites will experience.

We settle into our home shelter in the land of Jacob like we had never left. We stroke the walls lovingly and sit at our table while we remember the precious hours with our Master here. Laying our heads down for the night we close our eyes and smile at the familiar sounds and smells of the time spent here.

MOVING TO EGYPT

Genesis 46: 1-7

1. So Israel took his journey with all that he had, and came to Beersheba, and offered sacrifices to the God of his father Isaac.

2. Then God spoke to Israel in the visions of the night, and said, "Jacob, Jacob! And he said "Here I am."

3. So He said, "I am God, the God of your father; do not fear to go down to Egypt, for I will make of you a great nation there.

4. "I will go down with you to Egypt, and I will also surely bring you up again; and Joseph will put his hand on your eyes."

5. Then Jacob arose from Beersheba; and the sons of Israel carried their father Jacob, their little ones, and their wives, in the carts which Pharaoh had sent to carry him.

6. So they took their livestock and their goods, which they had acquired in the land of Canaan, and went to Egypt, Jacob and all his descendants with him.

7. His sons and his sons' sons, his daughters and his sons' daughters, and all the descendants he brought with him into Egypt.

After we have shared our morning meal in the land of Canaan with Master, He tells us we will begin our journey to Egypt today. He shares with us that Jacob is a bit uncomfortable as he remembers Elohim had instructed his father Abraham to stay away from Egypt. He had instructed Isaac the same. Jacob is going to need some personal assurance from Elohim so they will be stopping in Beersheba for confirmation.

Genesis 46:26 tells us that there are sixty-six people, as we start our journey to Goshen. This number does not however, include Joseph and his family, already living in Goshen. Not far into our journey we arrive in Beersheba where Jacob stops the entire caravan to offer a sacrifice.

As Jacob prepares his sacrifice and his descendents you remember that this is the place where Hagar fled to when she left Sarah in **Genesis 21:14.** I add that Abraham made a covenant with the Philistine princess in this place in **Genesis 21:32.** Raising your finger you continue, reminding us that Abraham lived here after offering up his son Isaac in **Genesis 22:19.** Master is pleased with our remembering and reaches out to squeeze our hands. I love His touch as my entire being responds with goose bumps. As He does so, He assures us that many more memories will be made in this place as we journey further through our scriptures. You mention that Jacob has come such a long way with Yahweh. We remember when he left the home of his parents, he was not concerned at all what Yahweh had to say. Now here we are experiencing the God filled man Jacob.

What a mighty work Yahweh has done in Jacob's life!

What a mighty work He is doing in my life!

Jacob offers his sacrifice as his descendants look on. You and I join them as we bow ourselves before the "God of Jacob's father Isaac." And I whisper a praise of thanksgiving for Elohim's growing and nurturing in my life.

Jacob chooses to spend the night here in Beersheba so we along with all his descendants seek a comfortable resting place. As we close our eyes the Hebrew song of praise rolls in our minds and you begin to sing as the full assurance of Elohim's guidance of Jacob and his family fills our hearts.

It is before sunlight when Master awakens us and invites us to follow Him. As we approach Jacob's shelter Master explains that Jacob is having a vision of Elohim. We look to each other through what had been sleepy eyes, now fully awake and excited. We are miraculously able to hear but we see nothing as Elohim calls to Jacob two times. You and I drop to our knees at the sound of His voice as it fills the air all around us. Then Jacob obediently slides onto his knees as he replies, **"Here I am."** I think he is still asleep! With the voice of Elohim in my ears, I rub them to be sure I am hearing. He declares to Jacob that **"I am God"**. These words cause my breath to catch and goosebumps to rise covering all of me.

Master whispers that we are hearing 'El.' I grab your hand and pull you closer to me, the same time my shaking hand reaches for Master's hand which is always available. Then El adds that He is **"the God of your father."** Without lifting my head, I hear my own voice quietly say, "Elohim is in this place!" I am weeping now, my hand holding my own chest, shaking, I realize the voice I hear in my ears is indeed the voice I have been hearing every day along this journey. The voice of Elohim, El Shaddai, Yahweh, El Elyon, Jehovah, MASTER! The very voice that holds my hand now! My thoughts are broken as I am drawn back to Elohim speaking to Jacob.

The first assurance Elohim gives Jacob is to not be afraid and to go to Goshen in Egypt. I smile knowing that is what Jacob asked of **"the god of his father Isaac."** Then Elohim reminds Jacob of the promise he made to him years ago, that He will make from Jacob a great nation. I am surprised when I hear that this great nation is going to be accomplished in Egypt. As I think on this, the Spirit of God reminds me that I had asked why Jacob is not called Israel in scriptures. I recall, as the Spirit enlightens me to understand, that this group, I am traveling with now will be the beginning of 'the Children of Israel'. Understanding now, I thrill to know that this name was not about Jacob but his descendants. The name "Israel" is about setting apart a people, not just a man, for Elohim's purposes. I remember the lessons about precept upon precept and I cannot wait to talk this one over with you.

I bow motionless, in the presence of El (Elohim) my Master!

I am beyond thrilled when I hear Elohim say that He will go to Egypt with Jacob. I remember so clearly when Elohim refused to go into Egypt with Abraham and Sarah. The words, **"I will also surely bring you up again"** causes a huge breath of relief to fill my lungs as I remember when Abraham came back from Egypt he couldn't have walked any faster on his way, headed back to Canaan.

Then I hear the words, **"Joseph will put his hand on your eyes."** Before I can even form the question the Spirit of God offers. Elohim is promising Jacob that Joseph will be present at Jacobs death and burial to place his fingers on Jacob's eyes in the final farewell.

As with each time we hear from Elohim, He is gone quickly and the world around us is not the same. Master walks with us back to our shelter. We are without words at His presence, His words, His grace toward Jacob, and us. We retire to our sleeping mats and lay there without speaking. Tears of joy and excitement are running into the very ears that had just heard the voice of Elohim! Without a sound we lay there until sleep overtakes us.

We awaken with the sun and hastily prepare for our journey. When we begin to walk, Master suggests that He would like to visit with us about this man Jacob, we quickly position ourselves on either side of Him to not miss a word.

Before beginning, Master points out that Jacob left home with only his staff, a few servants, and his camels. He compares this to a man of God who is living in the flesh where there is not a thought for God's position in his life. He suggests that this is Jacob's life in Haran. This is when he was serving Laban, the father of his wives Leah and Rachel. Master reminds us that Jacob left Haran running from his father-in-law and afraid to see his own brother Esau.

We do not respond but nod our heads in agreement as Master considers Jacob in Canaan and how, in that land, Jacob was fighting life in his own strength. No consideration for God's hand on him until he had a dream. There he fought with the Spirit of God until he acknowledged his own name and sin. At that time Jacob's mind began to change, but it still has taken some time.

Now, here we are with Jacob who is a refined man of God who will follow the God of his father wherever He leads. Jacob is not walking in his own strength, he is not running away, nor is he fighting.

You ask Master how this applies to us.

There is a time in our lives when we hear the word of God and we turn to it.

There is a time when we struggle with the word of God because it does not fit into what we assumed our lives would look like. Sometimes this takes many years.

Then we realize His grace and seek His knowledge, we begin to walk by faith. We are no longer moving through life on our own understanding or strength.

We are pleased at this understanding and the visual that Jacob's life offers. You say, "Precept upon precept."

Today I feel honored to walk among these people toward Egypt. "The Children of Israel." As I look around at them, I know they have no understand of the impact they will have on the world throughout eternity.

WHO ARE THE CHILDREN OF ISRAEL?

Genesis 46:8-12

8. Now these were the names of the children of Israel, Jacob and his sons, who went to Egypt; Reuben was Jacob's firstborn.

9. The sons of Reuben were Hanoch, Pally, Hezron, and Carmi,

10. The sons of Simeon were Jemuel, Jamin, Ohad, Jachin, Zohar, and Shaul, the son of a Canaanite woman.

11. The sons of Lebi were Gershon, Kohath, and Merari.

12. The sons of Judah were Er, Onan, Shelah, Perez, and Zerath (but Er and Onan died in the land of Canaan). The sons of Perez were Hezron and Hamul.

13. The sons of Issachar were Tola, Puvah, Job, and Shimron.

14. The sons of Zebulun were Sered, Elon and Jableeel.

These were the sons of Leah, whom she bore to Jacob in Padan, Aram, with his daughter Dinah. All the persons, his sons and his daughters, were thirty-three.

15. These were the sons of Leah, whom she bore to Jacob in Padan Aram, with his daughter Dinah. All the persons, his sons and his daughters, were thirty-three.

In Goshen Master takes us to a beautiful spot under a wide spreading tree to look at our scriptures with Him. The grass is lush and green, and the landscape is scattered with streams and small ponds. The few people already living here are welcoming and the Children of Israel are finding their places and getting settled. There are no hills in this area so we can see for miles except then the tall clusters of palm trees stand in the way.

As we get comfortable Master opens a scroll with names of a genealogy carefully scripted on it. My first response is that I will maintain a good attitude and I will learn everything Master brings us about these people.

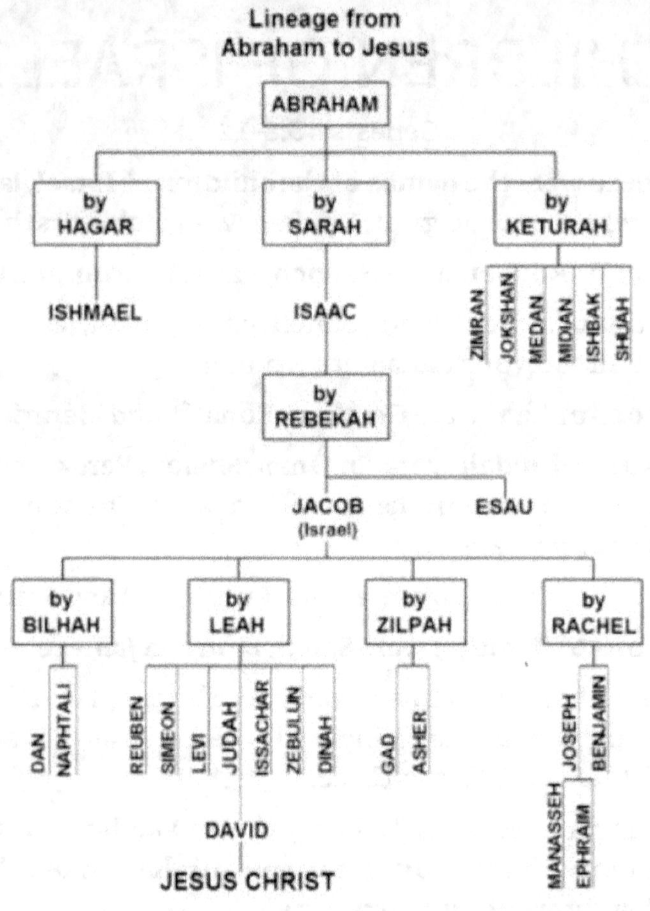

He places four rocks on the corners, and I lean closer to examine the chart with you.

Descendants of Reuben,

Son of Leah.

Oh wow, this will not be uninteresting as the others because I see these people right before me. I hear them talking and can observe their lives right here. Master looks up at me and I say, "I remember that you love all the people in the genealogies we have explored, therefore I love them." He smiles at me indicating that He knows me too.

Reuben is the firstborn of Jacob and Leah. He married a Canaanite wife named Eliuram. He has a son Hanoch meaning 'initiation.' You mention that this is an interesting name for a firstborn. Master agrees and shares that Hanoch will be the father of the Hanochite people who will live near Midian.

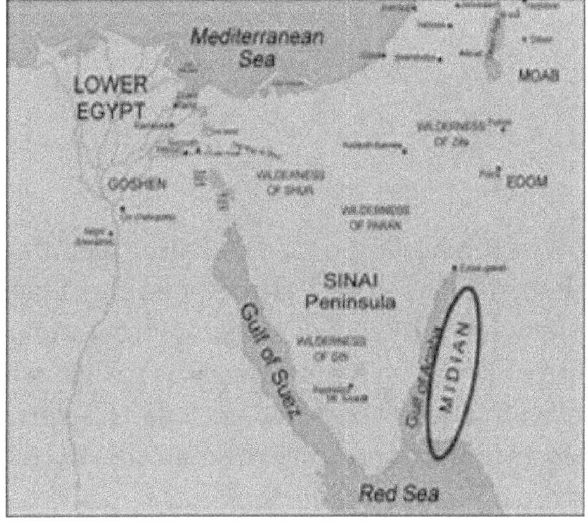

Bible Maps.com

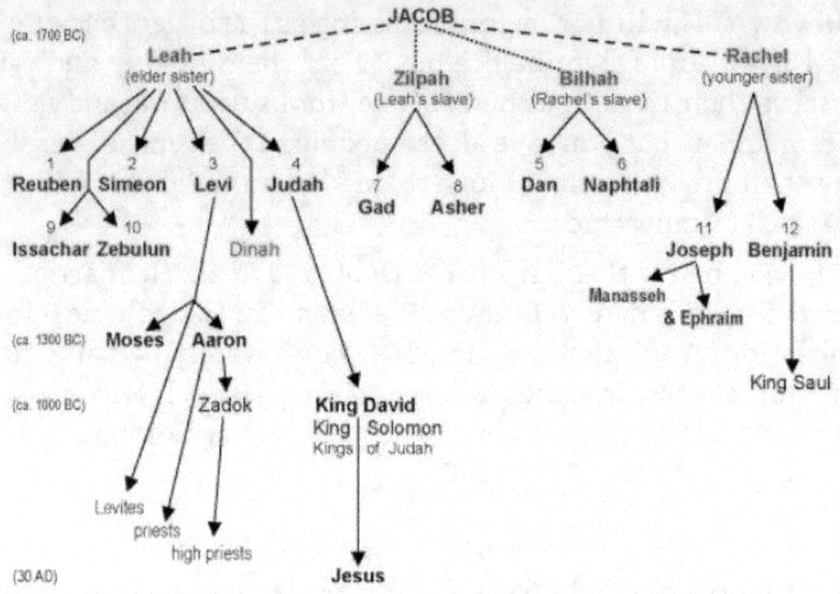

The next son of Reuben recorded is Pallu, meaning 'distinguished', and he will father the Palluite people. They will produce the people who will war against Moses and Aaron under the leadership of Korah in **Numbers 26:5-11**. He reminds us that this is the war where the LORD opens the earth and it will swallow two hundred and fifty men along with Korah. However, the children of Korah live.

Reuben's third son is Hezron and Master points him out to us as he walks by. It is fun to see his name on this chart and see the real person. His name means 'enclosure' and unfortunately that is all we know of his life. I watch him walk away and wish I could talk to him and at least get an idea of his life up to this point.

Next, Master introduces Karmi the fourth son of Reuben. Master, looking across the many people getting settled, tells us that all we will know of him.

Descendants of Simeon

Son of Leah

Moving His hand, Master takes us to the second son of Jacob and Leah, Simeon. Master takes us to the sons of Simeon. You remind us that he, along with Levi, massacred the entire settlement of Hittites living in Shechem because the prince raped Dinah his sister. I note that this event was recorded in **Genesis 34:24-31.** I mention that it was horrific and violent.

Simeon will have six sons but most of his descendants will disappear. Simeon's sons are Jemuel and we will not know the meaning of his name. He will also be known as Nemuel in **Numbers 26:9,12 and 1 Chronicles 4:24.** Master reminds us that we will recognize him as one of the brothers who will lead the violent uprising against Moses and Aaron.

Simeon's second son is named Jamin, meaning 'right hand.' It is unfortunate we will know nothing of him or his descendants.

Ohad is Simeon's third son and we will not know the meaning of his name. We will see him again in **Exodus 6:15** where he will be listed as a head of his father's house when the Children of Israel prepare to leave Egypt.

Jachan means, 'he will set up. Master points out to us his settlement that is taking shape not too far from where we are today. He will be the father of the Jachanite people mentioned in **Numbers 26:12.**

The fifth son of Simeon is named Zohar and Master tells us that in the future we will know nothing of what he will do with his life. I mention that this is a sad thought for me, and I am impressed that I must make my life count for something.

The sixth son of Simeon is Shaul who will forever be referred to as "the son of a Canaanitish woman." His descendants will be called Shaulites and will be considered 'mixed blood.'

Descendants of Levi

Son of Leah

Next Master moves us to the sons of Jacob's son Levi who is neatly listed under his name. We know a little more about Levi as he was born in Haran and he joined his father on the return to Canaan. Levi joined his brothers in the plot against Joseph and now we see him bowing before him as Joseph's dreams had prophesied. We will witness Levi when he dies at the age of one hundred and thirty-five as recorded in **Exodus 6:16.** Master adds that in spite of Levi's involvement at the massacre in Shechem; Levi and his descendants will be blessed as recorded in **Deuteronomy 33:8-11.**

The first sons of Levi are listed as Gerson, Master points that his family is settled closest to us in the plane of Goshen. We are excited to hear that his descendants will have an active part in the wilderness traveling of the Children of Israel as recorded in **Numbers 3:23-25; 4:21-28.** As we look in the direction of this busy tribe, Master adds that they will be prominent in the service of the Temple of Solomon specifically as singers. Smiling at you, I wonder if they will sing for us now or if this will be just the descendants who will do that.

The second son of Levi is Kohath and we can see his encampment across the stream from where we are. Master is excited to tell us that this man will be an ancestor of Moses. We are even more amazed when He tells us that they will care for the Ark of the Covenant, the table, candlestick, altars, and vessels of the sanctuary. He adds that they will carry all of these on foot, there will be no wagons for them. As we sit staring at the chart before us, Master encourages us to seek out these people because they are interesting and very visible in biblical history.

Merari is Levi's third son. His name means 'bitter' to which you and I have a definite facial reaction. To our reaction, Master tells us that he is the patriarch of the tribe of Levi. The

Merarites will have the responsibility for the woodwork of the tabernacle in its journeys as recorded in **Numbers 3:17, 33-37.** He adds that when the Children of Israel occupy the Promised Land the Merarites will hold twelve cities in Reuben, Gad and Zebulum territory **Joshua 21:7, 33-34.**

Descendant of Judah

Son of Leah

Master's expression changes as He points to Er, the first-born son of Judah. You ask why the change in expression and He takes us to **Genesis 38:7 But Er, Judah's firstborn, was wicked in the sight of the LORD, and the LORD killed him.** I draw in my breath and put my hand over my mouth wondering, without asking details how old he was, what was the wickedness? There is no further explanation, Master just moves His hand to the next son.

Judah's second son is Onon. Master cautions us that there is tragedy in this man also. Again, He takes us to **Genesis 38:8-10 And Judah said to Onan, "Go in to your brother's wife and marry her, and raise up an heir to your brother." But Onon knew that the heir would not be his; and it came to pass, when he went in to her brother's wife, that he emitted on the ground lest she should give an heir to his brother. And the thing which he did displeased the LORD; therefore He killed him also.** I remember that this act started a whole chain of ungodly events. You suggest that sometimes scripture seems too real and hard to understand.

When we look back, Master is ready to talk about Shelah whose name means 'a petition.' He tells us Shelah's descendants will be called the Shelanites.

Master looks at us as He says the name Perez, meaning 'breach.' He tells us that Perez is one of the twins born to Jacob by Tamar, his daughter-in-law. We have no discussion about this boy other than he will also be called Phares later in **Numbers**

26:20-21. This will be when Moses is taking a census of the Children of Israel.

Zerah is Tamar's other twin, meaning 'rising.' We will see his descendants, called 'Zerahites' in **Joshua 7** when Jacob's descendant, Joshua, takes Jericho and the Children of Israel take possession of **"accursed things"** from Jericho. Joshua then will lead them into Ai to conquer that land. Joshua will discover that, because the Children of Israel placed those **"accursed things"** among their own possessions, God will not fight with them unless they destroy these things. Joshua vows to find them and destroy the man and family who has possession of it. It is found with Achan of the tribe of Judah. Master then encourages us to read this chapter and consider if there is any unclean thing we are possessing that is not acceptable in His sight. Then He reminds us that He cannot stand with us if we choose to hold on to these things. You ask if He will reveal these things to us and He assures us He will.

I am not certain I am ready to continue, but Master is so He leads us to Hezron the grandson of Judah by Tamar and Jacob by Perez. We will know nothing more of him.

Also listed is a son named Hamul meaning 'spared.' Master tells us that all we will know of him is that his descendants will be called Hamulites.

Descendants of Isschar

Son of Leah

Isschar's firstborn son is Tola. We are excited when Master points out his camp just the other side of a stream behind Jacob's tent.

Master moves his hand to Puvah the second son of Isschar. We understand that his name is also spelled Phuvah in **Numbers 46:13** and **1 Chronicles 7:1.** He shares with us that there will be a later descendant also called Tola who will be the seventh judge in Israel for 23 years and he is mentioned in **Judges 10:1-2.** I mention that it is refreshing to find a godly descendant among these sixty-six people setting up their homes around us.

The next name on the scroll before us is Job. Master assures us that this is not the Job of our bibles as we remember that the Job lived during the time of Abraham. I am a bit frustrated when I know that we will know nothing about this Job. I do, however, determine that with all these names I am seeing on this chart, I hope to see some of them during our stay in Goshen.

Next on the scroll is Shimron which means, 'a guard.' Master tells us that the only information we will have of Shimron is that he is the fourth son of Issachar, son of Jacob.

Descendants of Zebulun

Son of Leah

Zebulun's firstborn son is Sered, whom we have no individual information about. I ask Master, "How can it be we have no information about these men, they are so important?" He assures us that the importance is not about these individual tribes but about the Children of Israel as a whole, and how they serve Elohim. You ask if the tribes they produce are important individually." He asks us to stay with Him and assures us their part as an entire group is important, but the individuals are part of a bigger picture or body. I am beginning to think of my part of the bigger picture, in the "body of believers."

Elon is Zebulun's second son. Master again shows us that this is all we know of him. However, we are beginning to understand that they are real people and there is purpose in their lives.

Master continues with Jahleel. Not even knowing the meaning of his name, we are guided to be content that we know nothing more of him. Master does, however, point out that he is walking not far from us with young girls carrying flowers. I imaging that the flowers are for their mother.

Master tells us that all these sons and daughters, including Dinah, were born in Padan Aram. You suggest that they were all born when they were living under the household of Laban. As I begin to count the names we have listed on the scroll, Master shares that there are thirty-three.

ZILPAH'S SONS

Genesis 46:16-18

16. The sons of Gad were Zipion, Haggi, Shuni, Exbon, Eri, Arodi, and Areli.

17. The sons of Asher were Jimnah, Ishuah, Isui, Beriah, and Serah, their sisters. Ahd the sons of Beriah were Heber and Malchiel.

18. These were the sons of Zilpah, whom Laban gave to Leah his daughter; and these she bore to Jacob: sixteen persons.

After we have taken a short break for our noon meal Master leads us back to the scroll. However, we have moved our location to a more comfortable flat rock where we can sit on our wraps and use the rock as a table. As we sit down, I remember the snake that slithered out from under the rock where we met Noah and I make more noise that is necessary. The air is clean and warm, the grass is soft and welcoming, and our Master's presence is sweet and precious. I am blessed to be in this place.

We begin with the sons of Gad the first son of Zilpah and Jacob, His name is Ziphion meaning 'watching.' Master informs us that he will also be known as Zephon the father of the Zephonites.

Haggi is Gad's second son. Master shares with us that he will be the father of the Haggite people. You ask, "Why are we interested in who these people are 'the father of' if we know nothing more about them." He adds that it is important whose family you belong to. It is like attaching a last name. Mankind finds great security in belonging and this gives them that. It also gives others recognition of where they belong.

Master now takes us to Shuni, the third son of Gad. He is camped right next to our camp and in fact is very friendly.

Sliding down the list of the sons of Gad we come to Ezbon. We do not know the meaning of his name, but we do know that he will also be called Ozni in **Numbers 26:16.**

Eri is the next son of Gad whose name means 'my watcher.' As I look at the scroll, I notice the intricate lettering and the exactness of each letter. I wonder at the skill it takes to write this and who penned this. The preciseness amazes me when we know nothing more about this man.

Looking again to the scroll, Master points to Arodi who will also be called Arod. We both look to Master as He tells us he will be the father of the Arodite people.

Gad's seventh son is called Arell who is also called Areli. He will be the father of the Arelite people. Master adds that we will know nothing more of this man. However, his people will be mentioned in **Numbers 26:17** when Moses is counting the Children of Israel.

DESCENDANTS OF ASHER

Son of Zilpah

Jimnah is the firstborn of Asher. Master tells us that his name means 'good fortune.' However, we will not know if his name proved to be true because we know nothing more of Jimnah.

The second son of Asher is Ishuah whose name means 'he will level.' You ask Master what that phrase means but receive no answer as He continues.

Isui is the next name and we both struggle to pronounce his name. Master tells us that his name can also be spelled Ishui. He also cautions us to not confuse this Ashui with the son of Saul in **1 Samuel 14:49** and smiling, He adds that they are years apart.

Master leads us to Beriah. We see that Beriah has two sons Heber and Malchiel. We are told that Heber means 'associate', but we know nothing more of him. We are excited to hear that Malchiel's name means 'God is my king." His name gives us hope for these people.

These boys have a sister named Sarah whose name means 'princess', but we do not know if she really was like one. We know nothing more of her. We also do not understand why a female is listed, especially as we do not see a future reference to this Sarah.

Before you can begin counting, Master tells us that there are sixteen descendants by Zilpah.

SONS OF RACHEL

19. The sons of Rachel, Jacob's wife, were Joseph and Benjamin.

20. And to Joseph in the land of Egypt were born Manasseh and Ephraim, whom Asenath, the daughter of Poti-Pherah priest of On, bore to him.

21. The sons of Benjamin were Belah, Becher, Ashbel, Gera, Naaman, Ehi, Rosh, Muppim, Huppim, and Ard.

22. There were the sons of Rachel who were born to Jacob: fourteen persons in all.

Master moves on, placing His mighty hand on the next few verses. We see the familiar name of Joseph and beside him is Benjamin. We have seen them several times walking together, talking. I did not hear what they were saying but my mind imagines many things as they were only boys when they were together last.

There with the boy's names is Rachel, the desire of Jacob's heart. Oh, the years that have passed. I consider the honor Master has offered us, allowing us to experience Jacob's sin and repentance, his failures and God's grace and blessings on his life. I look up at Master and find Him looking at me smiling. He knows my every thought. With that, He suggests we look at these boys. Of course, I am more than excited to see these men through His eyes.

You remind me that Joseph's name means, 'may God add'. I remember well when he was born and Rachel's words at seeing a son, **"The LORD shall add to me another son." In Genesis 30:24.** I loved that she considered the sons of her maidservant

Bilhah her own. I do still struggle with the custom of giving a maidservant to a husband, but I understand why they did this. Master shares with us that Joseph will be the ancestor of the two northern tribes of Manasseh and Ephriam. Reminding us of the covenant Yahweh made with Joseph at an early age, Master asks if we see the fulfillment around us. We agree that we do, and He shares that it is not yet complete. There it is again; Master motivates us to look for His plan to be revealed before us as we journey through His word. You ask if we will always see Joseph as a leader and the great man of passion that he is today. Master again, placing His hand on yours, encourages you to be patient.

precept upon precept

Then He adds that there are still more lessons to come from Joseph.

I ask about Benjamin and what he will have for us. You say, "Let us see if I remember correctly, Rachel named him Benoni meaning 'son of my sorrow or agony'. Master nods agreement but continues looking for you to add something. After a moment's thought you say, "Yes, Jacob renamed Benjamin after Rachel died. He called him Benjamin 'son of my right hand'." With a nod and a smile this time, Master is pleased with your memory. You also add that Benjamin played no part in the sale of Joseph into slavery. I add to our picture that Benjamin is a favorite son of Jacob and this has been a problem for the entire family. Master points to Jacob's tent and we see Benjamin along with one of his children, sitting with Jacob and laughing joyfully.

As we are watching, Master reminds us that Joseph is married in Egypt to Asenath the daughter of a pagan priest of On. Asenath gave Joseph a son whom he named Manasseh meaning 'one who forgets'. You and I look at each other and I say that this child was set up from the beginning. Master adds that Manasseh's brother Ephriam will be greater than him. We look at each other wondering what this means. Just as you are about to ask, Master continues with the sons of Benjamin.

Ephriam means 'double fruit' and you and I imagine that it means he will inherit both his and Manasseh's blessings, but we know we must wait on Master to guide us through this. Master tells us that there will be a tribe called the tribe of Ephriam among the tribes of Israel bringing them to thirteen tribes.

What?!

Master promises He will explain this all to us soon but now we are looking at the genealogy of Jacob's sons and we do not want to miss anything here.

The oldest son of Benjamin is Belah. He will be mentioned again in **Numbers 26:4** as the head of the Belahite family but we know nothing more of him.

The second son of Benjamin is Becher which is the term used for a young camel. This prompts a slight giggle from both of us, but you hold back a comment. Master tells us that his family will find no place in the registry of families in **Numbers 26:38** or in **1 Chronicles 8:1-6**. You ask why and Master graciously leads us to understand that, in the beginning, there will be too few of them to form a tribe. However, later his nine sons will build the family to twenty thousand and more as recorded in **1 Chronicles 7:8-9.** Looking to Master, you ask if this is because in the beginning Becher had only daughters and they are not counted in a census. With no definite response Master tells you that He loves your searching for reasons and answers.

Ashbel is Benjamin's third son and Master shares with us that the only thing we will know of him is that his descendants, the Ashbelites will be listed in the census in **Numbers 2626:38.**

Moving His finger Master points to Gera the next son of Benjamin. He tells us that his name means 'grain' and you cannot help but comment that Benjamin is not too creative with his children's names. Master adds that we will know nothing more of Gera.

Naaman is the next name of the scroll, meaning 'pleasant'. Master tells us that Naaman is Benjamin's grandson by Bela but is listed as his son here. We remember learning that the relationship for son and grandson is often referred to the same. I remember that I found this confusing until realizing it is easier than keeping all the different relationship possibilities straight. You ask of his lineage, as we have not seen a man named Bela in the genealogy of Benjamin. Master does not seem to hear you, but we are certain He does because He hears our every thought. However, we do not get an answer currently. Master continues that he will be the father of the Naamanite people.

Master moves to Ehi meaning 'union'. He tells us we will know him as Ahram or Ahra in **1 Chronicles 8:1.** At that we agree to not question further these names or their position. We are honored to be going through this scroll with Master and pleased that He is sharing what He is.

Master guides attention back to Jacob and Benjamin telling us that the young man with them is Rosh, Benjamin's sixth son. This is the only mention of Ehi in scripture.

You and I look at each other and cannot help but giggle as Master brings us to Muppim. We find his name funny but when we consider the other names and how foreign they are to us, I guess they are all a bit 'funny'. Master shares that later is scripture we will see him called Shupham in **Numbers 26:39** or Shuppim in **1 Chronicles 7:12, 15.** He is also called Shephuphan in **1 Chronicles 8:5.** Master explains that names change through scripture as people are in different areas and different languages pronounce or spell them differently. I understand that as I know this happens with my own name in different languages.

Next, we come to a group of people who will settle on the coast, they are descendants of Huppim, Benjamin's eighth son. We are disappointed to hear that we will know nothing more of him. I was hoping to know if he and Muppim were twins. You and I look at each other and what starts with a grin bursts into laughter at the names of these men. Master giggles with us as we fight to control ourselves enough to move on. Just when we have controlled ourselves by not looking at each other, master mentions the next grandson.

Ard is Benjamin's grandson by Bela also. That tears it and you burst out with "Huppim, Muppim and Ard." We have lost control again and out of the corner of my eye I see that Master is not offended but laughing with our joy. After a few minutes of side-splitting laughter, you lift your head from the rock table, and we take a few breaths to compose ourselves again. Master is waiting patiently for us knowing that with the intense information we are trying to take in, we needed a good laugh. Without saying the name Ard, He continues to instruct us that this man will also be known as Addar later in scripture, but we will know nothing more of him or his descendants.

Master tells us that Benjamin will add to the family of Jacob fourteen persons. I wish I had been keeping track of the totals of each family but assume they will be totaled for us later.

THE SONS OF DAN AND NEPHTALI

Genesis 46:23-25

23. The son of Dan was Hushim.

24. The sons of Naphtali were Jahzeel, Guni, Jezer, and Shillem.

25. These were the sons of Bilhah whom Laban gave to Rachel his daughter, and she bore these to Jacob: seven persons in all.

We are feeling restless, but Master encourages to remain with Him through these two verses before we move on. He promises a rest and change of focus soon, so we agree to abide with Him here.

His scroll is spread before us and He moves His hand to point to Dan the fifth son of Jacob. Master catches our attention again when He shares with us that Dan's descendants will be given the responsibility of being the rear guard when the Children of Israel leave Egypt during the Exodus. This information is recorded in **numbers 10:25 Then the standard of the camp of the children of Dan (the rear guard of all the camps) set out according to their armies; over their army was Ahiezer son of Ammishaddai.** It is fascinating that only one son of Dan is mentioned here because at the time of the Exodus the tribe of Dan will equal sixty-two thousand seven hundred men. He tells us that the portion of the Promised Land that will be given to Dan's descendants will be the land between Judah and the Mediterranean Sea. Master adds that this is the land of the Philistines. You ask if Dan's descendants, the Danites, will conquer the Philistines. Master replies that they will not but that it is a journey for a later time.

The only son of Dan mentioned in this scripture is Hushim but unfortunately, we will find nothing recorded about his life. Master does tell us that he will also be called Shuham in the census of **Numbers 26.**

Naphtali is the second son of Bilhah, Rachel's handmaid, along with his older son Dan. Master tells us his name means 'fight' or 'struggle'. Master tells us we will be there when Jacob blesses Naphtali and that blessing will be all we will know of him personally. However, we will see his descendants throughout the Old Testament.

Naphtali had a son and named him Jahzeel and, without lifting His head, Master tells us we will know nothing of him either. then He moves his finger to Naphtali's second son.

The second son is called Guni who will not leave a legacy for us to explore.

Master tells us that Jezer is the third son of Naphtali whose name means 'purpose'. The meaning of his name gives us hope that there will be a great plan for this man, but Master tells us we will know nothing more of him.

The last son of Naphtali is named Shillem who will be called Shallum in

1 Chronicles 7:13. You ask, "Are these the Shulamite people mentioned in **Solomon 6:13 Return, return, o Shulamite;**

Return, return, that we may look upon you!

What would you see in the Shulamite-

As it were, the dance of two camps?

At that question, Master looks up from His scroll to caution us to not try too hard to tie these people to their family lines. He tells us these are not the same people and that trying to trace any family lines but the 'scarlet thread' is wasted. Then He adds that, if we need to know the ancestors of a people, He will tell us. He finishes by stating that we will know nothing more of the family of Shillem.

Closing this section, we understand that these two men and their families are the sons of Bilhah, Rachel's maidservant. There are seven persons.

SHEPHERDS

Genesis 46:26-34

26. All the persons who went with Jacob to Egypt, who came from his body, besides Jacob's sons' wives, were sixty-six persons in all.

27. And the sons of Joseph who were born to him in Egypt were two persons, all the persons of the house of Jacob who went to Egypt were seventy.

28. Then he sent Judah before him to Joseph, to point the way to Goshen. And they came to the land of Goshen.

29. So Joseph made ready his chariot and went up to Goshen to meet his father Israel; and he presented himself to him, and fell on his neck and wept on his neck a good while.

30. And Israel said to Joseph, "Now let me die, since I have seen your face, because you are still alive."

31. Then Joseph said to his brothers and to his father's household, "I will go up and tell Pharaoh, and say to him, 'My brothers and those of my father's house, who were in the land of Canaan, have come to me.

32. 'And the men are shepherds, for their occupation has been to feed livestock; and they have brought their flocks, and herds, and all that they have.'

33. "So it shall be, when Pharaoh calls you and says, 'What is your occupation?'

34"that you shall say, 'Your servants' occupation has been with livestock from our youth even till now, both we and also our fathers,' that you may dwell in the land of Goshen; for every

shepherd is an abomination to the Egyptians."

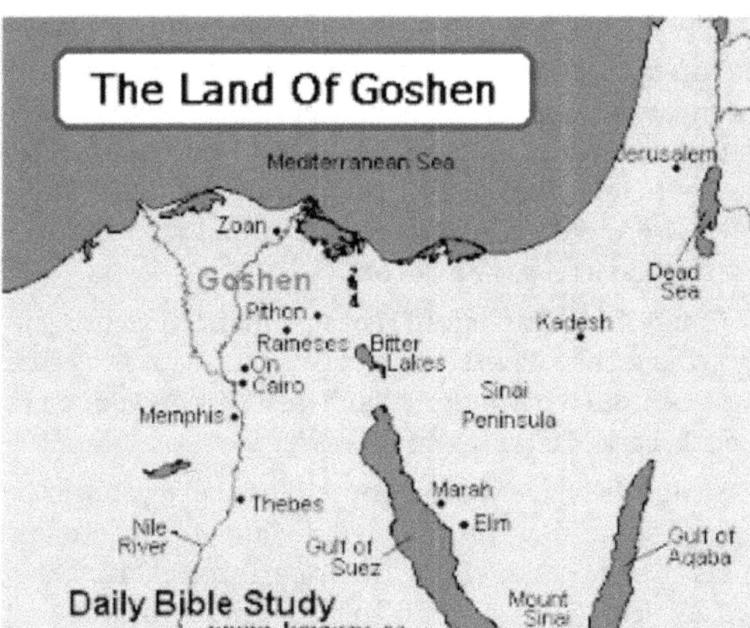

We awaken to the sounds of people bustling about preparing their morning meals. Mothers are talking with their children, encouraging them to hurry to prepare before their father returns from caring for their flocks. When I roll over on my sleeping mat, the sound of a nearby stream whispers of the joy of being in the presence of my Master and the unfolding of history before me. I whisper a silent prayer of thanksgiving as I rest my head for one last deep breath before joining you outside. I can hear you talking with Master but cannot discern what is being said. I am certain He is sharing a truth designed just for your ears and I smile knowing He is such a personal God.

The table is set with fresh fruit, fish, and goat milk when I exit our shelter. I thank both you and Master for Your care of me and He holds his hand out to you telling me it was all you this time. I thankfully nod in your direction.

As soon as Master finishes sharing the scripture for today you ask why they did not count the wives of Jacob's sons when numbering the people. His short answer is that it is not custom-ary to number women in a census.

You follow the previous question asking another, "Why the scriptures still numbering Joseph separate from his brothers and Jacob." Graciously He reminds us that man is known by his place of origin. I remember we did talk of this when we wondered why Rachel was called an Edomite even though she was a relative of Jacob.

You tell me that before I got up Judah left to bring Joseph to Him where they have settled in Goshen. I am excited to see him again united with his father and brothers. As I pop a grape in my mouth, I ask Master if Jacob is excited.

As soon as I have washed myself for the day, I hear people gathering behind me. You grab my arm and urge me to hurry as Joseph is coming. He is riding in his personal chariot, the very one we witnessed Pharaoh gift to him. This is the one that sets Joseph apart as the second in command in all of Egypt. Looking around we see uncertainty on the faces of the Children of Israel. You suggest that most of them have never seen such splendor and have always considered Egyptians 'the enemy.' Joseph is led right up to the front entrance to Jacob's home and, leaving his chariot behind, rushes to his father's arms. The arms that for so long have remained empty are now bathed in tears of joy. I look at you and see we are both weeping with excitement. Jacob is now called Israel as he says to Jacob, **And Israel said to Joseph, "Now let me die, since I have seen your face, because you are still alive."** Turning momentarily to face Master, you ask, "Why is Jacob called Israel now?" He asks you if you remember what the name Israel means, you silently shake your head 'no'. You offer that Jacob means 'supplanter' but do not remember what Israel means. He offers that Israel means 'God preserves.' A sigh escapes me as I realize that Jacob the supplanter has become the child of God who now lives by faith. God has done His work in Jacob and Jacob is the man God intends him to be.   All those days of not knowing, hoping, praying for his son are completed in this one statement.

Joseph's brothers have gathered, each knowing that the relationships between Joseph and them is completely restored. Joseph instructs them that he will go before them to Pharaoh and explain that they are shepherds and that they can be honest with Pharaoh when he asks them what they do and why they live in Goshen instead of closer to the palaces. Joseph adds that shepherds are an abomination to the Egyptians because sheep eat the grasses so close to the ground leaving no food for other animals. Master adds that Egyptians feel so strongly about sheep that mutton is seldom, if ever, used in the Egyptian diet. I offer that just as Jesus Christ will refer to Himself as the shepherd, he will also be an abomination to those who will not follow Him. You offer me a high five as Master reaches for my other hand in approval.

As He is holding my hand, I am completely in awe and repentant as I acknowledge that He did exactly what He promised to do. I know I doubted Him, and in fact more than once insisted that He "Do something." His understanding smile floods me with peace and I once again marvel at the big picture He is painting right before me in His scriptures.

We watch as Joseph leaves the camp of his father and you and I agree to go for a walk. I want to put faces to the names from the scroll Master shared with us in this chapter of His word. He encourages us to look for banners as each of the twelve sons will soon be raising their family banner to mark their encampments. That is an exciting thought as I remember the banners from the book of Exodus. Are we really going to see them?

I guess we are.

JACOB'S FAMILY HONORED

Genesis 47:1-6

1. Then Joseph went and told Pharaoh, and said, "My father and my brothers, their flocks and their herds and all that they possess, have come from the land of Canaan; and indeed they are in the land of Goshen."

2. And he took five men from among his brothers and presented them to Pharaoh.

3. Then Pharaoh said to his brothers, "What is your occupation?" And they said to Pharaoh, "Your servants are shepherds, both we and also our fathers."

4. And they said to Pharaoh, "We have come to dwell in the land, because your servants have no pasture for their flocks, for the famine is severe in the land of Canaan. Now therefore, please let your servants' dwell in the land of Goshen."

5. Then Pharaoh spoke to Joseph, saying, "Your father and your brothers have come to you.

6. "The land of Egypt is before you. Have your father and brothers dwell in the best of the land; let them dwell in the land of Goshen. And if you know any competent men among them, then make them chief herdsmen over my livestock."

Master joins us on our walk, and we are thrilled to be alone with Him again. He has barely finished stating the scriptures for us when you ask Him why we only see Canaan and Egypt in this famine. You want to confirm that the famine was over all the known land, which He affirms as true. He suggests that we go with Joseph and his brothers to meet Pharaoh and we are more than excited. It has been a long time since we were in the presence of Pharaoh or in his magnificent palace.

We are pleased to see that the first verse Master shares with us shows the respect Joseph holds for his Pharaoh, his friend. Even though they work as a ruling team, God has blessed them as friends also.

Joseph arrives before Pharaoh with five of his brothers. You suggest that these brothers must have felt some apprehension coming before this ruler. I suggest that they are trusting Joseph and that this is amazing. I almost hold my breath when Pharaoh asks them to state their occupation. I ask Master if this is a trick question or is he interested. Master shares with me that this is a customary greeting that shows the intent to find common ground. Almost as if rehearsed one of the brothers' steps forward to tell Pharaoh that they are shepherds. With a sigh of relief, he steps back in line with the rest of his brothers

Pharaoh addresses Joseph with a sly smile as he confirms that Joseph's entire family is united. He knew this has been the desire of Joseph's heart since the two had met years ago. You and I stand to the side of the great hall listening. I cannot help but look around for the cheetah who had been here when we left this palace last time. I catch Master's eye and mouth the words, "Where is the cheetah?" He seems amused with my wondering mind and nods my attention back to Pharaoh and Joseph. The brothers respectfully listen, they seem unsure of what is happening. Then they hear Pharaoh state that they may also "rule over his cattle." There is silence in the room as Joseph considers this invitation. It seems that the air has become cooler with this consideration. Without answering Pharaoh, Joseph nods to his brothers and they leave the court of the Pharaoh without turning their backs. They remain in silence with only the sound of their leather sandals on the stone floor until they are on the front steps of the palace. We follow, also in silence even though our minds are a whirl with forming questions. Will they be in the employee of Pharaoh? Will they be held responsible for cattle who cannot survive the famine? Are they able to care for both their sheep and Pharaoh's cattle?

A BLESSING FOR PHARAOH

Genesis 47:7-12

7. Then Joseph brought in his father Jacob and set him before Pharaoh; and Jacob blessed Pharaoh.

8. Pharaoh said to Jacob, "How old are you?"

9. And Jacob said to Pharaoh, "Tow days of the years of my pilgrimage are one hundred and thirty years; few and evil have been the days of the years of my life, and they have not attained to the days of the years of the life of my fathers in the days of their pilgrimage."

10. So Jacob blessed Pharaoh and went out from before Pharaoh.

11. And Joseph situated his father and his brothers and gave them a possession in the land of Egypt, the best of the land, in the land of Rameses, as Pharaoh had commanded.

12. Then Joseph provided his father, his brothers, and all his father's household with bread, according to the number of their families.

Master offers no answers to our questions and we arrive back at the home of Jacob. Joseph bids his brothers a gracious farewell before approaching his father. After a short visit with Jacob, Joseph guides the aging man to his chariot and helps him step into it. Together the two head back to Pharaoh's palace. You and I notice the smile on Jacob's face as the wind blows gently in his white hair and beard. He is nestled safely in front of Joseph between his strong arms. You say that you think he enjoys traveling this way.

We follow closely as Joseph helps Jacob up the steps of the palace. We do not want to miss even one reaction from Jacob as he experiences this place. He is shaking and I do not know if it is fear or he is weary from the journey. Master assures us that Jacob feels perfectly safe holding Joseph's arm.

We find our place in the palace and it seems Pharaoh has been conducting other business while we were away. When it comes to Joseph's time to address the ruler, he brings Jacob in through the towering heavy doors and stands beside him.

Leaning forward on his throne Pharaoh asks Jacob how old he is.

There was no coaching of Jacob before he came as there had been with his five sons. When he opens his mouth you and I witness a different Jacob than we had known all those years previously. There is no boasting, no defense, no lies, no pride. Here stands a man humbled by God and out of his mouth comes a blessing on the Pharaoh.

What?!

Suddenly I feel honored to have been witness to the transformation Yahweh has performed in Jacob's life. My heart swells with joy in my Master as tears well up in my eyes. Once again, He has performed what He said He would do. Why does my heart and mind ever doubt Him?

Jacob, with his strongest voice, tells Pharaoh that he is one hundred and thirty years old. Master whispers that we will soon see that Jacob will live seventeen more years after this day. I imagine he is strengthened in part by the fact that his family is all together and thriving. Continuing, Jacob tells Pharaoh that his life is really nothing to boast about. He does not brag about pulling the trick on his brother, or his service to Laban for the wife he loved, nor that he was an important man in Canaan. Instead he tells Pharaoh that he has not lived up to the greatness of his fathers. Glancing at you, I see you are as amazed as I am. Jacob is giving glory to God for his life without taking credit for one moment of it.

You whisper that Jacob is a sinner, saved by grace just like us. Master, pleased with your comparison, takes us to **James 3:13-16. Who is wise and understanding among you? Let him show by good conduct that his works are done in meekness and wisdom. But if you have bitter envy and self-seeking in your hearts, do not boast and lie against the truth. This wisdom does not descend from above, but is earthly, sensual, demonic. For where envy and self-seeking exist, confusion and every evil thing are there. But the wisdom that is from above is first pure, then peaceable, gentle, willing to yield, full of mercy and good fruits, without partiality and without hypocrisy.** With this verse you and I again are reminded with without our Master we are evil in every breath.

The scripture tells us that Jacob blesses Pharaoh, but we are not told what he is saying. You ask Master if we will be aware of the blessing that Jacob is giving Pharaoh, but He does not give us an answer. This sets my mind to wondering if the fact that Jacob came with such grace and presence of God is the blessing. I may never know the answer, but I am content with this thought.

After the blessing of watching the encounter in the court of Pharaoh, Joseph gently transports his father back to the camp where the family is establishing themselves under the permission of Pharaoh. Joseph stands a little taller and the expression on his face is less stern as he has witnessed God's hand on his father's life. He has witnessed the answered prayers from all these years of being separated from his family.

Joseph's God is powerful and good!

After confirming with his brothers that Goshen is exactly where they are permitted to settle, Joseph serves his brothers by providing each of them with bread for their families.

Before leaving this section of scripture, Master points out that our scripture states that the Children of Israel are settling **"in the land of Rameses"** as Pharaoh commanded. Hearing this, you question why this area is called "Rameses because he will not be born for five hundred years from now. Without turning to Master for guidance, you begin to reason out loud. As you do, I look from Master to you, wondering if He is going to stop you and explain the answer to your question. You suggest that maybe Rameses is the name of a region and not the name of a man. Or is our scripture giving us a glimpse into the future referring to the land where Rameses will be raised? Is there more than one Rameses and this one is not the Rameses of the time of the Exodus? Master startles you when He interjects into your questions. History will show there will be eight men called Ramesses. Snapping your head in His direction your eyes plead for answers. Master faces you as he explains that the term Rameses is used to identify a region and Rameses II, whom we are talking about in reference to the Children of Israel reigned in this region of Egypt. His reign was the second longest reign in Egyptian history spanning from 1279 to 13 B.C. He takes us to **Exodus 1:11 Therefore they set taskmasters over them to afflict them with their burdens. And they built for Pharaoh supply cities, Pithom and Raamses.** Then He guides us to **Exodus 12:27 Then the children of Israel journeyed from Rameses to Succoth, about six-hundred thousand men on foot, besides children.** Being content with your new understanding, you ask what the name Rameses means and grinning He tells us that Rameses means 'child of the sun' or 'created by Ra'. Then, so we can follow this region through our journey in scripture, He shares with us that Rameses may also be spelled Ramesses in addition to Rameses as we just saw in the Exodus scripture. Opening his hand to us, He shows us a familiar picture. Right there in the palm of His hand is Rameses II whom we will be concerned with when we study Exodus.

Bing.com/images

Again, I am beside myself with wonder as I reach out to touch the picture that seems to float in His hand. My finger passes right through the picture.

Master is pleased at my delight.

THE FAMINE IS TOO SEVERE

Genesis 47:13-21

13. Now there was no bread in all the land; for the famine was very severe, so that the land of Egypt and the land of Canaan languished because of the famine.

14. And Joseph gathered up all the money that was found in the land of Egypt and in the land of Canaan, for the grain which they bought; and Joseph brought the money into Pharaoh's house.

15. So when the money failed in the land of Egypt and in the land of Canaan, all the Egyptians came to Joseph and said, "Give us bread, for why should we die in your presence? For the money has failed.

16. Then Joseph said, "Give your livestock, and I will give you bread for your livestock, if the money is gone."

17. So they brought their livestock to Joseph, and Joseph gave them bread in exchange for the horses and flocks, the cattle of the herds, and for the donkeys. Thus, he fed them with bread in exchange for all their livestock that year.

18. When that year had ended, they came to him the next year and said to him, "We will not hide from my lord that our money is gone; my lord also has our herds of livestock. There is nothing left in the sight of my lord but our bodies and our lands.

19. "Why should we die before your eyes, both we and our land? Buy us and our land for bread, and we and our land will be ser-

vants of Pharaoh; give us seed, that we may live and not die, that the land may not be desolate."

20. Then Joseph bought all the land of Egypt for Pharaoh; for every man of the Egyptians sold his field, because the famine was severe upon them. So, the land became Pharaoh's.

21. And as for the people, he moved them into the cities, from one end of the borders of Egypt to the other end.

Bing.com/ Egyptian coin image

With the reading of the scriptures before us we understand that the famine in the land is severe and it is hard for us to watch the people so desperate. Today you and I sit with Master near our shelter as we watch a young mother trying to nurse her infant, but she has no milk. She seems to be trying to satisfy him with all she has to offer. The flocks are few as they have not had enough grassland to sustain them and the water that had once flowed through the land seems to have dried up. The people are thin and slow, the excitement of a new settlement has left them, and fathers are discouraged. They cannot supply for their families which brings a man to desperation. I ask Master how much longer until this seven-year famine is complete, He assures me that it will end soon.

We watch as men come to Joseph telling him that with the failing economy, they cannot buy grain for bread. Joseph wants to help them, so he offers a trade, grain for their livestock. As we watch this bargaining Master tells us that throughout time many will say that Joseph is taking advantage of these men. He has the grain and could gift it to them rather than have them starve. He explains that when a man is put in a position of receiving gifts to support his family, his self-worth is destroyed. These men would never recover their drive to care for their families if Joseph simply gifted them the supplies. So, they bargain. Master points out that Joseph did not take advantage of them as the exchange carried these men and their families a full year.

It is a hot day and a dry wind is blowing the dust around in this once fertile area. We watch as men we do not know approach Joseph. They appear to be spokesmen for their individual groups of people. They are telling Joseph that they have nothing left to trade for food but their land and themselves.

Tears fill my eyes and as they roll down my cheeks, the dust fills them, causing them to stick to my face in streaks. Master, "How much longer must these people suffer?" I grasp His hand seeking hope for these people as they are desperate enough to sell themselves into slavery in exchange for food. Then it strikes me, this is when the children of Israel begin their slavery in Egypt! They are not being captured into slavery but are offering themselves up in exchange for food. Turning to face Master I ask Him, "Is this what this famine is all about, so You can rescue them from slavery five hundred years from now? Is this your plan to draw them to you? Oh, Master it is hard for me to understand a love like this."

Not only does Joseph buy up the land and the people of Canaan and Egypt but he moves them closer to the food supplies, to the cities. Joseph knows that the famine will end in the next year, but the people cannot sustain themselves that long.

The emotions of the desperation have exhausted us as we lay our heads on our sleeping mats seeking rest for the night. Tears roll from my eyes as I suggest to you that these people are being made ready to declare whom they will serve? You remind me that in Moses' time they will be called to paint their doorposts with blood from lambs, setting them apart as believers in the one true God. Later they will have to be bold enough to stand with those leaving Egypt with Moses. You add that often mankind seeks other men's wisdom when they are in desperate circumstances, instead of seeking God who sustains them. We agree that the men around us now are obviously seeking Joseph instead of the God of their fathers. With closed and weary eyes, I whisper that I have done this very thing. I listen to people moving about outside our shelter, seeking a place to establish themselves. The land has become crowded and noisy with settlers. As I drift into sweet sleep, I seek Master's face for assurance that this is His will for these people.

SLAVERY

Genesis 47:22-26

22. Only the land of the priests he did not buy; for the priests had rations allotted to them by Pharaoh, and they ate their rations which Pharaoh gave them; therefore they did not sell their lands.

23. Then Joseph said to the people, "Indeed I have bought you and your land this day for Pharaoh. Look, here is seed for you, and you shall sow the land.

24. "And it shall come to pass in the harvest that you shall give one-fifth to Pharaoh. Four-fifths shall be your own, as seed for the field and for your food, for those of your households and as food for your little ones."

25. So they said, "You have saved our lives; let us find favor in the sight of my lord, and we will be Pharaoh's servants."

26. And Joseph made it a law over the land of Egypt to this day, that Pharaoh should have one fifth, except for the land of the priests only, which did not become Pharaoh's.

The heat of the day awakens me along with the sound of you and Master sitting together outside our doorway. It is so hot my bedding sticks to me as I arise and fight off the bedding, attempting to not miss one precept that Master offers. I haphazardly comb my hair with my fingers, pulling it back from my face. The humidity is sticky on my skin. I do not stop to straighten my damp clothing as I get dressed. I hear you laughing, and I know I am missing something I trip exiting our shelter. Face first in the dirt I look up to see my Master's smiling face as he suggests I go wash the dirt off myself and clean myself up for breakfast. Oh, I am torn to leave you two even to wash, but the suggestion was fair as I consider myself.

The fresh sprinkling of water on my already damp skin is cool and refreshing. We are cautious with the stored water, so I splash just a little on my face and in my hair. Refreshed, I return to find our table blessed with mutton, berries, and water. You and Master share that you and He have been reliving your life in His presence and on this journey. I feel a bit guilty for desiring to intrude but I do so enjoy praising Him.

As I pop the last of the nuts in my mouth, Master asks if we are ready to continue. Without hesitation, we both lean toward Him.

He reads the next passage of **Genesis 47** Speaking of the **'land of the priests.'** You interrupt and ask who these priests are. You ask if they are the ones we will see in the Levitical cities. He is pleased to explain that these priests are priests of Egypt in this day and not of the tribe of Levi. Master explains to us that the land He is showing us has been set apart for the priests of Egypt who have already sworn allegiance to Pharaoh. Pharaoh made an agreement that he will care for their needs.

Joseph is instructing those whom he has already moved to closer settlements. We move in as close as is comfortable. We hear him tell them that Egypt is providing them crops and that they are to till the land and grow crops to feed their people. He adds that when they harvest their crops one-fifth will go to Pharaoh and Egypt. The slaves may keep four-fifth to feed their own families and to plant for next season's crops.

We find a place to sit in a small patch of shade from a large rock. Sitting cross legged you suggest we consider what has happened to these people.

1. Pharaoh had the dream that Joseph told him revealed seven years of plenty followed by seven years of famine.

2. The people knew the dream and that the famine was

> coming but none stored up food or prepared in any obvious way. However, Joseph stored enough for everyone.
>
> 3. It didn't take long into the famine that the people needed help and Joseph was there with his supplies. The people bought what they could but soon there was no money left to purchase food.
>
> 4. When there were no other options, the people traded their animals and then their land, and finally themselves (as slaves).

We know that hard times are coming as we read in our scriptures. Master, You tell us to store up our treasures in heaven, but we are not taught how to do that. Your word says by doing 'good works', but we are not even certain what those are without guidance. You add that in our day we are told about our armor to protect us from satanic attacks but are not taught how to put it on. By the time we live, scriptural lessons will be so non-confronting that sin will no longer be called sin but will have different names, it does not offend. Master, "We need the Spirit of God to dwell in us so completely that we recognize the famine, and mostly so we can recognize you and your voice." "It is frightening to face the world with limited relationship with You!" "Master, I understand why these people around us surrendered to Egypt, I don't understand why people in my day, living in abundance, surrender to the evils of the world."

He reaches out to touch our hands, assuring us that He will NEVER leave us. It is a covenant between Him and us. Turning, we see written on the rock sheltering us; **Hebrews 13:5 Let your conduct be without covetousness; be content with such things as you have. For He Himself has said, "I will never leave you nor forsake you."** As this verse slowly fades from view another appears; **Matthew 6:33-34 "But seek first the kingdom of God and his righteousness, and all these things shall be added to you. Therefore do not worry about tomorrow, for tomorrow**

will worry about its own things. Sufficient for the day is its own troubles.

Still holding our hands, Master impresses
on us that He will teach us.

JOSEPH'S PROMISE

Genesis 47:27-31

27. So Israel dwelt in the land of Egypt, in the country of Goshen; and they had possessions there and grew and multiplied exceedingly.

28. And Jacob lived in the land of Egypt seventeen years. So the length of Jacob's life was one hundred and forty-seven years.

29. When the time drew near that Israel must die, he called his son Joseph and said to him, "Now if I have found favor in your sight, please put your hand under my thigh, and deal kindly and truly with me. Please do not bury me in Egypt.

30. "But let me lie with my fathers; and you shall carry me out of Egypt and bury me in their burial place." And he said, "I will do as you have said."

31. Then he said, "Swear to me." And he swore to him. So Israel bowed himself on the head of the bed.

We are still seated by the rock with Master when He shares with us the scripture of Joseph's promise to his father Jacob (Israel). He invites us to walk with Him back to Jacob's shelter to share in the tender moments between Joseph and his father.

Realizing that he is old, now one hundred and forty-seven years, Jacob calls for Joseph to make a last request. Master shares with us that Jacob knows his sons have their home here in Egypt (Goshen), and he knows this is not the land of promise for them. His sons are comfortable here with all the charms of the city that once lured their grandfather Abraham.

He also assures us that Jacob has not forgotten the covenant Yahweh made with his fathers and himself concerning the land of Canaan. You remind us of the covenant made between Yahweh and the descendants of Abraham.

1. The promise to "Make you a great nation" in **Genesis 17:8**

And that "I will be their God" in **Genesis 17:8**

2. The promise to father "Numerous descendants" in **Genesis 17:16.**

3. The promise of personal blessing fulfilled in two ways;

Temporarily as recorded in **Genesis 13:14-15, 17, 15:18** and

24:34-35.

Spiritually as recorded in **Genesis 15:6** and **John 8:56**

4. To make Abraham's 'Name great" as recorded in **Genesis 12:2.**

5. Abraham "Shall be a blessing" also recorded in **Genesis 12:2.**

Abraham was promised that; "I will bless those who bless you and curse those who curse you" as recorded in **Genesis 12:3.**

He was promised that "All the families of the earth shall be blessed", through him.

The belief in this same covenant draws Jacob's heart to Canaan. The Spirit of God whispers in our hearts that the hope of the Old Testament saints is when the Messiah's kingdom is established in the "New Jerusalem," they will reign with Him. I understand that believing these things guides Jacob's desire to be near to the New Jerusalem as possible when Christ comes to establish that city. Jacob is expressing his faith in what Yahweh has promised.

Jacob has become a man of God.

ISAIAH

LAST WORDS OF WISDOM

Genesis 48:1-9

1. Now it came to pass after these things that Joseph was told, "Indeed your father is sick;" and he took him with him his two sons, Manasseh and Ephriam.

2. And Jacob was told, "Look your son Joseph is coming to you." And Israel strengthened himself and sat upon the bed.

3. Then Jacob said to Joseph: "God Almighty appeared to me at Luz in the land of Canaan and blessed me,

4. "And said to me, "Behold, I will make you fruitful and multiply you, and I will make you a multitude of people, and "give this land to your descendants after you as an everlasting possession."

5. "And now your two sons, Ephriam and Manasseh, who were born to you in the land of Egypt, are mine; as Reuben and Simeon, they shall be mine.

6. "Your offspring whom you beget after them shall be yours; will be called by the name of their brothers in their inheritance.

7. "But as for me, when I came from Padan, Rachel died beside me in the land of Canaan on the way, when there was but a little distance to Ephrath; and I buried her there on the way to Ephrath (that is Bethlehem)."

8. Then Israel saw Joseph's sons, and said "Who are these?"

9. Joseph said to his father, "They are my sons, whom God has

given me in this place," And he said, "Please bring them to me, and I will bless them."

It is early afternoon when Joseph arrives with his two sons at the camp of Jacob. Master tells us that Jacob sent for him. Jacob is not well and knows he is near death. You suggest that this is such a gracious thing on Yahweh's part to give them this time together before Jacob joins his fathers in death. I am pleased when Master moves us into position where we can both see and hear the conversation between these men. As Joseph and bis sons arrive Jacob musters the strength to sit upright on his bed. He is old and his eyes are weak, but his spirit is strong. He has purpose in his voice. You remind us that Jacob's father Isaac's eyes are not strong in this his last days.

We remember along with Jacob as he tells Joseph about the covenant Yahweh made with him when he was at Luz (Bethel) many years ago. Joseph sends a knowing glance at his sons. You suggest that Joseph has heard of this before and that he has told it to his sons. It is unexpected when Jacob says, **"God appeared to me there, and God blessed me."** I remember the verses in **Genesis 35: 9 -10** where Yahweh changed Jacob's name from Jacob to Israel even before he would be called by the name Israel. I remember the humility Jacob showed that day, and our watching to see if he would be a more godly man after that encounter. You add that it took Jacob a long time to become a 'godly man' but he has become all that Elohim saw in him that day. I marvel now at the hope Jacob's spiritual growth gives me in my own life. You ask if we can read this encounter again and Master quickly recites; **"Then God appeared to Jacob again, when he came from Padan Aram, and blessed him. And God said to him, "Your name is Jacob; your name shall not be called Jacob anymore, but Israel shall be your name." So He called his name Israel.** You add that this is when Elohim restated the covenant that He made with Abraham promising him the land for himself and his descendants. I love hearing this again and am reminded how honored I feel to know the covenants God makes with the people of the bible. I am excited to see them fulfilled!

Master tells us that the reason we can journey through our Bible now and in our day is because Elohim will have fulfilled two-thirds of this covenant by the time we live. He adds that an unstable treaty will allow the children of Israel possess part of the land promised to them. When they do get to inhabit the entire land, they will live in peace, own property, and pay no taxes. You ask when this will be, and He tells us to look to the times described in the book of Revelation and throughout the scriptures which we will journey through later.

In awe we listen as this old man of faith tells Joseph and his sons, Manasseh and Ephriam the blessing Elohim had given him. No sooner has Jacob stated the blessing than he added his desire to bless Manasseh and Ephriam. He tells Joseph that even though these sons were born in Egypt they are included in the covenant of Elohim. They will each become a tribe among the Children of Israel. However, any born after the death of Jacob will be Joseph's descendants alone.

You ask Master why Manasseh and Ephriam will have tribes that now make thirteen sons of Israel instead of twelve. He reminds us that Levi will not own land. His descendants will be a tribe but not share in the inheritance of the land. We acknowledge that these two boys are over the age of seventeen because we know that they had been born before Jacob arrived in Egypt. I ask, "Why does Joseph not inherit land?" The reply is that, by Manasseh and Ephriam receiving land, Joseph is getting a double portion of the inheritance.

Again, you inquire why the double portion and Master takes us back to **Genesis 49:3-4 Reuben, you are my firstborn,**

My might and the beginning of my strength,

The excellency of dignity and the excellency of power.

Unstable as water, you shall not excel,

Because you went up to your father's bed;

Then you defiled it –

He went up to my couch.

Master continues instructing us that parents have a special duty of pronouncing blessing on their children. By custom, the firstborn would receive a double portion as he would hold the most responsibility in the family. Joseph in these scriptures has received a double portion of the blessing usually intended for the firstborn. Jacob took that blessing from Reuben because of his actions with Jacob's wife. Now he has passed this 'Double portion" blessing on to Joseph and has given each of Joseph's sons a portion.

We are before Master with our mouths open in awe.

Nothing to say.

Amazed!

Jacob's heart cannot speak of Ephrath (Bethlehem) without remembering his beloved Rachel and he reminds his son and grandsons that he buried her there.

MANASSEH AND EPHRAIM

Genesis 48:10-22

10. Now the eyes of Israel were dim with age, so that he could not see. Then Joseph brought them near him, and he kissed them and embraces them.

11. And Israel said to Joseph, "I had not thought to see your face; but in fact, God has also shown me your offspring!"

12. So Joseph brought them from beside his knees, and he bowed down with his face to the earth.

13. And Joseph took them both, Ephraim with his right hand toward Israel's left hand, and Manasseh with his left hand toward his right hand, and brought them near him.

14. Then Israel stretched out his right hand and laid it on Ephraim's head, who was the younger, and his left hand on Manasseh's head, guiding h is hands knowingly for Manasseh was the firstborn.

15. And he blessed Joseph, and said:

"God, before whom my fathers Abraham and Isaac walked,

The God who has fed me all my life long to this day,

16. The Angel who has redeemed me from all evil,

Bless the lads;

Let my name be named upon them,

And the name of my fathers Abraham and Isaac;

And let them grow into a multitude in the midst of the earth."

17. Now when Joseph saw that his father laid his right hand on the head of Ephraim, it displeased him; so he took hold of his father's hand to remove it from Ephriam's head to Manasseh's head.

18. And Joseph said to his father, "Not so, my father, for this one is the firstborn; put your right hand on his head."

19. But his father refused and said, "I know, my son, I know. He also shall become a people, and he also shall be great; but truly his younger brother shall be greater than he, and his descendants shall become a multitude of nations."

20. So he blessed them, that day, saying, "By you Israel will bless, saying, 'May God make you as Ephraim and Manasseh! And thus he set Ephraim before Manasseh.

21. Then Israel said to Joseph, "Behold, I am dying, but God will be with you and bring you back to the land of your fathers.

22. "Moreover I have given to you one portion above your brothers, which I took from the hand of the Amorite with my sword and my bow."

This old man Jacob is not laying on his death bed but is sitting on the edge of it leaning on his staff as Master guides us to Hebrews 11:12 **By faith Jacob, when he was dying blessed each of the sons of Joseph, and worshipped, leaning on the top of his staff.**

We are standing nearby when Jacob reaches out to take the hands of Manasseh and Ephriam and asks Joseph who these boys are. Jacob proudly introduces them, probably not for the first time, as Jacob pulls them close and kisses their cheeks and hugs them. You ask about this 'kissing' and Master explains that this is a show of attachment or kinship, acceptance in the family. This much touching is not usually done in the Egyptian culture and the boys shy away but Joseph gently moves them toward their grandfather. He purposely places Ephriam on Jacob's left hand and Manasseh on his right because Manasseh is the older. Remembering that the one on the right hand will be the leader over the one on his left and the heir to the family inheritance. When Jacob begins to bless the boys, he crosses his hands over and blesses Ephriam with his right hand and Manasseh with his left.

What just happened?

Master tells us that in the book of Numbers we will witness Ephraim's superiority over Manasseh. We will later see that the tribe of Manasseh will march under the banner of Ephriam as told in the book of Numbers. He also tells us that Joshua, along with several great leaders, will come from the line of Ephriam.

You ask Master why Jacob switched the blessings and in this way. He reminds us that Jacob was the younger brother also. He tells us that God does not follow our customs and that spiritual things are on an individual basis. God knows the potential in each of these young men, as He does in all of us, and applies blessings as He sees fit. I wonder why Joseph would question his father's actions as he himself was not the firstborn and yet Master just showed us that Joseph's sons will receive the Reuben's blessing of the firstborn. Joseph even tries to correct his father's perceived mistake in giving the better blessing to Ephriam.

I mention to Master that I love hearing Jacob speak of Elohim as, **"The God who has fed me all my life long to this day."** What an honor for me to be witness to His amazing work in the life of Jacob! What an honor for me to hear him say these words and acknowledge that Elohim has been there all along. I confess that I am learning to see His hand in my life also, and how He guides, pursues, and draws me to be more like Him. To be more holy and righteous as He is holy and righteous.

It is fun when Jacob mentions the **"Angel who has re-**

deemed" him. I had recently noticed Jacob walking into his tent, still bearing the limp from the night he wrestled with the Angel in **Genesis 34:24-30.** That was surely an exciting night for us, being witness to Elohim fighting for the soul of Jacob, knowing that He will do the same for us.

You notice that in the last words of blessing on these young men Jacob places Ephraim's name before Manasseh's. This wording sets in stone the priority blessing on Ephraim's life.

Removing his hands from the heads of Ephriam and Manasseh, Jacob turns his face to Joseph and tells him that he will have his inheritance in Canaan. Master offers his hand to raise us from our knees and we welcome His touch. Joseph looks surprised at this declaration as he has made a wonderfully comfortable life here in Egypt and he cannot imagine leaving here. What you and I understand, and Joseph does not now understand, is that it will be his descendants that will inhabit Canaan. Jacob continues with a personal gift to Joseph and Master takes us to **John 4:5 So He came to a city of Samaria which is called Sychar, near the plot of ground that Jacob gave to his son Joseph.** As Master expressed this verse, you, and I both are amazed that this gift is revealed so many years later that this blessing is specific for Joseph. It will be a ridge near Sychar where Joseph will be buried on a piece of land that Jacob brought from the Amorite in **Genesis 14,** during the time of the conquest of Sodom and Gomorrah. He adds that Sychar is the place of Jacob's well where Jesus will meet the Samaritan woman. Master adds one more point to our understand that this piece of land in our day will be a place of controversy as Israel will fight to build on what will be called the "West Bank."

Jacob is obviously tired, and Joseph assists him to recline in his bed. Ephriam and Manasseh kiss their grandfather goodbye and they return to Egypt in their royal chariots. I stand watching the dust rise behind them, wondering if they will see Jacob alive again and if they understand the blessing that has been placed on them. As I wonder these things the Spirit of God whispers in my heart, "Does any man understand the blessing that has been placed on their lives?"

What an amazing Master you are!

Master walks back with us to our shelter as the sun is setting. What started out as a hot, humid day is now cooler and my mind is filled with wonder.

I will sleep well tonight.

BLESSING REUBEN

Genesis 49:1-4

1. And Jacob called his sons and said, "Gather together, that I may tell you what shall befall you in the last days."

2. "Gather together and hear, you sons of Jacob,

   And listen to Israel your father.

3. Reuben you are my firstborn,

   My might and the beginning of my strength,

   The excellency of dignity and the excellency of power.

4. Unstable as water, you shall not excel,

   Because you went up to your father's bed;

   Then you defiled it –

   He went up to my couch.

Master greets us in the morning with a table set before us. You mention what a loving gesture this is. He reminds us that it is important for us to spend time with Him in the start of our day. We agree and thank Him for His presence almost as though we think He might leave sometimes, which He never does. I can think of Him at any moment and He is there ready to answer my questions, instruct me in new truths or just to be with me. It is an incredible thing I have learned through this journey.

I will never be the same!

The hot wind is blowing the flap on our shelter and the dust of the ground is being lifted into large clouds moving across the land. I shelter my eyes and secure my wrap around my head to cover my mouth and nose as Master invites us to Jacob's tent for what I am certain will be an exciting lesson.

Entering Jacob's tent, we find that all his sons are here. It is crowded and hot and we find a small bench to the side where the wind is lifting the side of the tent a bit to let fresh air find its way in. Master tells us that Jacob has requested his sons join him as he wants to tell them, **"what shall befall you in the last days."** Looking around this room I see Jacob's twelve sons, all born over a period of approximately twenty-three years through four different mothers. The Spirit of God whispers that these twelve boys will provide insight into the ancestry of the Hebrew people. As is done in Hebrew tradition each of these men will have a banner with a symbol on it that represents them, the 'symbols of these men will be displayed in works of art, tapestries, jewelry etc. throughout the ages. The 'last days' for Israel will be different than those of the New Testament believers (the church). He shares with us that scripture is revealing truths about the earthly nation of Israel. Master instructs us that we must watch the prophecies concerning the nation of Israel and compare them to the prophecies concerning these twelve tribes. Specifically, He wants us to watch how they NEVER contradict, they are always in harmony. You respond that it is an amazing miracle to blend all these lives without a discrepancy.

I glance at you as you survey these men and ask Master what it means to 'bless' someone. He teaches us that Jacob will identify the character of each son and therefore the character of his tribe. He adds that the phrase 'last days' means the following years and not any specific span of time.

The love and respect for this man Jacob is great in this room, and I thrill knowing that he truly has his heart aligned with Elohim. I thank Master that He has granted Jacob this opportunity to gather and bless his sons in these last days of his life, and for him to be so comfortable and vocal about the care of Elohim in his own life. We thrill when we hear Jacob sharing with them that Yahweh is guiding their lives also.

Reuben is standing on Jacob's right side of Jacob when he breaths his name. "Reuben you are my first born." Then as Jacob pauses, Reuben glances around at his brothers waiting for the announcement of his inheritance and his blessing. I imagine that Jacob is remembering the joy of his birth and his first wife Leah. Reuben speaks again and acknowledges that Reuben is much like his father, so much like him that Jacob sees his own might and strength dignity and power in his son. Possibly, Jacob remembers the dreams he held for this boy. Master quickly reminds us that Hebrew tradition says Reuben will receive double the inheritance of his brothers as recorded in **Deuteronomy 21:17 "But he shall acknowledge the son of the unloved wife as the firstborn by giving him a double portion of all that he has, for he is the beginning of his strength; the right of the firstborn is his."**

Reuben is standing taller now as all his brothers listen carefully and watch between Jacob and Reuben. Jacob tells Reuben that he is **"unstable as water and that he will not excel."** What kind of blessing is that? You whisper quietly. Reuben looks around at his brothers again, this time disbelieving what he is hearing. Jacob continues as he looks directly at Reuben. Jacob clearly and plainly explains to Reuben why he will not receive the blessing of the firstborn. Then he quotes **Genesis 49:4** again, "**Because you went up to your father's bed;**

Then you defiled it –

He went up to my couch.

You and I reason that more than twenty years have passed since this sin and Jacob has never brought it up until now. And, apparently Jacob didn't confide in Reubens brothers either because this is the first, they have heard this. Reuben is not standing as tall now and appears embarrassed and ashamed.

You ask Master to please tell us more of the meaning of being **"unstable as water."** He responds by telling us that only two of Reubens descendants will be mentioned in scripture as being bold in any way, Dothan and Bairam, mentioned in **Numbers 16** when they will rebel against Moses and Aaron. Then later is scripture the descendants of Reuben will remain on the East side of the Jordan River rather than enter the Promised Land and enjoy what God had for them there. This event is recorded in **Numbers 32.** To be certain we understand, Master tells us that Reuben lost his birthright and leadership position because of his instability! **James 1:7- 8** says **"For let not the man suppose that he will receive anything from the Lord; he is a double–minded man, unstable in all his ways."** Master encourages us to learn two things from the blessing Jacob has pronounced on his son Reuben.

1. The act of sin can have long range effects on our lives.

2. Our sins can be forgiven, but the effects of our sins often must still be experienced.

To this He adds **Proverbs 6:32-33 Whosoever commits adultery with a woman lacks understanding; He who does so destroys his own soul.**

Before we move on to the blessing of Simeon and Levi Master cautions us that God forgives and forgets – it is often much harder for us and those we offend to forgive and forget as He does.

SIMEON AND LEVI

Genesis 49:5-7

5. Simeon and Levi are brothers;

Instruments of cruelty are in their dwelling place.

Let not my soul enter their council;

Let not my honor be united to their assembly;

For in their anger they slew a man,

And in their self will they hamstrung an ox.

Cursed be their anger for it is fierce;

And their wrath for it is cruel!

I will divide them in Jacob

And scatter them in Israel.

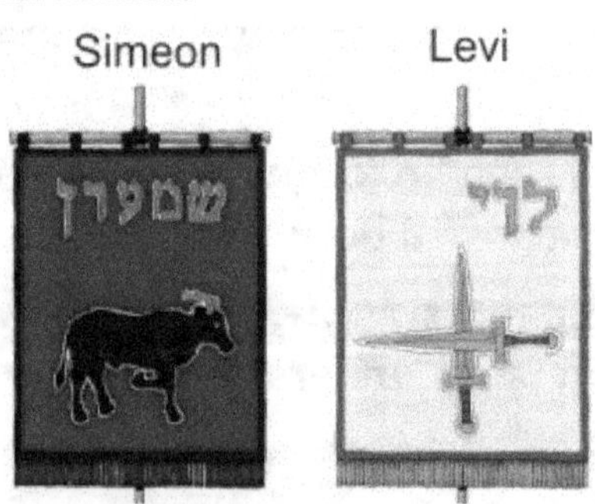

Simeon is next and is standing beside Levi, we are surprised when Jacob speaks to them together. Master reminds us that in **Genesis 34** these two brothers teamed up to avenge their sister Dinah's offender. Jacob describes their angry killing of the all the peoples of Shechem as 'Hamstringing an ox'. You ask what that phrase means, and Master instructs us that it is the same wording as 'digging down the walls of a fortified city'.

Their anger is fierce, and their wrath is cruel! They apparently were partners in crime always because that is how Jacob approaches them. He also reminds us that they are the second and third sons of Leah.

It is heartbreaking and I reach for your hand as Jacob describes them as cruel even in their dwelling place. This is who they are! The look on their faces tells us that they thought Jacob was not aware of the things they do. You whisper that it must be horrible in their homes.

Still holding your hand, we witness Jacob as he states that even as he knew their evil deeds, he refused to let his soul be drawn into their council for the sake of his honor among men. Master suggests that Jacob's shame of these boys is great. He adds that many achievements for God can be destroyed by one violent outburst or an uncontrolled temper. Then He takes us to **Proverbs 25:28** and encourages us to hide this verse in our hearts.

Whoever has no rule over his own spirit

Is like a city broken down, without walls.

In a desire to really hide this verse in your heart you ask Master what it means, and I nod in agreement. He shares with us that self-control is a fruit of the spirit and so it is a gift to us. We can accept this gift and use it in our lives to His glory. A person who choses to have no self-control or declares "This is just who I am" is lying to you or has not chosen to have the Spirit of God with him. I ask, "Is there a time for passionate responses or actions within this 'self-control?'" Master lovingly tells us that He loves our passion when it is used for His glory, but not when it is used to inflict harm on another person.

Our attention is drawn back to Jacob as he pronounces his sentence upon these two men who stand before him, looking like guilty men before a judge. He declares that they will have no land granted to them from the land Elohim as promised to the descendants of Abraham. Instead they will be scattered among the other brother's land. The boys are looking around at their brothers and I imagine they are wondering who will take them after their fathers' harsh description of them.

Master tells us that Simeon's descendants will primarily reside within the tribe of Judah. **Joshua 19:1-9** will describe where they will dwell. They will have seventeen scattered cities including their suburbs. However, these cities will be in arid and barren region that we will know as the Negev where nothing grows. There is not enough that grows thee to sustain life. Master adds that during the wilderness wandering the Tribe of Simeon will decrease in size. They will continue to decrease partly because they are so involved in the worship of the idol Ball-peor who was a god of agriculture whom they sacrificed body parts to. You laugh at the thought of these people offering body parts to try to get crops to grow in the barren land they will inhabit.

Throughout history the Hebrews will consider all poor Hebrews came from the tribe of Simeon. Simeon appears upset that the rights of the firstborn did not fall to him as he looks to Levi who may soon hold these rights.

Turning his gaze to Levi, Jacob assures him that what he has said of Simeon is his to claim also. However, Master leads us to **Deuteronomy 10:8-9 At that time the LORD separated the tribe of Levi to bear the ark of the covenant of the LORD, to stand before the LORD to minister to Him and to bless in His name, to this day. Therefore Levi has no portion nor inheritance with his brethren; the LORD is his inheritance, just as the LORD God promised him. The Levites will be given the honored position of representing the other tribes before the Lord and the right to care for the hold articles of the Tabernacle.**

Master reminds us that the Levites will be given the honored position of representing the other tribes before the Lord and the responsibility of caring for the articles of the Tabernacle. From Levi will come Aaron, the priest of many who will be privileged to offer sacrifices on behalf of the people. The descendants of Aaron will be financially supported by the tithes of the people so they can spend all their time ministering before the Lord as told in **Deuteronomy 18:1-5.**

I ask Master how it happens that a blessing that becomes a curse for Simeon's descendants will be a blessing for Levi's. Master tells us that the explanation to us that is found in **Exodus 33** which records the incident with the golden calf in the wilderness. Then He adds that we will get to that. He also shares that when Jerusalem is destroyed in 70 A.D. all the tribal lineage of the tribe of Levi will be destroyed so Jewish people in our time will not be able to trace their ancestry back to the priests. You add that at this time Levi does not know these future events and does not understand how his descendants will live with no land. Jacob tells him that they will have cities along with Simon's people. Master adds to your observations that it is the grace of God that takes an evil man like Levi and makes him the head of a priestly tribe. They will be scattered for the purposes of God. You mention that it is only by God's grace that we are transformed from our evil selves into priests before God. My own mind reals with the sin that engulfs me and the grace that raises me above that sin, into acceptance before Him.

Master whispers that this is an important lesson to focus our passion on Godly things and purposes, not on our own selfish plans.

JUDAH

Genesis 47:8-12

8. Judah, you are he whom your brothers shall praise;

Your hand shall be on the neck of your enemies;

Your father's children shall bow down before you.

9. Judah is a lion's whelp;

From the prey, my son, you have gone up.

He bows down, he lies down as a lion;

And as a lion, who shall rouse him?

10. The scepter shall not depart from Judah

Nor a lawgiver from between his feet,

Until Shiloh comes;

And to Him shall be the obedience of the people.

11. Binding his donkey to the vine,

And his donkey's colt to the choice vine,

He washes his garments in wine,

And his clothes in the blood of grapes.

12. His eyes are darker than wine,

And his teeth whiter than milk.

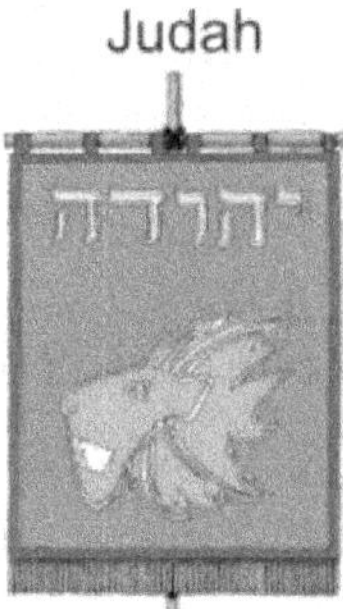

As Jacob shifts his position, he begins again blessings his sons and the brothers look at Judah in shock. I am thinking that they believe all the blessing will rest on Judah and they do not understand why. Master whispers that Judah will be given the family leadership inheritance. Nodding in understanding, we continue.

Master guides us to understand four blessings that Jacob pronounces on Judah.

1. <u>Judah will be the leader of his brothers.</u> You offer that his name does mean 'praise'.

   A. Master reminds us that he did convince his brothers to spare Joseph's life in **Genesis 37:26-27**.

   B. Then when they went down to Egypt Judah was the spokesman for the group in **Genesis 44:14-34**.

   C. We will see in the future that when the Children of Israel are marching through the wilderness, Judah will lead them as told in **Numbers 10:14**.

   D. After conquering the land of Canaan, the tribe of Judah will be the first to receive their allotment of land which will be the most desirable land in **Joshua 15:1**.

   E. The tribe of Judah will consistently be the largest tribe among the Children of Israel.

Master shares with us that in reference to **Joshua 10:24,** and the statement of putting their feet on the necks of the enemy, reminds us of a custom of later Germanic tribes who put an arm around another person's neck as a sign of superiority over that person. You mention that this custom has survived in some form to our day. You mention that you did this to your brother until he cried 'uncle.'

Master offers a fun fact concerning the Hebrew people in our day. When they are asked what tribe they belong to they will always respond that they are of the tribe of Judah. A Hebrew will say, "I am a Jew" which is the shortened version of the name Judah that came into existence after the return of the Children of Israel from the Babylonian Captivity. You ask if other tribes were present at that time and Master tells us that they were, but the tribe of Judah was dominate so all claimed that tribe. That is why the land is called Judea and the people there called Judeans, shortened to Jew.

1. <u>Judah will be a great conqueror.</u> You suggest that possibly this is what it means when Jacob states that Judah's hand will be on the neck of his enemies.

When Jacob tells Judah that his fathers' children shall bow down before him there is an obvious objection among the brothers without any of them saying a word. What they do not understand is that the Lord Jesus Christ will come from Judah's line and that all mankind will bow before Him.

A.   King David, a descendant of Judah, will prove to be the greatest conqueror in the history of Israel. Master suggests we look at **2 Samuel 22:41 You have also given me the necks of my enemies, So that I destroy those who hate me.**

B.   Judah is compared to a lion's whelp indicating that though his descendants who will have come from slavery will come a mighty warrior who will be feared if any dare to come against Him. Judah's banner will bear the symbol of a lion and from them will come the term, "Lion of Judah." Master guides us to

Revelation 5:5 But one of the elders said to me, "Do not weep. Behold, the Lion of the tribe of Judah, the root of David, has prevailed to open the scroll and to loose its seven seals."

Wow!

This vision of majesty carries all through my bible! In this scripture the Lion is a reference to Jesus Christ the Messiah who is, by descent, a member of the tribe of Judah.

2. <u>Judah will produce a royal line of kings.</u> Master points out that the first king of Israel will be Saul who will be from the tribe of Benjamin as recorded in **1 Samuel 16:1-13.** However, God rejected Saul and appointed David to be king of Israel. Then He adds that all legitimate kings of Israel will be descendants of Judah. This is what the phrase "The scepter shall not depart from Judah, nor a law giver from between his feet. You ask about the phrase, "until Shiloh come" and Master is pleased to say that this is a promise to Judah that the kingship will remain with him until Jesus comes and the people bow down to Him as king. You add, "From the line of Judah." You also state, "Shiloh means 'rest, and tranquility' which is what the Messiah will bring.

3. <u>Judah will produce the Messiah.</u> Master instructs us that Shiloh is one of the names of Messiah. He also tells us that there are at least three detailed interpretations concerning Shiloh but we will not cover them now. He promises that as we go through our scriptures it will become clearer how the word Shiloh is used.

Master shares with us that a 'scepter' is used as a symbol of authority. However, there is no record either in scripture or ancient writings of any Jewish king ever using a scepter.

Continuing, in verse eleven and twelve Master teaches us that in scripture the term 'Shiloh' is generally understood as being the title for the Messiah. By far most bible scholars believe that it is a reference to Jesus coming into Jerusalem riding on a donkey offering Himself as the Messiah, the King, and the Savior. Jesus washed his garments in wine (blood). This was His own blood and when He returns, He will be wearing garments stained with the blood of His enemies. This is a prophecy concerning His second coming when He returns in judgment.

Taking us to **verse 12** of this chapter, Master instructs us that the reference to milk is a reference to abundance and blessing, especially when it is combined with the word honey. Then Master offers a caution in this part of scripture, asking us to beware that the things that God blesses us with do not become more important that He himself.

ZEBULUN

Genesis 49:13

13. Zebulun shall dwell by the haven of the sea;

He shall become a haven for ships,

And his border shall adjoin Sidon.

Jacob is moving around the circle of sons and comes to Zebulun. It appears that since the last two sons' blessings were not as harsh as the first, Zebulun is not already defensive. We wonder at the shortness of the blessing on him since it says nothing more than that he will be a sea merchant or possibly live near a seaport. Master shares with us that the location of Zidon is the same as the city Sidon in the land of Phoenicia, which in our day will be in Lebanon. Master adds that seaports are a profitable place to live.

Adding more information to the blessing Master shares with us that Zebulun's descendants will not reveal any notable individuals. However, there will be one named Elon who will judge Israel for ten years as recorded in **Judges 12:11-12.**

You ask if we will learn anything more of these people

later in time. Master tells us that a reference in **Judges 5:18 Zebulun is a people who jeopardized their lives to the point of death,**

Naphtali also, on the heights of the battlefield. I am pleased to hear that they are a brave people, willing to risk their lives for others. Then Master adds that in **1 Chronicles 12:33** tells us that they will be unwavering when the goal is set before them. We are thrilled to know that later they will be a people committed to the God of Abraham, Isaac, and Jacob. Because of this commitment they will be successful in conflict, they will possess unwavering commitment to the goal.

ISSACHAR

Genesis 49:14-15

14. Issachar is a strong donkey,

Lying down between two burdens;

15. He saw the rest was good,

And that the land was pleasant;

He bowed his shoulder to bear a burden,

And became a band of slaves.

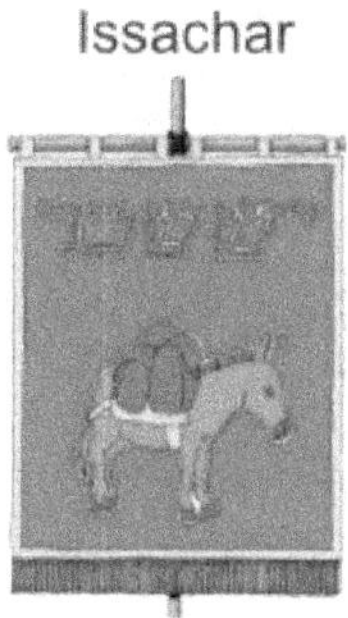

Turning our attention to Issachar you whisper that he is Leah's fifth born son. Jacob compares him to a donkey meaning he will be a burden bearing man for hire. Master reminds us of Leah's statement when he was born as recorded in **Genesis 330:17-18 Leah said, "God hath given me my wages, because I have given my maid to my husband. So she called his name Issachar.** Master adds that there is little information about him and that most we will hear will be Hebrew traditions and rumors. What we will know is only from the blessing Moses will give him in **Deuteronomy 33:18 And of Zebulun he said: "Rejoice, Zebulun, in your going out. And Issachar in your tents!"**

From this verse man will conclude that Zebulun will be a merchant and Issachar student of the Torah. In this time a donkey is a valuable beast, transporting goods and the burdens can be understood as saddle bags hanging on either side of the donkey carrying valuable cargo. He adds that in **Judges 5:15** and 1 **Chronicles 7:1-5** the descendants of Issachar are praised for their powerful assistance and valiant men of might, patient in labor and invincible in war. They will be considered men of great insight and men who carry other burdens.

You ask Master if these two men Zebulun and Issachar are men of commitment to work and care for other workers. His nod tells us that that is what He is telling us.

DAN

Genesis 49:16-18

16. "Dan shall judge his people

As one of the tribes of Israel.

17. Dan shall be a serpent by the way,

A viper by the path,

That bites the horses heals

So that the rider shall fall backward.

18. I have waited for your salvation, O LORD!

Dan

Reminding us, Master shares that Dan is Bilhah's son that was given to Rachel when she could not bear a child. You add that he must have grown up feeling less than one of the beloved sons because you remember Rachel's statement when he was born, "**Genesis 30:6 Then Rachel said, "God has judged my case; and He has also heard my voice and given me a son. Therefore she called his name Dan.** "I add that Dan means, 'judge and serpent'.

Master tells us, **"Dan shall judge his people as one of**

the tribes of Israel." He explains that even though the practice of handmaids bearing offspring for their masters is a common practice tolerated by God during this time, there is still an attitude of less acceptance by the families.

Jacob states here that Dan is accepted as a son of Israel.

Jacob calls Dan a "serpent". Currently as well as in our day a serpent reminds us of Satan and his influence in the world. Our scriptures and archeology will show us that the people of Dan will be heavy into idol worship and in fact will erect large idols in their cities. Jacob is indicating that satanic influence will be dominant in Dan's descendants. Master adds that Samson will be the descendant of a Danite, Manoah of Zorh as recorded in **Judges 13:2**.

He also explains that the battles that the Danites encounter, mostly with the Philistines, will be fought with cunning rather than by military might. They will be a tribe of few against larger opponents. He indicates the battle the Danites entered in **Judges 17** as a sad time indicating the character of these people. In **Judges 18:27-31** the idol worship is evident as the tribe of Dan conquers the people of Laish.

As a final note Master shares with us that the tribe of Dan will have a diminishing place among the Children of Israel, beginning with the twenty listings of the tribe. The tribe of Dan will be far down the list if not last. In the wilderness they will be the last to be given their land of inheritance in the Promised Land. In **Revelation 7:4-8** the tribe of Dan will not be mentioned among the one hundred and forty-four thousand sealed in the tribulation. Probably because of their problems with idolatry throughout history. Then Master causes us to notice that the tribe of Dan will receive a tribal inheritance in the Millennial Kingdom as recorded in **Ezekiel 48:1-2**.

Jacob then closes his blessing on Dan by stating that he has waited to see the salvation of Dan and his family. He states this as a prayer, so it is a half prayer half plea for Dan to surrender.

It occurs to me that this is the plea of so many parents' hearts and it must be especially intense when a parent can see a glimpse of their son's future.

GAD, ASHER, NAPHTALI

Genesis 49:19-21

19. Gad, a troop shall tramp upon him,

But he shall triumph at last.

20. Bread from Asher shall be rich,

And he shall yield royal dainties.

21. Naphtali is a deer let loose;

He uses beautiful words.

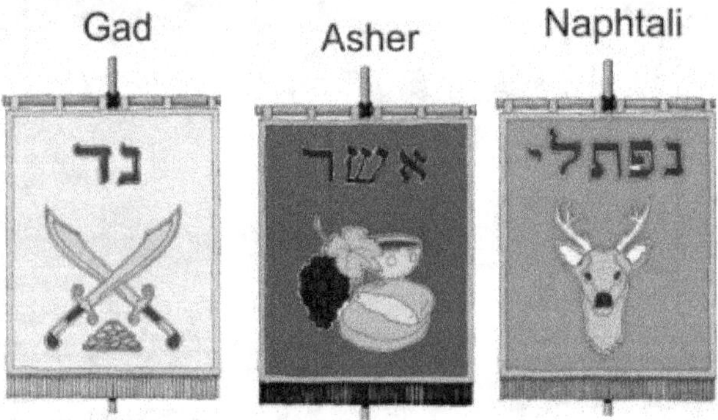

I am surprised when Jacob lumps these three men together, and they appear to be also as they move closer together to hear what their father has to say about them. There is suspense in the room as the blessings have been so different and precise.

Master is quick to point out that these are the other sons of Rachel's maidservants Bilah and Zilpah.

Beginning with Gad Jacob speaks of his being a warrior.

Master takes us to Moses description of his descendants in **Deuteronomy 33:20 And of Gad he said:**

"Blessed is he who enlarges Gad;

He dwells as a lion,

And tears the arm and the crown of his head"

He adds that there will be no notable people in the line of Gad, with the exception of a Jewish tradition which states that Elisha will be of the tribe of Gad.

You ask Master what we will learn from Gad in scripture and He tells us that there are only six references to him but there are lessons to be learned.

1. He will graduate from the school of hard knocks. His toughness comes from those experiences.

2. The hard knocks Gad experienced show that through troubles we can come out as refined gold. To add to this thought Master takes us to **Psalm 119:71 It is good for me that I have been afflicted, that man learn Your statutes.**

3. Gad's spiritual readiness teaches us that we must always be ready to meet our enemy. With that He takes us to a scripture written by Paul.

1 Peter 5:8 Be sober, be vigilant; because your adversary the devil walks about like a roaring lion, seeking whom he may devour.

4. The promise to Gad is that in the end he will overcome. Pointing out that Gad is an overcomer, Master takes us to John's definition of overcomer. Triumph is found in **1 John 5:4-5 Whatever is born of God overcomes the world. And this is the victory that has overcome the world—our faith. Who is he who overcomes the world, but he who believes that Jesus is the Son of God?**

I find myself breathing a big sigh of relief to hear that one of

Jacob's sons will "triumph" as a believer in the Messiah, the Son of God. I glance at Gad to see he has the same reaction as I have, and I smile.

Jacob shifts his attention to Asher who is standing next to Gad. You mention that Asher and Gad are full brothers and Asher is Jacob's eighth son.

You go on to remind me that his name means 'happy'. Master smiles at you, pleased that you have hidden these things in your heart.

Smiling, Jacob declares that, "Asher shall be rich." At that, all the brothers look his way as Gad pats his shoulder. This is especially precious news as they have just experienced the agony of surrendering all they have and are to Egypt as they go into a life of servanthood. Before we get carried away imagining, Master stresses that the bread from Asher will be rich. This means that he will enjoy rich produce and supply the tasty foods for the tables of kings. He takes us to **1 Kings 4:7 And Solomon had twelve governors over all Israel, who provided food for the king in his household; each one made provision for one month a year.** You and I laugh a little at the thought, the king must have anticipated the meals from Asher's tribe.

Master shares with us that Asher will not be recorded as ever engaging in a battle. The most famous Asherite in scripture will be Anna, the prophetess who will greet the infant Jesus in the Temple in **Luke 2:36-38.** Through this reference Master points out that in time of Anna the Hebrew people still maintained their tribal identities. It also verifies that representatives of the ten northern tribes still existed over seven hundred years after the Assyrian captivity. Proving that the ten tribes were not lost as some believe.

Pointing to the word 'rich' in verse 20 of our scripture, Master tells us that this word is also translated 'oil'. At the same time, He shows us where Moses is blessing the tribe of Asher in **Deuteronomy 33:24 And of Asher he said: "Asher is most**

blessed of sons;

Let him be favored by his brothers,

And let him dip his foot in oil.

He explains that this oil is olive oil which has an abundance of uses such as cooking, lighting, medicine, anointing. He assures us that when we get to the land that Asher inherits it is a land of abundant olive groves. You offer that the blessing of Asher is that he will share his abundance with others, and I agree with a confident, "Yes", Master touches our hands in agreement. Then He adds that 'oil' is also associated in scripture with the Holy Spirit. We all smile as we understand what He is telling us.

Naphtali is anxious to hear his father's blessing as his brothers' have been favorable ones. I am also anxious with him and find myself smiling at him. The blessing is brief, and the anticipation is captivating me. Master points out that Naphtali is a deer, also known as a hind or a female deer, or doe. You can't not contain your comment and say that a 'hart' is the word for a male deer, or buck. I have come to love your added information and I admire how you retain it.

Master tells us that Naphtali will be known for his speed and agility; he will be known as a swift runner. Hearing this Naphtali puts his weight on both feet, causing him to stand a little taller and firmer. He seems to already know this but loves having his father notice.

Speaking of the beautiful words of Naphtali Master tells us that Barak is from the tribe of Naphtali and will be mentioned in the "Song of Deborah" in **Judges 5:1-31**. Master also adds that when Jesus calls his disciples, many of them will be from the land of Naphtali's descendants. He asks us to consider that these twelve men carried the 'beautiful words' of the gospel as a 'deer let loose'.

What a fun image!

With that, Master desires we consider the three lessons

we can learn from Gad, Asher, and Naphtali, the sons of maidservants.

Gad: BE READY.

Asher: BE FRUITFUL.

Naphtali: BE SWIFT.

JOSEPH

Genesis 49:22-26

22. Joseph is a fruitful bough

A fruitful bough by a well;

His branches run over the wall.

23. The archers have bitterly grieved him,

Shot him and hated him,

24. But his bow remained in strength,

And the arms of his hands were made strong.

By the hands of the Mighty God of Jacob

(From there is the Shepherd,

The stone of Israel).

25. By the God of your father who will help you

And by the almighty who will bless you

With blessings of heaven above, Blessings of the deep that lies beneath,

Blessings of the beasts of the womb.

26. The blessing of your father

Have excelled the blessings of my ancestors,

Up to the utmost bound of the everlasting hills.

They shall be on the head of Joseph,

And on the crown of the head of him who was separate from his brothers.

Jacob's countenance changes as he addresses the son of his beloved Rachel. There is a softness in his voice that was not there with the other men and they seem to recognize it, as I do. You whisper without looking at me that his name means, 'may He add', indicating that Rachel wanted another son after Joseph.

Master points out that Jacob calls Joseph a 'fruitful bough' and we will see his descendants will be fruitful, also indicated by the comment of his branches running over the wall.

You ask Master if the comparison in our day of Joseph being a 'type of Christ' is a valid comparison. His response is that the New Testament does not mention Joseph as a type of Christ. He also tells us that Joseph will continue to trust God through every trial.

When Jacob mentions the abuse, Joseph endured at the hands of his brothers they all look at the floor before looking back at their father. It appears they have believed Jacob did not know what they had done.

Master desires that we note the five titles of the Lord mentioned in this passage and He takes us to each one.

1. The mighty God of Jacob

2. The Shepherd

3. The Stone of Israel

4. God of thy father

5. The Almighty – Shadddai, The all-Sufficient One, The Sustainer

This is who carried Joseph!

Master tells us that He wants us to understand the lesson from the life of Joseph is that almost every time Joseph speaks, he mentions God.

Our scripture mentions Joseph being 'set apart' in reference to the long time Joseph was removed from his family.

Master is showing us clearly that the patriarchal blessing that would have traditionally gone to Reuben is being laid on the head of Joseph. I remember that this a double portion of the inheritance. You ask Master what effect will this double blessing have on Joseph's descendants. He reminds us that Jacob has already blessed Joseph and Asenath's sons Manasseh and Ephriam, and that is where the two portions will go.

Master shares with us that the precept to learn from Joseph is in **Matthew 25:21.** This is in Jesus own words. **"His lord said to him, "Well done, good and faithful servant; you were faithful over a few things, I will make you ruler of many things. Enter into the joy of your lord. '**

BENJAMIN

Genesis 49:27

27" Benjamin is a ravenous wolf;

In the morning he shall devour the prey,

And at night he shall divide the spoil."

It is strange to me when Jacob describes Benjamin as a "ravenous wolf." I thought Benjamin was so dear to him that he would have nothing but praise for his youngest son. Master explains to us that the comparison is to Benjamin's warlike attitude. Still, I wonder if Jacob is speaking from his heart or if this is the prophecy of the Spirit of God, and maybe Jacob is even surprised at his own words. You add that you have said things that you knew came from the Spirit of God and not from you. I can also identify with that experience and it is strange and thrilling at the same time.

Master reminds us that Rachel died giving birth to Benjamin, so he has lived his whole life with the emotions of not knowing his mother. In her last breath she named him Benoni meaning 'son of my pain'. However, Jacob renamed him Benjamin meaning 'right-hand son'.

It looks to me that Jacob is describing Benjamin as a ravenous wolf who tears his prey to pieces. Master urges me to be patient and He will show me how this prophecy will hold up in Benjamin's descendants. In the land of inheritance for Benjamin there will be many cities known throughout the Bible; such as Jericho, Bethel, Gibeon, Ramah and Mizpah. But most notably is Jerusalem where God will build His temple.

Master asks us if we would like to hear an interesting fact about Benjamin, and we both respond that we love the facts that accompany His word. He proceeds to share with us that left-handedness will be a common trait among the Benjaminite people. This will become an asset for them when they are in battle because the enemy will not expect a left-handed attack, which aided in their victories. Master takes us to **Judges 20:16 Among this people were seven hundred left-handed; every one could sling a stone at a hair's breadth and not miss**. Laughing, you reply that Jacob had named him his "right-hand son".

Also, in Judges 20 we will see revealed the viciousness of the way the Benjaminite people do battle.

Master shares with us that a notable descendant of Benjamin will be Saul, son of Kish. Then, Saul's son Jonathan was also a great warrior although his zeal was channeled for the Lord as recorded in **1 Samuel 12:6 and 12.**

Included in the descendants of Benjamin we will find Paul of Tarsus who was first zealous against Christ and then zealous for the cause of Christ. There are several Benjaminite's recorded in scripture and Master encourages us to watch for them. They will usually fight for God's glory.

Encouraging us to not ever lose hope in any person, Master shares that He can mold and utilize any temperament for his glory. You and I determine that we want to be a molded for His glory, ready to tear apart the armies of darkness.

As we watch Jacob sitting on his bed, weak from his blessings, he has one last request of his sons.

THE TWELVE TRIBES OF ISRAEL

Genesis 49:28-33

28. All these are the twelve tribes of Israel, and this is what their father spoke to them. And he blessed them; he blessed each one according to his own blessing.

29. Then he charged them and said to them: "I am to be gathered to my people; bury me in the cave that is in the field of Ephron the Hittite,

30. "In the cave that is in the field of Machpelah, which is before Mamre in the land of Canaan, which Abraham bought with the field of Ephron the Hittite as a possession for a burial place.

31. "There they buried Abraham and Sarah his wife, there they buried Isaac and Rebekah his wife, and there I buried Leah.

32. "The field and the cave that is there were purchased from the sons of Heth."

33. And when Jacob had finished commanding his sons, he drew his feet up into the bed and breathed his last, and was gathered to his people.

It is a sad solemn scene before us as Jacob says good-bye to his sons. They listen attentively as he makes his last request, but I think they already knew what he would ask them to do for him. As tears run down my cheeks, I remember the boy leaving home alone at his parents' request, his first glimpse of Rachel and then his disappointment when he realized he had married Leah instead of Rachel. I think of Rachel hiding her father's idol and Jacob wrestling with the angel of the Lord at Peniel. Even in the last weeks I have watched him walk with a limp that is his constant reminder of who is LORD in his life.

Jacob was so afraid when his sons went to Egypt to purchase food as he watched his own world crumbling at the fierceness of the draught. I think of his joy when he saw Joseph again and then realized he had more grandchildren here in Egypt. Now I see the man of God laying here, totally trusting his Elohim and in turn trusting his sons. I consider the honor of experiencing his life with him and the gracious care of Elohim every step of his life. Thank you Master, Jacob's life has blessed and challenged me!

Quietly they leave their father as he has now breathed his last. He is now re-united with his father Isaac and mother, Rebekah. As I leave the tent, I whisper that I will meet him one day in the house of God.

The sons are a flurry of conversation, each one expressing their opinions and some questioning the wisdom of this old man. And yet, they know the value of this blessing and they know their father to be a godly man who speaks the words of Elohim. They also know that what their father has spoken cannot be changed or altered.

As Master walks with us back to our dwelling, it strikes me that Jacob was making sure that he would be in the land Elohim, the land of promise when his LORD returns. His desire is that he is there when Elohim fulfills His promises to the nation Israel. Master reminds us that Jacob has asked to be buried by Leah and that Rachel was buried up in Bethlehem.

You mention that it is impressive how much Jacob knows about his family history. Master assures us that he knows everything, and that he has passed it down to his sons. We know that either they will remember and pass it along, or that it will be record it in written form for Moses to write out for us. What an amazing God we serve that can preserve these records so exactly that they can be proven and called truth.

As we arrive at our dwelling, somewhat subdued at the passing of Jacob, Master shares **Hebrews 11:13** and reminds us how Jacob will be seen in years to come. **These all died in faith, not having received the promises, but having seen them afar off were assured of them, embraced them and confessed that they were strangers and pilgrims on the earth.** At that, we embrace master before retiring as we humbled say.

Amen.

JACOB'S BURIAL IN CANAAN

Genesis 50:1-14

1. Then Joseph fell on his father's face and wept over him, and kissed him.

2. And Joseph commanded his servants and physicians to embalm his father. So the physicians embalmed Israel.

3. Forty days were required for him, for such were the days required for those who are embalmed, and the Egyptians mourned for him seventy days.

4. Now when the days of his mourning were past, Joseph spoke to the household of Pharaoh, saying "If now I have found favor in your eyes, please speak in the hearing of Pharaoh, saying,

5. My father made me swear, saying, "Behold, I am dying; in my grave which I dug for myself in the land of Canaan, there you shall bury me." Now therefore, please let me go up and bury my father, and I will come back.'"

6. And Pharaoh said, "Go up and bury your father, and he made you swear."

7. So Joseph went up to bury his father; and with him went up all the servants of Pharaoh, and elders of his house, and all the elders of the land of Egypt,

8. And there went up with him both chariots and horse-

men, and it was a very great gathering.

10. Then they came to the threshing floor of Atad, which is beyond the Jordan, and they mourned there with a great and very solemn lamentation. He observed seven days of mourning for his father.

11. And when the inhabitants of the land, the Canaanites, saw the mourning at the threshing floor of Atad, they said, "This is a deep mourning of the Egyptians." Therefore it's name was called Abel Mizraim, which is beyond the Jordan.

12. So his sons did for him just as he had commanded them.

13. For his sons carried him to the land of Canaan, and buried him in the cave of the field of Machpelah, before Mamre, which Abraham bought with the field from Ephron the Hittite as property for a burial place.

14. And after he had buried his father, Joseph returned to Egypt, he and his brothers and all who went up with him to bury his father.

Master, standing with us outside our dwelling, informs us that even now Joseph is with his father's body, weeping and mourning. The thought breaks our hearts as we later prepare for bed in silence. Once we are on our sleeping mats, we talk ourselves to sleep with the memories of Jacob we will never forget.

It is important that we understand that in the years Jacob lived in Egypt he became a beloved man. I suggest that perhaps he brought to Egypt the same spirit of prosperity and peace that had been seen in Joseph years ago. You and I acknowledge that we remember that spirit and the Spirit of God in his life. You remind me of the first blessing Jacob's father placed on him when Jacob deceived him in **Genesis 27: 28-29 Therefore may God give you**

Of the dew of heaven,

Of the fatness of the earth,

And plenty of grain and wine.

Let peoples serve you,

And nations bow down to you.

Be master over your brethren,

And let your mother's sons bow down to you.

Cursed by everyone who curses you,

And blessed be those who bless you!"

At Joseph's request the most skilled physicians and servants prepared Jacob for his burial which will take place in Hebron. Master adds to our thinking that this process will take forty days. Wow! I am intrigued at the thought. Then He adds that they mourned him for seventy days. I ask if there is significance in the number of days required by the Egyptians. He shares with us that in our day, it will be presumed that the forty days are required for the care of the body itself. But He instructs us that the ceremony begins with soaking and wrapping of the body which takes thirty days. Then there is an additional thirty days when there will be much singing, music, and worship in honor of the deceased, preparing them to enter the next life.

We notice that Joseph respectfully requested of Pharaoh that he be allowed to take his father to his burial place in Canaan and was granted permission. You ask if the Egyptians went with him to ensure he would come back or out of respect for Jacob. Master does not answer the question but continues to show us that this is an exceptionally long funeral procession. People along the way noticed, and in fact they renamed the place where the procession camped at a place called 'Atad'.

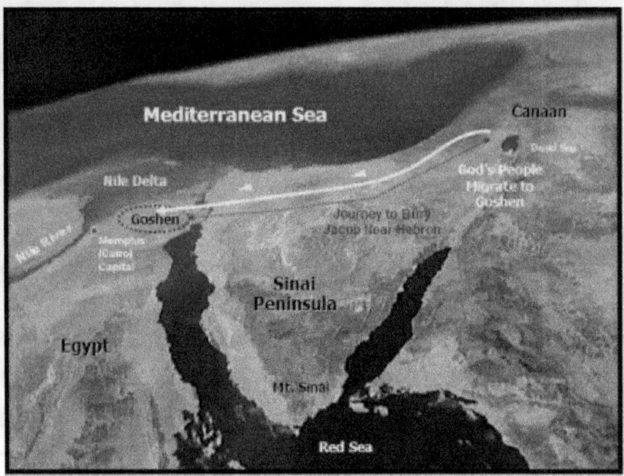

Bing.com images

Master shares with us that Atad means 'threshing floor' and you follow by asking what a threshing floor is? He explains that it is a place where grain is processed, separating the wheat from the chaff. Sheaves of grain are spread on the hard clay packed floor and trampled by oxen pulled sleds.

He then adds that the Canaanites there changed the name of the place as a result of the mourning going on here. I imagine that it is a strange thing for them to see the Egyptians carrying on so. Master shares that the change of name means, 'funeral from Egypt'. The Egyptians are there seven days and the degree of Egyptian authorities with their chariots and horsemen made quite an impression on the people of Canaan. He adds that in our day we will not know exactly where this location is.

As we stand at the site of Jacob's burial, I wonder at the people surrounding me. The Egyptians, are they just here on order of the Pharaoh or did they know and respect Jacob? Joseph's brothers and family, their lives totally turned upside down in the last few years. Here they are back in Canaan at the sacred burial place of their ancestors. Myself an observer, as some others may be, curious and seeking, sharing in the mourning for a man of God. Turning to Master I tell Him I am honored to be barefoot before Him in this place.

FEAR GRIPS JOSEPH'S BROTHERS

Genesis 50:15-23

15. When Joseph's brothers saw that their father was dead, they said, "Perhaps Joseph will hate us, and may actually repay us for all the evil which we did to him."

16. So they sent messengers to Joseph, saying, "Before your father died he commanded, saying,

17. "Thus you shall say to Joseph: "I beg you, please forgive the trespass of your brothers and their sin; for they did evil to you." 'Now, please, forgive the trespass of the servants of the God of your father." And Joseph wept when they spoke to him.

18. Then his brothers also went and fell down before his face, and they said, "Behold, we are your servants."

19. Joseph said to them, "Do not be afraid, for am I in the place of God?

20. "But as for you, you meant evil against me; but God meant it for good, in order to bring it about as it is this day, to save many people alive.

21. "Now thereforre, do not be afraid; I will provide for you and your little ones." And he comforted them and spoke kindly to them.

As we are walking, Master leads us to three scriptures. We are not told whether this event happened before they left Egypt. Perhaps during the seventy days of mourning, or on the journey back. I believe it happened as the brothers passed familiar land and places, maybe even people. Memories flowing freely as fear gripps them. Master adds that memories can bring us fear as they are often distorted or unresolved. Wherever and whenever this event happened, it deeply upset Joseph. He openly weeps in front of whomever is there. He is reminded that the prophecy of his his youth, stating that his brothers will bow down before him, is repeated over and over throughout the years.

Master points out that at each reoccurance of this prophecy Joseph gives the glory to Elohim.

You point out that Joseph's commitment to his brothers is unique and gracious. Master adds that this is a commitment that can come only from Elohim and His love for His people.

He concludes this section of scripture by showing us that Joseph did just as he promised his brothers and in fact Elohim allowed him to share in the lives of his descenants to the third gereration.

Wow! That is a blessing.

JOSEPH'S LAST DAYS

Genesis 50:22-26

22. So Joseph dwelt in Egypt, he and his father's household. And Joseph lived one hundred and ten years.

23 Joseph saw Ephram's children to the third generation. The children of Machir, the son of Manasseh, were also brought up on Joseph's knees.

34. And Joseph said to his brethren, "I am dying: but God will surely visit you, and bring you out of this land to the land of which He swore to Abraham, to Isaac, and to Jacob."

25. Then Joseph took an oath from the children of Israel, saying, "God will surely visit you, and you shall carry my bones from here."

26. So Joseph died, being one hundred and ten years old; and they embalmed him, and he was put in a coffin in Egypt.

Today, you and I witness the announcement by Joseph that he is dying as he instructs his family about his burial. You and I stand near by in the cool breeze listening with his children. Joseph assures them that the covenant Elohim made with them will still apply after he is gone to be with his ancestors. Master takes us to that covenant spoken to Jacob (Israel) in **Genesis 35:11-12 Also God said to him: "I am God Almighty. Be fruitful and multiply; a nation and a company of nations shall proceed from you, and kings shall come from your body. "The land which I gave to Abraham and Isaac I give to you; and to your descendants after you I give this land."**

This is another sad scene for us, but different because Joseph has lived a godly life and we know of his love and unfailing trust in Elohim. We agree that there is a peaceful joy in watching a child of God pass into His care. Joseph also believed completely in being buried in Canaan as his father's had. He knew his Redeemer would come for him and he desired, as his father had, to be where his Redeemer would touch His foot on the earth when He comes.

Master shares with us that Joseph will be embalmed in Egypt in a manner equal to his status and degree of respect. Joseph will be placed in an Egyptian coffin and put in a place in Egypt where he will wait for the day when the Children of Israel will be returned to the Promised Land.

Master takes us to **Hebrews 11:22 By faith Joseph, when he was dying, made mention of the departure of the children of Israel, and gave instructions concerning his bones.** This confirms to us that even Joseph, who trusted Elohim his entire life, was saved by faith as you and I are.

I kneel before my Master to thank Him for this man of faith who has touched my life in such a powerful way. I thank Him for the fathers of Joseph and the ancestors that have taught me more than I ever dreamed I would find here. He holds before me a map of each man's journey to be a man of God. Each location is familiar and filled with memories. I can't wait to meet these men in eternity and hear the details!

Without saying a word Master pulls our sandles from his tunic and hands them to us. With tears in our eyes we receive them with a promise that we will not have them long. He tells us that He has more for us and He will anxiously wait for our next adventure. As the map fades from His hands He encourages us to not forget what we have learned.